THE DEVIL'S JUMP

The Devil's Jump

PETER DOYLE

Criminy!
VERSE CHORUS PRESS

Cover image: courtesy, Justice & Police Museum Collection, Historic Houses Trust of NSW, Sydney, Australia

A Criminy! book
Published by Verse Chorus Press
PO Box 14806, Portland OR 97293
www.versechorus.com

FIRST AMERICAN EDITION

Cover design by Louise Cornwall
Book design and layout by Steve Connell/Transgraphic

Printed in Canada

Library of Congress Cataloguing-in-Publication Data

Doyle, Peter, 1951-
  The devil's jump / Peter Doyle. — 1st American ed.
    p. cm.
  ISBN 978-1-891241-20-8
  1. Black marketeers—Fiction. 2. Organized crime—Fiction. 3. Political corruption—Fiction. 4. Sydney (N.S.W.)—History—20th century—Fiction.
I. Title.
PR9619.3.D69D48 2008
823'.92—dc22

2007052904

For Biddy

1

WEDNESDAY, AUGUST 15, 1945

It was just after half past nine in the morning, and my working day was nearly over. I yawned as I drove along Oxford Street in Paddington, thinking it was maybe time to stop for some steak and eggs.

A factory hooter sounded, then another. Somewhere a bugle played a charge and nearby a church bell started ringing. Air raid sirens and car horns went off and a raggedy, swelling noise of shouts and cheers and hurrays rose up around me.

An old feller in a dressing gown ran in front of the car. I braked hard, pressed the horn, and made the appropriate gesture. The codger bowed to me, then skipped into a pie shop.

A tram stopped in the middle of the street. The driver got out and shook hands with passers-by. The old feller came out of the shop with a girl in an apron, and the two of them waltzed down the middle of Oxford Street. Another girl ran over to the Chev, leaned over and shouted something I couldn't make out. I wound down the window, and she leaned in and planted a big wet kiss on my cheek, then laughed and danced away. A feller took off his hat and dropped it on the ground, then sat down in the gutter and started crying like a baby.

A little kid ran by carrying a leering effigy of General Tojo. I got out of the car and grabbed his shoulder. "What's the mail, pal?" I shouted.

"The vile Jap bastards have surrendered. The war's over."

It was just as I'd feared.

"Watch your language," I said, and let him go.

I got back in the car, wound up the windows and turned on the radio. I sat there listening as Prime Minister Ben Chifley told the country in his gruff voice that there would be two days holiday to celebrate the peace, and would the men and women of Australia mind terribly not running completely amok.

I started the engine and moved off through the rapidly thickening crowd. Outside Paddington Town Hall a paper salvage bin had been set alight; the flames leaped up to twenty feet high as people danced in a big circle around the fire. The kid with the Tojo effigy had set it alight and was waving it in the air.

Under normal circumstances I'd have downed tools and joined in, but the previous evening I'd got a telephone call from my boss, Mick Toohey, publican, factory owner, and master black marketeer. He'd told me to get up before dawn, take his Chev out to the shed behind his printery at Botany, collect certain items and deliver them to various addresses around town. Then I was to pick up a suckling pig, a few rabbits, a dozen freshly killed chooks, some eggs, bacon, cigs, rum, and a case of genuine scotch whisky from the shed and bring all that to the Durban Club, Toohey's hotel in the center of Sydney.

I'd been less than keen, but Toohey said the State Parliamentary Joint Committee on Rural Bridge and Overpass Reconstruction was having dinner at his pub that evening, and he'd promised the worthy gents something special. If I did the right thing, he wouldn't forget it. But do the run while it was still dark, he'd said, so there'd be less risk of being sprung by the Rationing Commission, the Manpower Authority, the Military Police, the civil coppers, or anyone else who might stand in the way of rugged individualism.

I'd overslept, though, started late, and now I was in the shit.

Five minutes after Chifley's announcement, Oxford Street was completely blocked by crowds of crazy, shouting people. I got off the main street and threaded my way through south Paddington, skirted around Darlinghurst into Surry Hills, and down towards Central, looking for a way to get to the Durban Club, but every major street was thick with people moving in a roaring, swaying mass towards the city center.

I circled some more but got trapped by a mob in the Haymarket. A pair of lairs got up and danced on the bonnet of the Chev. I threw them off and edged slowly into the Chinese district, where it was all firecrackers, dragons, and lanterns, and crowds of laughing, cheering Chinese.

I pushed on through, hitting the horn, waving, smiling, begging people to clear a way, then came to a wall of people at the corner of Liverpool and Elizabeth Street. I backed up, and parked the car in a laneway. I took an old overcoat and a kit bag from the back seat, checked that no one was looking, then went to the boot and loaded the pig carcass, the chooks, the bacon, eggs, and the rum and whisky carefully into the kit bag. I put on the overcoat, stuck a rabbit in each pocket, filled the inside pockets with as many packets of cigs and bottles of whisky as would fit, then took off on foot into the throng.

I made progress for a while, and the kit bag turned out to be a bit of a lurk in itself—I was showered with undeserved hugs and kisses from comely revelers all the way. But the going got harder and the crowd got rowdier and drunker the closer I got to the city center. There were broken shop windows, kicked-in doors, and shopkeepers standing guard inside with axe-handles, ready to beat back looters, while outside people danced in wild circles, their eyes wide and unseeing.

I skirted a brawl between a big group of British and Australian soldiers at the corner of Park Street and headed into Hyde Park. I set the kit bag down behind some bushes and took a breather. A young soldier and a girl nipped through the hedge and crashed down next to me. The bloke asked did I have a cig. I slung him a pack. Did I know where they could get a drink? I opened a half bottle of scotch and passed it to him. They both took a big drink, then he put his hand under her dress and she threw her head back and laughed. I reclaimed the bottle and set off again.

I headed away from the uproar, towards College Street, took a short cut through the shrubbery and came out into a huge, silent crowd, kneeling with their heads bowed, facing St. Mary's Cathedral. I cut back left towards the Archibald fountain.

A deep thumping sound was coming from somewhere in the park. Then I heard a voice like an adenoidal bookie on the Randwick Flat, half-singing, half-talking: *You were thinkin' while I was sleepin'*. I followed the winding pathway through the park. The dull thump became the sound of a boogie-woogie piano, amplified through a public address system, and a drummer slamming a snare. Then that voice again: *I was snoozin', but you were creepin'*. I came around the corner. A gang of louts and good-time girls were jiving around a piano, drums and saxophone combo. The piano pounder was none other than my old pal, Max Perkal. *But soon I'll be laughin' and you'll be weepin'*.

Max saw me and immediately pointed at his open mouth. He mimed drinking from a bottle, then pointed at me and tilted his head, still playing the boogie-woogie bass pattern with his left hand. I shook my head.

The girls were wearing slacks with bright red or green cardigans; a few of the men had zoot suits like mine. Then I spotted a girl jiving on her own who stopped me in my tracks. I knew Molly Price, though not well. She saw me staring and came jiving over. She was wearing a gray overcoat; her hair was disheveled and her blue eyes were wide and bright, pupils the size of sixpences.

She shouted, "Come and dance with us." I shook my head, pointed to my wrist watch. She smiled slyly, turned her head to the side, looked out at me from behind her hair and then let her overcoat fall open. She was wearing black underwear—and nothing else. She laughed, snapped her garter belt, grabbed my hand and said, "Oh, come on, let's *live*!"

Somebody behind me gave me a push and I was flung into the mob of dancers. Then I thought, why not? I carefully placed the kit bag under the piano, took my overcoat off, folded it and put it on top, and said to Molly, "All right then sweetheart, let's show these mugs how to cut a rug."

Molly was a "hostess" at the Booker T. Washington Club, the nightspot set aside for black American servicemen stationed in Sydney, and the unofficial headquarters of the local jitterbugs. She had picked up some fancy moves, all right. But when it came to jitterbugging I was no slouch myself.

We jived around for a while. Molly kept her overcoat on, but left it undone at the front, so it fanned out when she swung herself around. A few of the other girls were dressed the same, just underwear or skimpy swimsuits beneath their overcoats.

The high spirits were getting to me. Dancing in the park with a pretty blonde in the middle of the day, good music playing, not a copper in sight—this really is the grouse, I thought.

We danced for what seemed like hours, then ducked into the bushes for a kiss and cuddle which soon turned serious. Molly gently took my hand out from under her overcoat and said, "We'll have to go somewhere else. Somewhere private."

I looked at my watch. "I've got some business to attend to. Will you wait here for me?"

"How long?"

"An hour or two."

She kissed me and whispered in my ear, "Meet me at the Rocket Club at eight. I'll be waiting for you. But don't be late."

When I got back to the bandstand the kit bag had disappeared. There was a bottle of rum on top of Max's piano and he was already half rinsed. Bottles of whisky were being passed from hand to hand. Then someone threw an egg and someone else retaliated. One bloke was jitterbugging with a plucked chicken, another wore one on his head. The pig was long gone.

I got my coat from under the piano. Miraculously, four bottles of whisky and a couple of rabbits were still in the pockets. I put the coat on. A nearby hooligan heard the bottles clinking in the inside pocket and turned to me with an evil grin. "Forget it sport," I said. "These are promised elsewhere."

He had other ideas, and as they say in the court reports, a scuffle ensued. I was outnumbered, and it was only with great determination that I managed to get away with any merchandise at all.

I pressed on through Philip Street. Confetti was raining down from the office buildings, thick as a heavy snowfall, settling ankle-deep on the ground. I grabbed at a piece of paper as it floated past—it was a torn up piece of index card.

Martin Place was the heart of the celebration. Ukulele players, hula dancers, fire-eaters, clowns, and acrobats lined the GPO steps, and all along the wide street people played two-up right out in the open. Hillbilly singers strummed guitars, and pipe bands marched around, each with its own crowd following behind. Orchestras from three or four different radio stations were playing in different corners of Martin Place, and from the harbor came a continuous hooting of sirens and foghorns.

As it got dark, couples started going the all the way in the shelter of doorways. The searchlights came on, lighting up the smoke from many bonfires.

By six thirty I'd had enough. I took what remained of the illicit goods, namely one rabbit in poor condition, around the corner to Toohey's hotel. But it was locked up and dark. A mob milled outside, drunk and aimless, looking for more booze. Someone was banging on the door to the public bar, yelling "Open up, you bastard. Give us a drink!"

I cut into the laneway, went around to the back door, and rapped on the glass.

A dim light came on inside, and Mick Toohey opened the door. He had a face that could scare littlies—bushy eyebrows, a large, square face and a mouth which was permanently turned down on the left side. The other side of his mouth was theoretically capable of smiling but had rarely been known to do so, hence his nickname, "Misery."

He looked me up and down and said, "What the hell happened to you?"

"I was beset by ruffians. But I fought tooth and nail to defend your property." I reached into the overcoat, took out the rabbit, held it out to him. It was squashed flat in the middle where a motorbike had driven over it, and the imprint of an army boot was clearly visible on its haunches.

"And the grog?"

"It didn't survive the journey. There was a melee."

"Where's the car?"

"In the Haymarket. Sorry Mick. Things got a bit out of hand, what with the war ending and all."

Toohey looked at me for a few seconds, but instead of hitting the roof he said, "You'd better come on through."

I followed him down the darkened passage. "So where is everybody?" I said. "What about the dinner for the Parliamentary Joint Committee on dick pulling or whatever it was?"

"Cancelled because of this damned peace," he said over his shoulder.

We went out to the back room, where on most nights a high-stakes card game was held. There was no game tonight; the curtains were drawn and a dozen or so grim-faced men were sitting around a circular table under a single weak light. A bottle of Johnny Walker and numerous bottles of beer littered the table.

A few of the blokes nodded my way—a taxi driver named Cyril, a former bookie named Darcy, a worn-out heavy named Ernest. The other fellers completely ignored me.

Mick signaled me to help myself to a drink. I poured a glass of beer, then took a seat away from the table.

Mick poured himself a shot of scotch and said, "Gentlemen."

They turned respectfully towards him.

"This is a black day. For all of us."

There were nods and murmurs around the table.

"We stand tonight on the brink of a troubling and uncertain future. Soon the big-spending Yanks will be gone, and the local mugs will have spent all their back pay." More nods.

"As if that wasn't enough, there's been talk of liberalizing hotel trading hours, and bugger me, I've even heard that certain socialists in the state house have plans to not only *legalize* off-course betting,"—someone muttered "Bloody shame"—"but to *nationalize* it, too!

"Well, the philosophers tell us all good things must come to an end, and I wouldn't want to sound like a whinger. We've had a good war, and blow me down if we didn't teach the damned slanty-eyed saber-rattlers a lesson they'll not forget in a hurry"— some half-hearted "hear hears"—"and each one of us can feel justly proud of the part he played in maintaining the morale of our fighting men and our hard-pressed civilian population through the trying days recently passed, regardless of what the wowsers might have said."

"So let's not get too gloomy, gents. Not *all* the news is bad, after all. I understand that Mr. Chifley intends to keep rationing in place for the indefinite future. I have it on good authority that the coupon system will be maintained for up to five years."

Grunts of approval.

Mick went to the sideboard and returned with a bottle of scotch in each hand. He put them down in front of two of the men at the table, and continued until every man had a bottle.

"So enjoy the peace, if you can. For my part, I'm going to the late thanksgiving Mass at St. Mary's. If any of you would care to accompany me, you'd be more than welcome."

Blokes looked at their watches and stood up, muttering about having to get home and feed the cat, or that Mum would be getting worried. Mick shook hands with everyone, gave a reassuring pat on the shoulder or a kingly nod, and said a few words to each of them as they left. When they'd all gone Mick turned to me.

I stood up, saying, "I, er, I have to be at, somewhere. I mean I don't think I can—"

"Come with me," he said.

I followed him out to the passageway and down narrow stairs into the darkened cellar. We crossed the room and came to a reinforced and heavily padlocked door. Mick unlocked it and pushed it open.

Boxes were stacked everywhere—booze, cigs, nylons, toys, shirts and footwear, but also outdated ration coupons, powdery chocolates, rusted tins of bully beef.

Mick sat in the leather chair behind the large desk in the center of the room.

"Sit down, William."

There was no other chair. I moved aside a carton of cigarettes and plonked myself down on an old wooden tool chest.

He leaned back, closed his eyes, rubbed the bridge of his nose and sighed. I sat there and waited. Outside I could hear the mob carousing.

Toohey opened his eyes and looked at me levelly. From outside came the sound of shattering glass, but Mick didn't blink. He waited another half minute, then leaned forward, put his folded arms on the desk and said quietly, "What kind of bloke are you, Bill? Really."

"I'm a Souths supporter."

"I mean deep down."

"So do I."

There was another crash of broken glass and a shout went up. A flickering red glow appeared in the glass brick skylight, but Mick's gaze didn't waver.

He spoke slowly and deliberately. "There are two types of people in this world. Those you can trust and those you can't."

I nodded.

"Most people put themselves on the trustworthy team. And they play the part. They'll pat you on the back and tell you you're a great feller. As long as you're buying the drinks, at any rate. But slip over for just a moment and see what happens." He pointed at me, and clamped his teeth together. "They'll kick you to death, and laugh at you while they do it."

I nodded, sneaking a sly look at my wristwatch. It was ten to eight.

He sat back again. "You see, Bill, a lot of those people who *seem* staunch, and who believe themselves to be, really aren't so at all. They've just never been put to the test."

The red glow lit up the dead side of Mick's face, but he kept his eyes on me.

"The only *real* way to find out what a man's made of is to give him a chance to do you harm, and see how he behaves."

"That's an interesting angle you've got there, Mick, but I—"

"It's a hell of a rub." His voice became lower, quieter. "Which is why I never do it, never give them the chance."

He went silent again. Outside a siren wailed.

"How old are you now?"

"Eighteen."

Toohey nodded. "I knew your father from when we were children together till when he died, in—what year was it?"

"1938."

"Christ, that's gone quick. Your father was a good man, Bill. He was a squarehead—and I say it with great respect—but he was staunch. Your mother too. In my book, the Glasheens are near enough to blood relatives. But what are *you* made of, Bill? Are you loyal comrade or a rat? Are you a man or a boy? I mean, do you have *character*?"

"Well, I'm—"

"Frankly, I don't know. And nor do you. You *couldn't* know. Not yet."

I took another peek at my watch. Three minutes to eight. The Rocket Club was five minutes away, if I ran.

"Well Mick, you've certainly given me food for thought there, no doubt about it, but I—"

He raised his hand and sat forward in his chair.

"You're going to get your chance to find out."

"That's great Mick, but I—"

"I'm taking some time off."

"Oh yeah? Where're you going?"

"Never you mind about that. I need someone to look after things."

"You want *me* to run the show?"

"Not *everything*. Obviously."

"What then?"

He opened the desk drawer, took out a notebook and dropped it in front of me. "I want you to act as my property manager."

I picked up the book. Columns. Names and addresses, amounts written in pencil: ten, fifteen shillings, a quid, thirty bob.

"This is . . . a rent book?"

Mick nodded.

"You want me to be a *rent collector*?"

"There's a damn sight more to it than that. This is a chance for you to learn how business is really done, from the inside. It's not the sort of chance many of *my* generation were ever given, I might add."

"How many of these . . . properties are there?"

"A couple of dozen—houses and a fish shop. It normally takes a couple of hours to do the whole round. Collect every Friday."

"And, ah, how much do . . . ?"

"I'll pay you a fair commission."

"Up front?"

"We'll sort that out when I return. You'll be keeping an eye on my slot machines, as well. There are some peep shows at Luna Park and a jukebox at the Cross. You'll empty the coin boxes each week. All right?"

"Yeah, I suppose so."

"This will be for three or four weeks, but after I get back, if all goes well, we might see about you attending to it on a more permanent basis. You could do all right out of this."

Then Toohey got up from behind the desk, walked over to the corner of the room, and moved a couple of Johnnie Walker cartons to reveal a battered tin trunk.

"Give me a hand with this, feller."

We lifted it onto the desk and he unlocked it. Some hand tools, sets of keys, spare locks, yellowed tradesmen's receipts pinned together, more battered booklets tied up in rubber bands.

"Everything you'll need is in here."

He took a folded sheet of paper out of the drawer, put it in on top. "There's a lot to tell you, but I haven't time, not tonight. I've written out instructions."

"Yeah, all right."

Mick put his hand on my shoulder. "I don't like to do things in such a hasty, unplanned way, but it can't be helped. I'm relying on you, Bill. I hope to Christ I'm not making a mistake."

"Relax, Mick. How hard can it be? When are you going?"

"Tomorrow or the next day. Now pay attention. You're to follow those instructions to the letter." He stood in front of me, pointed his finger at me. "Don't accept either threepence more or less than the exact rent for each property. Understand?"

"No more, no less. Yeah, got it."

"Don't let yourself be conned by any of those bludging tenants. But don't take advantage of anyone, either. Do you understand?"

"Don't con. Don't *get* conned. Check!"

"I'll ring you on Friday night to see that everything went all right."

"What if I need to ask you something before that, or—?"

"You'll just have use your common sense. Now go and get the car, so you can take this trunk home with you." He glanced at his watch. "It's ten past eight. I've got things to do for the next hour or two, so leave it a while, then meet me back here at say, ten."

"What about your Mass?"

He waved the idea away. "That was to get rid of the mugs. Off you go now."

Outside the pub the Civilian Maimed and Limbless Association kiosk was ablaze, with a mob of drunken men and women dancing around it and not a cop in sight. A hundred yards away a fire engine sat stranded with its tires deflated and its hoses unwound.

I fairly sprinted to the Rocket Club, where they let me in without question. Herb Atkins' jump band was on stage playing "Caldonia." Every table was full, and a packed crowd of jive fiends were dancing wildly under the mirror ball. I stood inside the entrance and scanned the room—plenty of nice-looking girls, but no Molly.

The song finished and Herb announced a short break. He put down his sax and came over to me.

"Hey, Billy Boy. How's things? Come and have a drink."

"I can't stay. I'm looking for Molly Price."

"She was here until a half hour ago. I saw her leaving with a Yank bloke."

I punched the door frame. "Damn my luck!"

"Yeah. Listen, Bill. You carrying any petrol coupons?"

Herb was fresh out of Long Bay Jail. He'd been put away a year ago after shooting a bloke at the 2KY Radiotorium, moments before his band was to play. There had been some difference of opinion over a truckload of illicit whisky, and Herb had emphasized his displeasure by brandishing his beloved US Army issue Colt .45. In the confusion of the moment the gun discharged, and the bullet went through the curtain and lodged in the leg of an audience member who'd been quietly sitting waiting for the show to start.

Now Herb was out of the slot, back in his zoot suit, working with three or four different combos, and ripe for mischief.

"Petrol coupons? I might have a few," I said.

"How many have you got right now?"

I thumbed through the coupons in my pocket and then said, "Ten quid's worth."

"I'll take them."

We moved away from the door, into a darker corner of the room. Herb looked left and right then dug out a tenner. I fronted him the coupons.

Herb smiled. "Come and meet the gang before you go."

"I've got things to do."

"Have a quick drink with us. You could do some business."

He led me over to a table where a Yank serviceman and an Aussie girl were sitting. She was small, and had the blackest hair and the reddest lips I'd ever seen. Herb introduced her as Lucy

Chance and me as "Billy Glasheen, the bloke who always knows where lightning will strike next."

Lucy Chance looked me up and down, then our eyes locked. Call it chemistry, call it instinct, but whatever the reason, we hated each other at first sight.

Herb said, "Lucy here's a singer. She's terrific."

"Is that right?"

"My oath. But you can hear for yourself. She's doing a guest spot with us later on. We're sort of easing her into the professional entertainment caper."

She was doing her best to look bored, but when she lit a cigarette it was with quick, nervous movements.

I checked my watch. "That's a pleasure I might have to forego this time."

"If any of you need *anything*," Herb said to the table at large, "that is, anything I can't get you, then Bill here's your man. Speaking of which, since he's here now, why don't we have a whip around and get ourselves a bottle or two of scotch and kick on at my flat after? What do you say?"

Lucy Chance shook her head and said, "A bottle of whisky? *Tonight*? I don't think so."

Herb said, "Don't be too sure sweetheart. Lightning Billy here will do the right thing by us."

She turned to me and said, "Is that so?"

"Try me."

"All right. Can you get us a bottle of genuine scotch whisky? Now?"

In fact, scotch was the one thing I had trouble getting hold of. Mick Toohey didn't mind me running around town delivering *his* black-market booze, but in deference to my late father's wishes he'd always actively discouraged me from consuming or dealing in spirits.

I said, "Yeah, no worries."

"The hell with whisky," the American bloke said. "I can get that from the mess."

I could have kissed him.

"What I could *really* use is a good cigar. I haven't seen a single one in this whole goddamn country."

Lucy Chance turned back to me, looking like she'd read my thoughts.

"Well?"

"Cigars? I'll get you cigars," I said. In fact, if there was one thing harder to get than good whisky, it was cigars, especially good ones.

"You can?"

"Yeah, sure."

"What, tonight?"

"When else? Cuban good enough for you?"

He laughed, and so did the girl. They turned away.

"I'm serious," I said.

He turned back to me, smiling, "You telling me you can get a Havana cigar?"

"They'll cost you ten bob each."

"You get me a Havana, I'll give you a goddamn *pound*."

"It'll take me a little while. I've got something to do first."

"Sure, pal, we're not going anywhere." He was still laughing.

I walked back to the Haymarket. The air was filled with smoke, and bonfires smoldered on the corners. There were still gangs of rowdies roaming around, but the crowds were moving now, in the direction of Kings Cross. I got the car and drove it back to Martin Place without any trouble.

I pulled into the laneway at the back of the pub right on ten o'clock. Mick Toohey stepped quickly out of the shadows. I was ready for him to go crook about the dents in the car roof, but he scarcely gave it a glance.

22

He unlocked the back door of the pub and signaled to me to park the car and come in.

We made our way to the office in the cellar. The trunk was there, still open. Mick was brisk now. He clapped his hands together. "All right then. Remember what I told you. And don't take any checks. All right?"

"What do I do with the rent money—bank it?"

"No banks! Just hang on to it. I'll get it from you when I return. You need to be absolutely discreet about this. Understand?"

"Yeah, no risk."

"And as far as the tenants are concerned, my name is Mick Daniels, and I'm just the feller who collect the rents for a third party."

A telephone rang up in the main bar.

"Wait here," Mick said, hurrying out.

Once I was sure he was out of earshot, I had a scout around the office. I checked the cupboards, looked under the desk, and went through the stacks of merchandise on the floor, but found nothing. I went to the filing cabinet, which was sort of out of bounds, but I was getting desperate. I found the cigars in the second to bottom drawer. I picked up two boxes of Havanas, one of which was already opened, buried them as best I could under the bits and pieces inside the trunk, and quietly closed the lid.

I heard the bolt slide back on the heavy door upstairs and then Mick speaking quietly. There were footsteps, and a minute later Mick came back into the room, moving briskly.

He picked up a box of chocolates and put them in the trunk. "Give those to your mother with my compliments." He snapped the padlock closed and handed me the key. "There's one more thing I want you to do for me."

"What's that?"

"There's been a change in plan. I'm leaving right now, and I'll need you to run an errand for me tonight. You know the

23

Mansions Hotel at the Cross?"

"Yeah."

"I want you to go there now. There's a bloke staying there, in room fifteen. Tell him I sent you. Tell him I said I've got the register and ask him to ring me here. You got that? Mick has the register."

"What's the register?"

"Never mind. Just tell that to the feller in room fifteen—in person. Anyone else asks you about it, you don't know what they're talking about. All right?"

"Yeah, all right. What's happening about the pub here?"

"Closed for repairs, as of now."

"Who's upstairs?"

"Don't be a stickybeak. Just do as you're told. Now get on the other end of this, will you."

We picked up the heavy trunk between us, lugged it upstairs. There was a light on in the ladies saloon bar, and I could hear a radio playing "I Can't Get Started."

We carried the trunk out to the laneway and put it in the boot of the car. I slammed it shut and got ready to drive off.

Mick came over to the window. "You know what you have to do. The ball's in your court now, Bill."

"Is everything all right, Mick?"

He looked at me with a strange, bright-eyed expression, like he was enjoying a very private joke. The side of his mouth that worked was smiling now. "Perfectly. Whatever happens, do as I told you and use your nous. As for me—" He paused. "For me, it's the Devil's jump." And then he laughed. Which easily ranked as the strangest thing that had happened that whole strange day.

"What?"

Toohey just shook his head, turned around, and walked back into the pub.

2

Bonfires were still smoldering as I drove through the city center. Drunks were sleeping it off in doorways.

I turned into William Street and came to a barricade of police cars and fire engines. A wall of coppers stood further up the street facing Kings Cross, where crowds of younger servicemen, girls, and fellers in zoot suits had reassembled.

A red-faced copper approached the car and waved at me impatiently. "Turn around, driver. No one past this point."

I leaned out and said, "I have an urgent message to deliver. I have to get through."

He straightened up slightly. "No more cars in there."

I grabbed a handful of coupons from the glove box, held them out to the copper and said, "Look, this is an emergency. Isn't there any way I can drive through?" I smiled.

The cop took the coupons and stared at them for a few seconds. He stood back, looked over the car, then zeroed in on me. I was wearing a tan zoot suit, silk tie, navy blue shirt. The car, despite the fresh dents on the bonnet, was a '38 model, which was near enough to being new at that point. Without taking his eyes off me, the cop slowly and methodically tore the coupons up into little pieces and threw them to the ground.

He leaned in and said in a voice I didn't care for at all, "How old are you?"

"Twenty-one." I was giving myself an extra three years, but I'd repeated the lie often enough that it almost felt true.

"All right mister twenty-one. Go home. Understand? If I even *see* you again, I'll slot you. Now piss off."

I reversed and drove through the back streets of Darlinghurst, all the way round to Bayswater Road, but ran into another barricade. Then I circled around through Elizabeth Bay, trying to get in from the Potts Point end—another roadblock. The Cross had been sealed off. The cops were letting people out of the cordon, to go home, but no one was getting in.

The Mansions Hotel was at the corner of Bayswater Road and Kellet Street, in the very center of the Cross. I could have parked the car and tried to make it up there on foot through the mob. But I figured that if I came back in an hour or two, I'd likely be able to drive right to the door to deliver the message.

I walked in to the Rocket Club with the cigar boxes under my overcoat. There was a large group sitting at Lucy Chance's table. I guessed she had already done her guest spot, because she was smiling broadly now.

I walked over and sat down next to the Yank. "All right then," I said. "You wanted a Havana? Be my guest." I opened the box and held it out to him.

Lucy Chance leaned over and reached inside. "What's *this*?" she said, holding up a folded sheet of paper. She sniffed it. "Hmm. Perfumed, too. What *could* it be?" She smiled and began to unfold the paper.

"Oh cripes," I said. She laughed as I snatched the paper out of her hand.

I put the letter back in the box, then ran my thumbnail through the seal on the other box. I felt my face turning red.

"I hope it's not your stamp collection in this one, pal," the

Yank said.

Relieved to see it actually contained cigars, and feeling more than a bit cranky, I said, "Take one."

"Don't mind if I do. Ten shillings you say?"

"Nah, stuff that. They're on me. It's only a cigar and I can get truckloads of them." And I handed the rest of them out around the table.

Lucy Chance turned to me, and smiled a big, false smile. "Shame on you, Mr. Glasheen! You came here to do business, but you've given all your merchandise away."

"Yeah. Something you wouldn't understand."

"I suppose that explains why you're still wearing a zoot suit."

"What's wrong with the suit?"

"Well, no offence, of course, but I would have thought they were just a little bit old hat now." She turned to the American. "Isn't that right, Tad?"

"Whatever you say, sweetheart. Hell, it's all darkie wear anyhow."

She turned back to me, patted me on the forearm. "Keep saving your pennies," she said. "I'm sure you'll get there sooner or later."

She got up, said to her companion, "Let's go, Tad."

The Yank stood up and shook my hand. "Hey, thanks for the cigar."

I sat around for another half hour. When the band finished up at one, Herb came over and said, "What happened to the gang?"

"They left."

He nodded, looked thoughtful for a moment. "You feel like earning a few bob?"

"Doing what?"

He reached in his pocket, then held out his open palm. He was holding two pennies. "Two-up."

I took the pennies out of his hand, turned them over, then picked one up by the edges, held it sideways against the light. "This one's dished."

He nodded. "They'll come up tails more often than not. It works best with two people. You in?"

"If anyone springs us, we'll have a blue on our hands."

Herb shrugged. "We'll just play against Pommies. Or Yanks. I'll toss, you back tails."

I looked at my watch. "I've got a message to run first. I'll be back."

When I drove back up William Street, the coppers were still there, but they weren't stopping cars. I drove through the crowd, which was thinner now, and parked near the Mansions. The plate glass in the guests entrance at the side was smashed, and a sheet of three-ply had been hastily nailed over it. I pressed the after-hours bell and heard a ring inside somewhere, but no one came. I called out a big hello, but still no one came. There were no lights on. I went around the front, banged on the door to the bar, then went back to the guest entrance and gave it a couple of whacks.

A group of soldiers and girls walked past, their arms linked.

"You won't do any good there, pal," one of them called out. "We already tried. They've battened down the hatches."

I went back to the Rocket Club and collected Herb. We drove up to Taylor Square, where there were plenty of people milling about, and started a two-up game in a side street. We did all right.

When I got back home to Marrickville at five in the morning, my pockets stuffed with pound notes, my mum was sitting up in the kitchen. She looked older than her forty years.

"G'day, Mum. Why are you up this late?"

"Your brother's back. Got in last night. He's sleeping in the sunroom," she said.

"Old Ronald himself, eh? How is he?"

She smiled. "He's good."

"Is there anything to eat?"

"There's bread, but no butter."

"What about those coupons I gave you other day?"

"I gave them to Mrs. Garside."

"You should have told me if you were running low. There's no need for us to run out." I pulled a handful of crumpled pound notes and ration coupons out of my pocket, whacked them down on the kitchen table. "There you go, put that towards the house-keeping."

She gave me a worried look.

My brother walked into the kitchen, looking leaner than last time I'd seen him, nearly a year before. He went over to the stove and set fire to a half smoked roll-your-own.

"How are you, William?" he said quietly, smiling a little, but not quite looking directly at me.

"Good. How was the war?"

"One big party."

He glanced at the money on the table. "How was the home front?"

"Hell."

He looked my way, still smiling. "But not so bad that it interfered with your supply of silk shirts."

"Got to keep up appearances, haven't you?"

"I suppose you have."

Mum stood up, filled the kettle and put it on the stove. Ron came over and stood next to me, looked at the top of my head. "What are you, now?" he said. "Five-ten? Middleweight?"

"Something like that."

Then he shaped up and threw a punch, pulled up short. I responded in kind.

Ron grinned and said, "You still haven't got my speed, though, have you?" He gave my shoulder an easy shake and sat down.

"So what are you doing for a crust?" he said.

Mum answered before I could. "He's got some very important responsibilities for such a young fellow," she said. "Mick Toohey says he's doing *very* well."

"Oh yeah," I said. "Mick sent you some chocolates, Mum. They're in the car."

Ron was still looking at me. "Important responsibilities, eh? And a motor car, no less." He nodded his head in mock admiration.

"I've been bringing in a quid, at least," I said.

Ron eyed the money on the table. "Very impressive." But his face went sour as he said it.

"But?"

"Nothing."

"Go on, speak your mind, Ron."

He turned away. "Well, I'm just back, and you're not a kid anymore, I know, and I probably shouldn't be sticking my nose in, but—oh forget it, mate."

"Spit it out, for Christ's sake."

"It's just that doing that sort of work—"

"Yeah?"

He looked at me. "Was that really the best choice you could have made?"

"You have a better idea?"

"You could have signed up, once you were eighteen. Still could, for that matter. I know blokes younger than you who did."

"And sat around in central Queensland playing draughts in an army camp? Swept up in Hiroshima for five shillings a day? It's been all over bar the shouting for the last year. Everyone knew that except the Japs."

"Try telling that to the blokes who died this last year. But

30

that's not what I meant, Bill. A bit of time in the service—away from the frontline—might just have done you some good. You could have learned a trade or something."

"Really?"

"And met up with some decent fellers. You know, *good* blokes. Instead of no-hopers."

"No-hopers?"

"You know what I mean. Mum filled me in. You're running around with that bloke Perkal, and that jailbird, Atkins."

Neither of us spoke.

"Oh for God's sake, stop it, both of you," Mum said. She picked up the money from the table, counted it out, and held out half of it to Ron.

He shook his head. "I don't want it," he said quietly.

"Yeah, I'm with him. I don't want him to have it, either," I said. "Or no, let him have it. I can make that two or three times over any time I like."

Ron left the room.

Mum looked at me and shook her head. "You shouldn't tease him like that, Bill." She said good night and went to bed.

I drank a glass of milk, and when everyone had settled down, I went and got the trunk from the car, and dragged it into my bedroom.

I fetched the cigar box I'd left sitting on the back seat, went to my room and shut the door. The letters in the cigar box *were* perfumed. I unfolded one and peeked at the first line.

My darling Mick,
I'm counting the days until we can be together again . . .

I laughed out loud. Some old sheila was writing gooey letters to Misery! And he was keeping them. I tried to picture her. It wasn't hard: a former blonde bombshell, well on the fade, a little wide in the haunches maybe, and wearing too much lipstick, but not too bad for all that. Perhaps a one-time Tivoli girl.

I thought what a hoot it would be to show the letter to Cyril and the crew back at the Durban Club. But maybe not—those old boys could get a bit sensitive about that sort of thing. Maybe they all had old girls tucked away who wrote them love letters. And I knew for sure Mick wouldn't take too kindly to me having a laugh at his love life. I carefully folded the letter again and put it back in the cigar box.

I slipped out of the house the next day at eleven and drove straight to the Mansions Hotel. Kings Cross was a mess, paper and rubbish and ashes and broken glass everywhere. Crowds were still carousing, though nothing like the night before.

There was a feller sweeping up in the foyer. I strode past him and straight up the stairs. He called out to me, but I ignored him. I knocked on the door of room fifteen. No answer. I knocked again, louder.

I turned around and the sweeper was coming up behind me, looking cranky.

"G'day, dad," I said. "I'm looking for the feller in this room."

He shook his head. "He's shot through!"

I stood there a second, not sure what to do. "When did he go?"

"He was gone this morning. He owes me two weeks board."

I started walking then stopped. "What was the bloke's name?"

The feller drew on the rolly in his mouth. "The dirty, rotten, filthy blighter! And you can clear out too."

When I got home mid-afternoon, Mum was wide-eyed and anxious. "Thank God you're back," she said. "The police have just been here."

"I always knew Ronny would come to a bad end."

"They were looking for *you*."

"Little me? Whatever for?"

"There's been a fire at the Durban Club. The place has been burned right out."

My heart thumped, but I did my best to look calm. "What did the cops want?"

Mum shook her head, pushed her hair back. "They wouldn't say. Oh God, Billy, what have you got mixed up in?"

"It's nothing to worry about, Mum. Fair dinkum. Mick Toohey's got something on, very hush-hush."

"The police want you to go in and see them. The chap in charge said if he had to come looking for you he'd be most put out."

"Oh yeah? Who was that?"

"A detective named Mr. Waters. You will go and see him, Billy, won't you?"

"Yeah, no worries."

"Ron's absolutely ropable."

"Don't worry about him," I said. "Listen Mum, I'm going into the city. If Mick Toohey rings, tell him I wasn't able to deliver his message last night. He'll understand."

"What message?"

"Never mind."

I drove back into town and cruised slowly past the burnt out Durban Club. A barricade had been erected in front of the door. The windows were smashed in, it was blackened inside, and wisps of smoke still rose from the ruins. Through the window I could see a lone fireman poking around. I didn't stop.

I remained in the city for the rest of the afternoon, played some more two-up. At six o'clock I rang home to check if there'd been any word from Mick Toohey. There hadn't.

At seven o'clock I slipped down to the Hole in the Wall cafe, the twenty-four-hour joint at Central, and ordered a mixed grill. I ate it ravenously. A man across the other side of the café was looking at me curiously. He had his hair cut short back and sides, and was wearing a rumpled blue serge suit. Possibly a member of the King's constabulary.

When I finished eating, he came over to my table and sat down. "What's your name, son?"

"My mum told me not to talk to strangers."

He tilted his head slightly, giving me another chance. I thought I'd better take it.

"Bill Glasheen."

"Address?"

"Hang on a second. Who are you?"

"Sergeant Jennings. You better come with me. They want to talk to you at the station."

"What made you pick on me?"

"That suit. Come on, now."

I could have chucked a turn, but I thought, best to get it over with. I picked up my hat, paid for my meal, and followed him outside.

"Who wants to talk to me?" I said.

He didn't answer, just pointed to his car parked right there on Pitt Street.

We drove up towards Darlinghurst Police Station. After a few minutes silence Jennings said, "Didn't you get the message to contact Detective Sergeant Waters?"

I didn't say anything. He turned around and said, "Answer me when I speak to you. Why didn't you come in and see us?"

"I was going to. Later."

He didn't say anything more. At Darlo I was made to wait in an empty room. I waited. And waited. Nothing happened.

Then two blokes came into the room. One of them was a fat-tish, ruddy-faced man in a double breasted suit. Ray Waters. The other feller was a younger, bigger bloke.

Waters sat down opposite me while the young bloke paced back and forth, his hands in his pockets. Waters looked at me for a couple of seconds, then said, "You do work for Misery Toohey?"

"Sometimes."

"When did you see him last?"

I hesitated.

"You don't need to think about it. Just answer the question."

"Last night," I said.

"Where and when, exactly?"

"At the Durban Club. I was delivering some rabbits."

"Of course you were," he said. "What time was that?"

"Around eleven."

"Did Toohey mention anything about going away?"

"Has something happened?"

Waters leaned forward. "Just answer the questions truthfully. Did Toohey say he was going away?"

I hesitated a moment too long. "No."

Waters nodded, looked at the other copper and smiled. He turned back to me and said, "Have you spoken to Toohey to-day?"

"No." Quickly this time.

"You're sure of that, now?"

"Yes."

"Do you have any idea of Mick Toohey's current where-abouts?"

"I wouldn't have a clue."

He nodded slowly. "I'm going to ask you a question now, Glasheen. I want you to think very carefully before you answer. Did Toohey say anything about a register?"

The other bloke had stopped pacing.

"What do you mean?" I said. "The *cash* register?"

35

Waters slowly shook his head. "I mean *the* register."

I felt suddenly hot and clammy. "I don't know what you mean."

He waited a second or two, looked at the other feller, then narrowed his small eyes. He didn't say anything, just kept staring at me. It was more unnerving than if he'd clouted me.

"Do you have a job, Glasheen?"

"Yeah."

"And where would that be?"

"I'm on the payroll at the Invincible Brass Foundry, at Redfern."

Which was true. I'd had a nominal job there since I'd swapped my school suit for a zoot suit back in 1942. I paid an intermediary five bob a week, and the foundry kept me on their books as a factory hand, which had kept me sweet with the Manpower Commission.

"What's the foreman's name there?"

I hesitated a second, then said, "Arthur, something. Arthur *Jones*, that's it."

Waters leaned forward. "You're a bullshit artist, Glasheen. Turn out your pockets."

I did so. He picked up my wallet, took out a wad of coupons and all my paper money. He looked at the coupons.

"You've got quite a bit more than the normal allocation here, Glasheen."

He counted the paper money. Twenty three pounds. He separated out twelve pounds, carefully folded it and slipped it into his top pocket, along with the coupons. He put the remaining money back in the wallet and handed it to me.

"Look, it's simple. If you can get me any information about the register, you'll be rewarded. But if you try to play silly buggers, you'll suffer. If you find the register, or if you hear anything about it, anything at all, then contact me and no one else.

You can ring here any time. If I'm not in, leave a message that you want to speak to me. That's all. Don't mention the register. Understand?"

I looked at the other bloke. He had his hands out of his pockets, ready to go the thump. I looked back to Waters and shrugged my shoulders.

The feller standing off to the side gave me a whack on the back of the head with his open palm.

"Answer Mr. Waters!"

"Yeah, I understand."

"All right then," Waters said. "You can fuck off now."

I didn't know if I'd handled it right or not. I badly wanted to talk to Toohey. But there was no word from him that night, nor on Friday morning.

The next afternoon was my first scheduled rent collection, and since there'd been nothing to indicate a change of plan, I acquainted myself with Toohey's written instructions, togged up, then set off after lunch to collect.

The properties were spread through an area that taxi drivers called "the Horseshoe," a ring of run-down districts which all but circled the city, from the Woolloomooloo waterfront all the way around to Pyrmont.

The first collect was easy enough, an old woman in Stanley Street. I told her who I was and showed her the authorization Toohey had given me. She gave me her eleven shillings; I wrote out a receipt. I cracked a little joke, but she didn't smile.

Next place there was no one home, nor at the one after that. Then I bagged two in a row. At five o'clock I knocked on a door in Palmer Street, the residence of one Jimmy Stevenson. I could smell cooking inside, and a light was on, but no one answered. I knocked again, then left, thinking, bugger it, I'll catch up next week. As I got back in the car I saw a little girl peeping through the front window from behind a curtain.

The next address was 36 Oxford Street, in Paddington. It was a barber shop. The cranky old feller inside told me to bugger off, he owned the property outright, and if I was trying on a bit of standover then I might just get more than I bargained for.

I went outside, checked my list. The address appeared to be correct. I worked my way around the Horseshoe, stuffing ten-shilling and one-pound notes into my jacket pockets. I stopped at a newsagent in Ultimo, swapped all my coin for more notes and pressed on. At six thirty I hit the fish shop in Glebe Point Road. The Greek behind the counter greeted me with a big smile, and said, "Hello, boss, you want some beautiful fish and chip?" The smile faded when I told him I wanted the rent. He took three pound notes from the till and passed them to me.

"How old you?" he asked suspiciously.

"Old enough, brother." I wrote out his receipt and left.

I checked my watch. Maybe Mick was able to do the rent round in a couple of hours, but I'd been on the job well over three and I was still only three-quarters done. I decided to leave the rest till the next day, and adjourned to the Toxteth Hotel up the road for a quick couple before closing time, then kicked on to the greyhounds.

I got in at ten. Toohey still hadn't rung.

I slept late the next day. At midday I went out to hit the last few collects, all in the Chippendale area. If you just went by the street names there—*Myrtle, Vine, Rose, Pine, Ivy*—you'd get the wrong idea about the place, like it was a cute little bungalow estate. It wasn't anything like that. These were narrow streets of dark ter-raced houses and decrepit weatherboard cottages. Clouds of coal smoke drifted in day and night from the Eveleigh rail workshops. The houses were all a grimy brown color, and every window sill and horizontal surface was coated with soot. There were bugger-all trees of any species to be seen.

I parked the Chev outside the first house in Rose Street. I got the rent all right and headed off on foot to the next house, forty yards along. People were in the street, out in front of their houses, chatting over the front fences. Somewhere I could hear a race being broadcast. Further down the street some young blokes were kicking a football. I copped cold stares from the loungers. I wished I hadn't worn the suit. A kid stepped in front of me, cheekily asked me to give him a zack. I told him I'd give him a clip under the ear if he didn't piss off.

The next collect on my list was one Jack Carmody, a wiry old leprechaun of a bloke. I told him I was the new rent collector.

He handed over the money and said, "So you've taken over from Misery, have you?"

"What?" I said.

The old feller shook his head. "The landlord. Mick Toohey."

"Oh," I said. "Mick just collects for . . . someone else."

He smiled. "Listen pal, I *know* Toohey owns this place."

"Whatever you say, uncle."

I went around the corner to the last two houses, collected all right from both of them, then walked back to where the car was parked, relieved to be finished. When I got there the blokes I'd seen kicking the football earlier were gathered around it.

A feller in a leather coat said, "Good car here, mate."

"Yeah." I stepped past him.

"Give us a drive, will you."

"Go and root your boot," I said.

He took a swing at me, but I was waiting for it, and dodged it. I got him with a left which settled him down a bit, but then someone whacked me from behind. I threw a wild punch which connected with nothing and then somebody hit me on the side of the head. I copped a kick in the shin and a punch in the stomach.

39

Another punch knocked me half silly. When I came to, I was lying on the deck, hands rifling my pockets.

The rifler grabbed the rent money, the whole two days worth. "You little beauty!" he said. I sat up, dizzy, and saw the thugs disappearing around the corner. The street was empty.

When I got home, I totted up how much of Toohey's rent money I'd lost. It was nearly fifty pounds.

I woke up Sunday thinking about the money, dreading my next conversation with Toohey. When I came out to breakfast my brother said, "So black marketeering wasn't enough for you? I hear you've become a bloody rent collector now."

Mum said, "Leave him alone, Ron."

"Who told you I was collecting rents?"

"A mate of mine saw you yesterday. Who are you working for?"

"None of your business."

"And why the hell were the coppers here yesterday? What's going on?"

Mum looked at me anxiously.

"That's all been straightened out," I said. "It didn't really concern me. Other than that I'm just doing my job and minding my own business."

"You're working for that reptile Mick Toohey, aren't you?

My mum said to Ron, "Don't be too hard on Mick Toohey. He was good to us when your father died."

"Don't be too impressed by friend Toohey, either of you," he said. "He's only out for himself. He's an exploiter and a profiteer. He takes and takes and puts nothing back."

"Get off the soap box, Ron," I said.

Ron laughed. "How much does he charge those people? Half their weekly wages? More? A working man can't get any sort of wage rise, even a small one, but the landlords keep hiking up the rents on properties that aren't fit for a dog." Ron was standing up now, almost shouting. "*This* is what I've come back to. Christ, it's bloody crook."

I took a seat at the table. "Well if you feel that strongly, Ron," I said, "Why don't you go down to the Domain, stand under a tree, and tell that to your red mates—and let me have my breakfast in peace?"

Ron was already around the table and about to go the thump, when a shuddering sob stopped him in his tracks. We both turned around. Mum was sitting at the end of the table, crying into a hanky.

Ron went over and put his arm around her shoulder. "Come on, Mum. There's no need for that."

She kept her head down, sobbing. Ron bent over and said, "Chin up, old girl."

She blew her nose and wiped her eyes. "Your father wanted you two to get along," she said.

He nodded in my direction. "Yeah, and he wanted young William here to be a decent sort, too, not some kind of bodgie American lurk merchant. I'm sorry, but it's about time *someone* gave him the mail."

"Shut up, Ron, and listen to me." Her voice was hard now. She looked from Ron to me, then back at him. "Get this straight, both of you. There'll be no fighting in this house. You don't have to like each other, but while you're under this roof you'll behave like brothers. If you can't do that, you can find somewhere else to live. That goes for you, too, Bill."

"Sweet with me," I said.

I went into the city that afternoon. Things had settled down since Victory in the Pacific Day, as it was being called, but there were still plenty of people about. The cold wind had died down and the sun was out. Couples were strolling in the park and around the Quay. There were men in uniform standing around in small groups, and others, recently demobbed, looking awkward in old civvies.

I ambled down to the Rocket Club, half-hoping to see Molly, though I knew it was probably too late to collect on her promise. She wasn't around anyway. The place was half full of dancers. I flogged some coupons to the head waiter then spotted Herb Atkins and Max Perkal sitting at a table in the shadows. Herb saw me and walked over quickly.

He drew me aside and said, "Billy, have you got any coupons?"

"How many do you want?"

"As many as you can get. A hundred. A thousand. Five thousand. Ten thousand."

"Strewth! I wouldn't have fifty."

"Well can you get hold of some? I've got a bulk buyer."

"It's tricky, Herb."

"Can't you just go to your bloke and place a bulk order?"

"That's not so easy at this particular moment." For the past ten months I'd been buying fake coupons from a sergeant with contacts in the army printery, but he'd been killed at Balikpapan six weeks before.

"My buyer's got cash money," Herb said.

"How do you know he's not an undercover man?"

"The Blighter vouched for him."

"Who?"

"You know, the Filthy Blighter."

"This is serious, Herb. We need to be sure of this bloke."

Herb slapped his forehead. "Blimey, what do you want me to say? The Filthy Blighter in person, to me, vouched for this feller. Christ, how much more do you need?"

"Oh shit. Right. The Filthy Blighter. To be honest I thought it was something like 'the man outside Hoyts,' or 'Dooley Franks from Parramatta,' or 'Blind Freddy' … You know, there's no such bloke, it's just a way of saying, 'mind your own business.'"

"Actually, there really was a Blind Freddy, but that's another story. The Filthy Blighter is a real feller all right. I'm surprised you don't know him. I thought everybody did. Anyway, he vouched for this buyer, and that's good enough for me."

"The coupon buyer, what's his name?"

Herb looked foxy. "Now, Bill, if I told you that, what sort of a mug would I be?"

"Well it's too bad, Herb. My supply has dried up."

We went over and sat down at the table with Max Perkal, who appeared to be dozing. The waiter brought us a plate of sandwiches and glasses of beer.

Then, without really meaning anything much by it, I said, "Of course, Herb, if we had any brains at all, we'd be printing our own coupons. That's the way to earn the real money. I mean, it's not like they're pound notes—just a bit of green cardboard and some printing."

"Easy to say," Herb said, "but you try getting near a printery these days without the Rationing Commission, or the Manpower Authority, or the cops, or the Department of Supply coming down on you."

"They leave Mick Toohey's printery alone."

"Yeah? Where's that?"

"Herb, if I was to tell you that, what sort of mug would I be? Anyway, forget it. We haven't got the right paper, we haven't got the plates, and we're not printers."

"Fuckin' hell," Max said, rousing himself. "I can operate a printing press."

Herb and I looked at him.

"What do you know about printing?" I said.

"Plenty. You learn these things growing up in a family of militants," he said. "Leaflets, handbills, newsletters—all that shit. You get me the right plates, I can get the paper, and I'll print your

43

bloody coupons."

Herb said, "I can get the plates."

Max and I stared at him now. "You can?" I said.

Herb nodded. As well as blowing tenor sax, Herb worked as a subeditor for the music papers, so it wasn't out of the question that he would know someone.

"If we were to do it," he said, "we could cut three ways. But what about the owner of your printery? Would we have to cut him in too?"

"If we move quick, that won't be necessary."

"So, we're on then?"

"Yeah," I said. "You get the plates and we'll see what we can do," thinking that would be the end of it.

I stayed and mingled for another hour, then before I left called Herb to one side.

"Listen Herb, this feller, the Filthy Blighter. What's his real name?"

"I wouldn't have the foggiest. He's just the Blighter. Why?"

"I need to get in touch with him."

"The coupon buyer is *my* contact, get that straight."

"No, this is something else. I was supposed to deliver a message to him, but I stuffed up."

"To tell you the truth, Bill, I wouldn't know how to find him. He gets down here sometimes. Or you see him at the Troc. Or the fights."

"What does he look like?"

"He's a pommy. At least, he talks like one. Ex-army or something. Tallish, thin, brown hair, a bit long."

"Age?"

"Oh, thirty or so. Hard to tell. Why are you asking me this?"

"Never mind. The Blighter, does he work?"

"Fucked if I know."

I had a feed at the Cross, then went up to the Mansions Hotel and banged on the side door. Eventually the old publican opened up.

"What do you want?"

"I was here the day after VP Day, looking for a bloke. But you told me he'd shot through. You called him a filthy blighter."

"What of it?"

"Did you mean the feller was a wretch and a scallywag, or did you mean *the* Filthy Blighter?"

"I meant he was a dirty rotten mongrel, and if you see him, tell him I want my fifteen quid. Now piss off."

I drifted up to the Roosevelt Club, then from there I kicked on with some Yanks, ended up in a poker game in a flat at Elizabeth Bay. I lost a bit of money at the start, then made a comeback. By midnight I was ahead by nearly enough to square up the lost rent money.

One bloke, a half-pissed supply sergeant, had already done most of his dough when we hit the big hand of the night. Everybody had a bet on the first round. I had a full house, three jacks and a pair of eights, and put down a big bet on the strength of it.

The others folded, but this sergeant thought he was on to something. I'd kept an eye on him all night. His facial expression always corresponded perfectly with how good his hand was. This time I guessed he had either two pair or three of a kind. I raised the stake by twenty quid to put him out. But he wouldn't go. He tried to borrow some money from his pals. They all refused, laughing, saying he already owed them more than he could pay.

He called them a bunch of lousy mean fucks who weren't worth shit. The bloke next to me said quietly, "Here we go again."

"Fuck all of you," said the sergeant. He turned to me and said, "I'm not out yet, pal. I'll write you an IOU. It's just till the end of

45

this hand, 'cause I'm going to whip your ass."

I shook my head. "You know the drill," I said, "you bet cash money or else you fold."

"Bullshit I'll fold. Will you accept goods in kind? I can beat you, Aussie, and if you don't give me a fighting chance then you're a rotten chickenshit."

"What do you mean, goods in kind?"

"Better than twenty crummy Aussie pounds, I'll tell you *that* for nothing."

"What is?"

"A shed full of good US war surplus, that's fuckin' what."

"Where? Guadalcanal? San Diego?

"No, smartass, nearby. I'll stake the whole shed against that pissant pot there. If I lose, which I won't, you have my guarantee. I might be a slob, but I've never welched in my life, and these guys will vouch for that."

"That's not how it's done."

At that the mood turned. I still don't know if it was a set up from the start, but suddenly I was one Aussie among a half dozen Yanks, all of whom were very strongly of the opinion that I should take the sergeant at his word. So I agreed.

He turned over a pair of aces and a pair of tens. I quickly took the pot and stood up.

"All right, then. This shed, where is it?" I said.

The sergeant stood up, too. "I said I've never welched and it's the goddamn truth. You got a car?"

Fifteen minutes later we were outside a padlocked shed in a back lane in Woolloomooloo. I didn't like it at all. There were three of them and just one of me. The sergeant opened the door and flicked a switch. The weak light revealed the shed to be empty but for a single battered crate. I turned to the Yank. "You mean all this is mine?"

He walked over to the crate. "*This* is yours."

I followed him over, peeked inside the box. Greasy dungarees. I picked up a pair. "What good are these?" I said.

There was silence. Then one of the Yanks said, "You ever decide to pick cotton, you already got a head start." They laughed.

The sergeant said, "There's a hundred pair here. Clean 'em up, sell them as war surplus. If you don't make twenty Aussie pounds with that, you can fuck me." More laughter.

There was nothing for it but to load them into the boot of the car and go home.

I was spared having to tell Toohey about his lost rent money all that week, because he didn't ring. Which was beginning to seem very odd, given how particular he was.

When I went out to collect the rents the next Friday, there were fewer defaulters. I knocked louder, persisted longer, gave less of an ear to hard-luck stories. But the Stevensons' house in Palmer Street still didn't yield, although again I was certain there were people inside.

I cruised past the barber shop at 36 Oxford Street and parked the car. I walked along Oxford Street, turned right at the Albury Hotel, then down Barcom Avenue and into Boundary Street.

A little way down, between a house and a block of flats, there was a rubble path that wound up the slope towards the rear of the shops that fronted onto Oxford Street. I trudged up the path and came to a T-junction. A narrow lane ran left and right along the back of the shops. I turned left, and at the end of the lane came to a gate and an old letterbox.

I walked through a small, overgrown yard to the rear of the barber shop. There was a whole residence tucked away back here. The door was locked. Through the window I could see an old kitchen and a hallway running off it. The place was obviously unoccupied.

I went around the front again and walked into the barber shop.

"That place I was looking for, it's out the back," I said.

The barber said nothing.

"It's joined to this shop."

"It's a separate title."

"People must have a bit of trouble finding it," I said.

"Yeah," he said. "But if they don't know, I say, bugger them. They've probably got no business there anyway." He winked.

"Yeah, I get you." I said. Old time Paddo. If you don't know what's what, then you can get nicked.

"Been empty for long, has it?" I said.

"A bloke used to live there on his own. Moved out a few weeks ago. Don't know what happened to him."

Again I called it quits after I'd collected from the Glebe fish shop, and adjourned to the Toxteth for a brew. It was packed and noisy. I took my beer to the end of the bar, sat down on a stool and looked over the form guide for the next day's races. Then the lights went out. A collective groan went up. The barmaids weren't put out; they had kero lamps and candles ready, and were soon pulling beers again.

"Bludging power workers," I said to a couple of blokes next to me. "Wouldn't work in an iron lung."

One of them nodded in the direction of my paper. "The printers are out too. It'll be the bread carters and slaughtermen next week. Cripes, we can only be thankful the barmaids haven't gone out yet."

"It's the bloody commos," he said.

I nodded.

The other feller said quietly into his beer, "We'll sort them out soon enough, though."

I turned around to face him.

He was a hard looking cove, with a healed-over dent on his forehead. He looked my way, then leaned closer and said quietly, "You did your bit during the war, did you, son?"

"Well, yes, I suppose I did."

He nodded slowly, then in a low voice said, "A few good returned men are getting together. We'll give the reds a good kick in the arse when the right time comes, depend on it."

"Fair dinkum?" I finished my beer. "Good for you. See you later."

He leaned over and said, "No names, no pack drill, all right?"

3

When I got home, Mum said Herb had rung four times already that afternoon. The phone rang again as she was talking.

"Thank Christ you're there," Herb said.

"What's the row? The Japs gone back to war or something?"

"I've got the plates. We're ready to go."

"Eh?"

"For the, you know, coupons. Max is all lined up. We can do it tonight, as soon as I finish playing."

"Tonight?"

"You said you could get us into your printery. That was true, wasn't it?"

"It's dinkum, don't you worry. But it's a bit sudden, isn't it? I thought we'd look into it a bit more first."

"Listen Bill, tonight's just right. The printers are out on strike. This is our best chance."

"It all seems a bit hasty. Where's Max?"

"He's here with me. Come on Bill, don't let us down on this. Are you on side?"

Mick Toohey was incommunicado, so there was no way for me to clear it with him. Which was difficult in one way—but if he remained in the dark about it, there'd be no need to cut him in.

"I suppose so."

"That's the spirit. We're working at the Rocket till nine. Come in and pick us up then."

They were both more than half shot when we finally left the Rocket Club, sometime after ten. We went first to the Perkal family newsagency in Stanmore to collect half a dozen stacks of hard-to-get green cardboard that Max had managed to pinch. From his dad, I guessed.

We loaded up, had sandwiches and a cup of tea in the kitchen, then drove off. It was a cold night, and the streets were empty. I turned the radio on. There was a live broadcast from the Hawaiian Club. I went to change the station and Max said, "Leave it on."

"I hate that Hawaiian stuff," I said. "Drives me bats."

"You probably haven't listened to it the right way," Max said. "I'll tell you what, comrade," —he reached into his jacket pocket and brought out a hand-rolled ciggy—"You have a go of that."

"Max, you know I don't smoke."

"This is different."

"What is it?"

"Gage."

"Eh?"

"Texas Tea. Mexican Spinach. Maitland madness. Loco weed. Indian Hemp. Gangster. Marijuana."

I looked at him.

"It's a reefer, Billy, for Christ's sake."

"Thanks all the same, but no."

"Why not?"

"I don't want to become a dope fiend. I saw a newsreel about it once."

Herb and Max both laughed.

"It's true," I said. "There was this girl. A good sort. She smokes a reefer and then another and then she gets hooked and has to become a prostitute so she can get more dope."

Max kept giggling.

I said to him, "Well, you're as silly as a two bob watch at the best of times, so it probably wouldn't make much difference to you. But that sort of thing's not for stronger-minded types." I turned to Herb. "That's right, Herb, eh?"

Herb just grinned.

"Well, isn't it?"

"To tell you the truth, Bill, it's not *exactly* like in the newsreel."

I was silent for a while. "You don't get hooked?"

"Not on this, you don't."

"But what about the coppers?"

"It's a hundred per cent legal. In Australia, anyway."

"Well give me some of the bloody stuff then."

Max said, "All right! Light that tea and let it be!" He lit the reefer, inhaled deeply, held the smoke in his lungs and handed it to me. We passed it back and forth until it was finished. Herb kept belting his flask of whisky.

We drove on for a while.

"I hope you didn't pay good money for that, Max," I said.

"Why?"

"Because it doesn't work."

The band on the radio was playing one of those sleepy tunes, like you were supposed to imagine the waves lapping on a moonlit tropical beach or some bullshit. Even though I didn't particularly like the style, the more I listened to the slippery guitar, the more I could picture that beach, the palm trees, the hula girls. The song finished, and then the band played "One O'clock Jump," Hawaiian style.

For some reason I locked in on the bass playing. I'd never really listened to the instrument before, but now I noticed that the bloke varied what he played for each chorus. It got so that I was waiting to hear how he'd do it next time round. Chorus by chorus he worked further and further up the neck of the instrument, then just when I was expecting him to go right up high to finish, he dropped down low and played an open string, like he was saying, "Tricked you, didn't I?" I laughed out loud.

Herb said, "That shit didn't work on you, eh?"

"No," I said, "Did nothing."

It was a bleak scene out at Botany. The factories and workshops were all dark; the only light came from a single lamppost fifty yards along the street.

We got out of the car. The air was full of the stink from the nearby tanneries and the swampy low-tide smell from the bay. Herb was molo; Max was wild-eyed and twitchy.

Herb whispered, "Which way?"

I took a bundle of keys from my coat pocket and nodded at the side door. The printery was half of an old factory which backed on to a big shed Toohey sometimes used. I had a key to the shed, and from inside you could unbolt the door to the printery.

The interior was dingy—and messy. Machinery, guillotines, and stacks of paper spread about.

"Looks like they just walked out."

"Wildcat strike," Herb said. "They're after the forty hour week."

"Doesn't anyone in this country know how to do a decent day's work anymore?" I said.

Max went over to one of the presses, walked around it.

Herb said, "Can you work that?"

He nodded, patting the machine. "A Heidelberg flatbed. It's old as the hills, but I should be able to get something out of the old girl."

Max produced another reefer from his pocket, lit it up. "You want some of this stuff, Bill?"

"Just a puff."

Herb came back with three sets of overalls he'd filched from the lockers. We put them on, brought the paper in and set to work. Max locked the plates in, inked them up, and started test pressing sheets. He showed me how to work the guillotine. I stuffed up a few but after a while got the hang of it.

We settled into a routine—Max did the printing, Herb brought the finished sheets over to me and I cut them. Even though none of us was at top form, we got into the swing of it, and after a couple of hours we had a very reasonable stack of rationing coupons neatly cut, wrapped, stacked, and ready to go.

At five o'clock we stopped. Herb sat down with his bottle, and Max lit another reefer. We sat around smoking the reefer, tired but feeling pleased with ourselves.

Max finished his smoke and said, "I think we're done."

We each picked up a big bundle of coupons and headed out the side door to the car.

We were a few feet outside when I said to Max. "Is it that reefer playing with my mind, or is something different out here?"

Then a searchlight came on, right in my eyes, and a terrifying racket began—banging and ringing sounds, and voices shouting, "Scabs! Scabs! Mongrel scabs!"

"Holy Jesus!" I said, and tried to shield my eyes. Max and Herb were in confusion behind me. A woman's voice screamed in my left ear, "You filthy scabs! You should be ashamed of yourselves!" I spun around.

We were surrounded by a dozen screaming women, all banging buckets and kettles. Behind the ring of women there was a group of men holding lengths of wood and chanting, "Out the scabs! Out the scabs!"

The men moved forward, past the women. Somebody threw a punch at me. I stepped backwards into Max, who fell over. Herb stepped in front of me, reached under his coat and pulled out a revolver, held it up and fired.

There were screams from some of the women and then a short silence. Herb aimed the gun at the blokes in front of us. They stopped, then started moving carefully backwards. I heard a man's voice say, "Go and get the .22 from the house!"

Dogs were barking, and lights came on down the street. Jesus, I thought, the coppers will be here in a minute at this rate. I helped Max to his feet, and we scurried back into the printery. Herb ran in after us. The mob closed in, booing and catcalling. Herb bolted the door.

"What are you doing with a gun, Herb, for Christ's sake?"

"I always carry it. And a good job, too."

"Jesus. So what's up with them?" I said.

"They think we're strike breakers."

"Where did they come from, at this hour of the morning?"

"Maybe they were keeping an eye on the place."

Outside the mob was chanting, "Scabs, come out!" I heard one voice call, "Nice car you got out here, you scab bastard!"

"Christ," I said, "We've got to sort this out, fast. One of you go out there and talk to them."

"Yeah, sure. And tell them what exactly?" Max said.

"Buggered if I know. Give them the secret commo handshake or whatever you do."

"All right." Herb stood up, unbolted the door, and called out to the mob, "Go and get fucked, the lot of you!" Then he fired a round off into the darkness.

Something thudded loudly against the door, and then there was a clatter of stones on the tin roof.

"Put that away, Herb. Max, give me your white shirt."

"What?"

"Give me your shirt!"

He undid his overalls, removed the shirt, and handed it to me.

"Look after it, padre."

I opened the door an inch or two, held the shirt out at arm's length and waved it about. Jeers and hoots. A lump of greasy clay hit the shirt. I nipped back inside, handed the shirt back to Max. "That'll wash out. Hey Herb, you got any more of that hooch?"

"I'm down to my last bottle."

"Give it to me."

I kicked the door wide open. There was light in the sky now.

Someone said, "What's that galah up to?"

I called out in the friendliest tone of voice I could manage, "Hello there. This isn't what you might think. Can we have a bit of a yarn about things?" I held the bottle up. "A *quiet* yarn."

I stepped back out of the doorway, but didn't bolt it.

Presently a rifle barrel came through the door, then a head. The bloke looked around.

Herb's gun was on the table.

"Come on in," I said. "It's all right."

The man stepped warily inside. Four others followed him. Big fellers, carrying cricket bats, and one older man, unarmed. They glanced around, none too impressed. Max and Herb were grinning and nodding at them.

"Let's all have a drink," I said. "I don't think you'll need the rifle or the bats."

I poured nips of scotch into the tin mugs we'd gathered from the smoko room, handed one to each of them.

"I'll tell you straight off," I said. "We're not strike breakers or scabs. Why, Max and Herb here are fully paid up members of the Musicians' Union . . . "

"*Musos?*" one of them said, the disgust plain in his voice.

"Yeah, and it's like this. We came out here to do a bit of a foreign order, just a private job for ourselves. And I can guarantee you, what we're doing here this morning isn't taking any work away from union members."

"So what *are* you doing then?"

"What are we doing?" I looked at Herb and Max. They weren't about to come to my rescue.

One of the others who had wandered off called out then from across the room, "Look!"

The others looked around. He was holding up a stack of coupons. "They're dirty rotten counterfeiters!"

The others turned back to me. "Sharpies!"

"I won't deny it," I said, nodding. "We're out here trying to turn a bob. That's true. But there's a bit more to it."

"Oh, really? And what would that be?"

I stared along the row of hard, angry faces, then past them to the older man. He seemed a bit different to the others—maybe I saw traces of kindness and reasonableness there. I looked him in the eye.

"Will I get a fair hearing?" I said.

The older feller said, "Go ahead, son."

I looked at the men. "First, let me ask you a simple question."

The bloke with the rifle said, "What?"

"Who won the war?

"Don't be smart."

"I mean, *we're* supposed to have won, right? But what have we got to show for it? Are we living in peace and plenty? And what's your missus been telling you about her shopping lately?"

"Eh?"

"I mean, can she get a pound of butter any time she wants it, or a piece of steak for your dinner, or shoes for the kids, or a frock or a new hat for herself? Can you buy a bottle of beer to take home whenever you feel like it?"

They stared at me. The old feller nodded slowly.

I directed my spiel right at him. "You and I can't get a bloody thing. Right? Austerity, they call it. But what about the nobs?

What about the North Shore crew? *They've* got their cars and their petrol and their new suits and their frocks and hats and their scotch and cigars and chocolates and what have you, no problem at all. I suppose *that* hasn't slipped your attention."

The old feller smiled a little now. I had him. But one of the others said, "Well, you've got a motor car yourself, and this scotch here tastes pretty much like the real thing."

"The car's just borrowed," I said. "And as for the scotch," I leaned in closer to them, pointed my thumb back at Max and Herb, "these blokes, they're slaves to the stuff. And worse."

A couple of concerned nods, glances back at the lads.

"Anyway, the way I see it, what we're *really* doing is helping to square things up a little. You could say we're striking a blow on behalf of the battlers."

The others glanced at the older feller, and I knew then that my guess had been right, that he was the senior man.

"As you can imagine," I said, "we were hoping to keep this quiet, what with the wowsers and coppers and sneaks and give-ups, and, ah, scabs getting around the place, it's not easy."

I paused for a second, looked the old feller in the eye and said, "So, brothers, I'm asking you straight out: can we count on your cooperation?"

The old feller looked to his comrades, then stepped forward. He put his hand on my shoulder and said, "I've heard some piss-weak bullshit in my thirty years in union politics, but by Christ, son, you really take the cake."

Then his smile disappeared. "We'll take half your coupons. If you don't like it, let's see you do something about it."

I turned to Max and Herb. They nodded.

"Jesus. All right then."

The old feller walked around the stacks of coupons, did a rough count and directed his fellers to take their share outside. When they'd gone he said, "Consider yourselves lucky. Now fuck off and don't come back."

He made to leave, then turned around and picked up the bottle of whisky. "We'll look after this."

I pulled up outside Herb's flat at seven in the morning. Max and Herb had both nodded off.

"Hey, wake up," I said. "Let's get these coupons inside, quick."

Herb opened his eyes and blinked. "Not in my place, pal."

"Why not?"

"I'm still on probation. I'd get ten years if I was caught with those. Take them to Max's place."

"Fuck that! What's my father going to say?" said Max. "Anyway, you're the one with the buyer."

"You'll have to take them, Billy," Herb said.

After I'd dropped Max off, I drove to Paddington and up the lane to the back of 36 Oxford Street. I found the right key on Mick's master key ring, and let myself into the empty house. It had a kitchen with a gas burner, then a small parlor and two bedrooms, one up one down. The joint was dusty and there was rat shit on the floor, but otherwise it was clean enough.

There was a bolted storage cupboard under the stairs in the smaller bedroom. I stacked the coupons inside it, locked and padlocked the front door, and went home.

I slept for an hour or two and woke up mid morning, still woozy from the reefer. I made a pot of tea, wondering if I'd become a drug fiend yet. The house was empty, and there was a strange overcoat in the lounge. I knew I was up for the day, so I tubbed, then headed off to finish the rent round.

It was easier this time. I collected the Chippendale rents quickly and wound up at the old bloke's place in Rose Street just before eleven o'clock.

One of the thugs I'd scrapped with the first week was standing outside Jack Carmody's house, leaning against a lamppost and smoking a cig. He wore his hair long and brushed back, like Cornel Wilde in *A Song to Remember*. He looked like a comic-book tough.

I got out of the car, and the feller smiled at me. "How you going, pal?" he said.

"Been worse." I stopped there, waiting.

"I'm glad I caught you," he said, "Since you're new around here, we have something to discuss."

I shook my head. "You're not taking my money again."

He walked over, still smiling, like we were great mates. "Let me put you in the picture about how things work around here."

I didn't say anything.

"Me and my mates. We're sort of well known. Infamous, in fact." He wheeled around and pointed towards the corner. "The publican down there at the Native Rose, the SP bookie in the front bar, the Chinaman in the corner shop over there, the butcher around the corner, the brothel in Vine Street, they all give us a little something each week." He paused. "It keeps us in milk shakes."

"Standover," I said.

"We take a little something, and give something in return."

"Is that so?"

"If anyone gives *them* any trouble, we sort them out."

"You robbed me blind. My first week on the job," I said.

He nodded. "That was a mistake. I told the blokes it was stupid. The way I see it, it's better to have a few fresh eggs every day than a chicken dinner once, if you know what I mean."

He pulled out a wad of folded-up notes and handed it to me. "So have it back."

I took the money from him.

"Now," he said, "I'd like to talk about you making a regular contribution."

"How much?"

"Give us twenty bob a week. Which is pretty reasonable if you ask me." He put his arm around my shoulder. "What do you say to that, old mate?"

I pulled away and turned to face him squarely.

"You're thinking of boxing on, right here and now?" He smiled. "Well, that's up to you. You might even do all right. But then what about next week, and the week after that? I'd be back with all my mates. What would you do then?"

He had a point.

"Twenty bob? What do I get for that?"

"Well, I could guarantee that the Surry Hills mob won't give you any bother."

"They don't as it is."

"But who knows what will happen? And I can probably persuade the mob from the Glengarry Castle not to flog you."

"Who are they?"

"Bad hombres. They've got their eye on you."

It might have been true and it might have been palaver. Maybe he was just saying it to give me a slightly dignified way of buckling under.

"Twenty bob's too much. The job isn't worth that to me."

"Well, feel free to make an offer."

"I'll sling you five bob."

He shook his head. "Make it ten and we're sweet."

"What about the other feller who gets the rents," I said. "I bet he didn't give you anything."

"That was different. If you want to keep coming around here, give us ten bob a week from now on. But it's up to you. And instead of me coming looking for you, how about you drop the ten shillings off at my hangout up the road?"

"And that would be where?"

"The Hi Society Milk Bar up there in King Street. If I'm not there, leave it with the dago behind the counter." He gave a mocking half-wave, half-salute, and sauntered off.

I watched him leave, then went into the old bloke's place.

Carmody opened his door before I knocked.

"You should keep away from the Abercrombie Street Boys," he said. "They're bad bastards."

"Yeah, I'll bear that in mind. Fifteen shillings rent, I believe."

He put his hand up. "Have you got a second? There's something inside that you should see."

I felt the strain of the previous evening catching up with me; I'd developed a bad headache.

"What?"

"It's the plumbing."

"Can't it wait till next week??"

"Just like the rest," he said, and went back inside, came back with his money. "There you are and be buggered," he said.

"Hang on, hang on," I said. I rubbed my forehead. "What's the problem, then?"

I followed him inside. An old blanket was pinned over the window, and instead of chairs and a table there were packing cases with newspaper laid on them. A coat hung on a nail hammered into the door jamb.

"Where's your furniture, dad?" I said.

"I pawned what there was after the wife died. I've never managed to get it out again."

The walls had rising damp, and big sections of plaster were missing. The floor in the corner of the parlor had a hole in it, and there was a bucket in the middle of the hallway to catch leaks. In the kitchen was a wood stove, a neat pile of splintered fence posts next to it. One kettle, one pot, a half loaf of bread, a tin of jam. And an old axe handle standing against a wall.

I pointed at it. "What's that for?" I said.

"The rats."

"Where's the tap?"

"There isn't one. Never has been."

"You get your water from the bathroom?"

He shook his head. "No bathroom."

"Where do you get your water?"

"That's the problem, you see. I used to get it from the tap in the backyard. But that's RS. I've been getting my water from next door for the past year."

"Didn't you tell Misery? I mean Mr. Toohey. Did you tell him about it?"

"Oh, I told him."

"And?"

Carmody shrugged. "He's a bit slow getting around to things."

"Look, uncle, I'll see if I can get a plumber and a carpenter around next week. I can't promise anything, but—"

"I'd fix the place up myself, if I had my tools."

I stopped. "You would?"

"My oath. I'd need materials too, though."

"I might be able to get the tools. But materials . . . What do you need?"

"Terra-cotta pipes, elbows and that. Some timber, corrugated iron, a bag or two of cement."

"Can you make a list?"

"I can do it now."

He went into the yard, paced out the distance from the kitchen to the back fence, then penciled something on the back of a brown paper bag. He counted the rotten floorboards inside and wrote down something else.

"Listen old feller, would *you* have any ideas where I might get the materials?"

"Could do."

"Care to tell me?"

"There's a bloke at Kensington. He might be able to help you out."

"I'm not going to pay profiteer prices, though. Mick would kill me."

"I'll write his name and address here." He scribbled on the back of the bag, then he handed it to me. "For the floor boards and the corro, tell him second hand will do, so long as the iron's clean, not rusty. Tell this feller—Les is his name—that you're buying on Mick Toohey's behalf. He'll probably do the right thing on the strength of that."

"So, let's be clear, I get the stuff, you do the work?"

He straightened up. "Yeah, I'll do what I can."

"All right then. Misery left some tools with me. I'll bring them along for you next week."

Carmody nodded.

I walked out the door, stopped and went back in. "How long have you been paying fifteen shillings rent?" I said.

"Forever."

"What's the official rent set at?"

"Half that. Seven and sixpence."

"Toohey charges you double?"

"Not just me. All Misery's tenants pay at least double the official."

I gaped at him.

"He's not the worst. Other landlords around here are charging three or four times the controlled rate."

I reached in my pocket, gave him back the difference. "Better keep it at the official rate, at least till we get the place fixed up."

"What will Misery say?"

"Leave that to me."

When I got up home Mum was at the stove, frying bacon and eggs, still in her dressing gown. She was whistling. My Uncle Dick was sitting at the table in his shirtsleeves, reading the *Telegraph*. His dark hair was slicked back, his thin mo trimmed.

"How's young Billy, then?" he said.

I told him he was pretty good, thanks.

After Dad died, Uncle Dick started popping by unannounced on an irregular basis, "just to see that everything is tickety-boo." He'd stay a few days, or a week, then be gone again just as suddenly. My brother and I had grown used to it.

"Where's Brother Ron?" I said.

Mum smiled. "He's gone to Katoomba for a few days. With a lass. Someone he met in the army."

"Well, bully for him," I said.

I went to my room and dragged Mick's packing trunk from under the bed. I unlocked it and took out the tools—a couple of spanners, multigrips, a hammer and chisel. Not enough for Carmody to do all the work, I thought, but they'd have to do for now.

Then I came across the cigar box I'd filched from Mick's office. I opened it and caught a whiff of that perfume. I wasn't a world authority on the subject, but this was obviously the good stuff. I opened the letter and started reading—then stopped, and folded it up again. None of my business. Then I thought, what if it contains something I needed to know—for instance, some clue as to why Mick Toohey had seemingly disappeared off the face of the earth? Maybe it was my duty to read it. Or maybe I was just being a stickybeak. I opened it and read it right through.

> *Royal Hotel, Brisbane*
> *August 8, 1945*

> *My dear Mick,*
> *I'm counting the days until we can be together again.*
> *Everything's done. I've got the Register. Please find the*

enclosed sample. Do your best with it. I'll arrive there on
Wednesday of next week with the rest of it.

I'm so frightened, but excited too, to think that what
we've longed for will soon be within our reach. Whoever said
you can't have money and love was wrong, and we'll prove it.
I know we'll be happy.

xxxx Lil

I reread it a couple of times, then unfolded the second letter, which turned out not to be a letter at all, just a blank sheet of paper folded around a piece of a photographic print. The fragment was about three inches square, with ragged edges, obviously torn from a larger sheet. It was an underexposed, shadowy photograph of a typewritten document. I could make out some place names—Fortitude Valley, Grafton, Roseville—and a few names and parts of names: "Reynolds, Thomas H. (Cpt.) 6th Div. Sigs. 49 Kinross St—," but that was all. I turned it over. Scribbled in pencil on the back, in Mick's handwriting, were the words: "The Blighter, FA 9014."

I put the letter back in the cigar box and the photo in my pocket. I found an ammo box in the back shed and put the tools in it, then stuck the trunk back under my bed.

I avoided Mum and Uncle Dick in the kitchen and went straight into the hallway where our telephone was. I took the photo out of my pocket and dialed the number written on the back. Nothing. I tried again; nothing. It was a defunct.

I went back to the kitchen. Mum and Uncle Dick were studying the form guide. I sat down and poured myself a cup of tea. After a few minutes, as casually as I could, I said to my mother, "How long have you known Mick Toohey?"

They both turned and stared at me.

"That's a funny question," Mum said. "I met him through your father, in nineteen, oh . . . a long time ago."

Dick said, "Mick Toohey went to school with your father and me. How is the old reprobate? Mick, I mean, not your dad, God rest his soul."

"He's all right, as far as I know. Has he got any family anywhere?"

Mum shook her head. "He was an only child. He married a lass from Bondi. In the early twenties. He was considered quite a catch."

"Toohey?"

"He didn't always have that paralyzed face. He was quite handsome once. Athletic, too. Surf club, all that."

Dick looked at Mum, smiling. "He chased after you at one stage, didn't he?"

Mum went all girlish. "Oh, he might have been a bit interested at one time."

"Where's the wife now?"

"She died a long time ago, before you were born. And there weren't any children. But why are you asking all this? Is everything all right?"

"Yeah. Tickety-boo. One more thing, I was wondering, Dick, have you ever heard of a bloke called the Blighter?"

He smiled broadly. "That'd be the *Filthy* Blighter! Yeah, of course. Now there's a rogue for you. What have you got to do with him, or shouldn't I ask?"

"Nothing. Someone mentioned him the other day, that's all. Would you happen to know what his real name is?"

"He's always been known as the Filthy Blighter, as far as I know. But I suppose he probably wasn't christened that."

"How would I go about contacting him?"

Dick shook his head. "Last I heard he'd gone outback somewhere."

4

Sunday morning I went to the address Jack Carmody had given me, in Cottenham Street, Kensington. It was a large bungalow, with a truck in the driveway. A sign stuck in the front yard said "L. Formica, Building Contractor."

A big, old feller in shorts and a tatty sweater answered the door.

"Yeah?" Slight accent.

"My name's Bill Glasheen. Jack Carmody gave me your name."

He nodded.

"We've got some building repairs to do. Jack thought you might be able to help us out."

He nodded again.

"It's for one of Mick Toohey's properties."

"You better come in mate." It sounded like *mite*.

Twenty minutes later, with a glass of rotgut wine under the belt, we'd made an arrangement. He'd deliver the stuff to Carmody's, for an only mildly exorbitant price, to be squared up after delivery.

I drove back through Darlinghurst, and on an impulse pulled up in Palmer Street, fifty yards from the Stevensons' place.

I walked down and knocked on their door. A feller answered almost immediately, a friendly, open-faced cove.

"I've come about the rent," I said.

He nodded enthusiastically. "Good on you, old sport. You must have your spies out."

"How so?"

"Because you've come at just the right time."

That's a turn up for the books, I thought. "Is that right?"

He nodded, reaching into his back pocket. "Yep, I'm having a bit of a good run," he said, opening a wallet swollen with pound notes. "Sorry to have fallen behind like that," he said. He took out a thick wad of bills. "How much are we up for again?"

"I make it six pounds, six shillings."

He nodded again, started counting out the notes. "Yes sir," he said. "Sometimes it's like you just can't go wrong, eh?" He separated a pile of ten shilling notes and handed them to me. "There you go, mate, plus the next month in advance."

I pocketed the money.

"Would you like to come in for a cuppa while you're here? Myra!" he called back in to the house. "We got a cuppa and a biscuit there for a good young feller? Come on in, mate."

I was inside before I knew it. His wife came out and shook hands. A pleasant, dark-haired woman. "Oh, Jimmy, I hope you're not overwhelming this young man, are you?" She smiled apologetically. "He had a bit of a win last night."

I was shown into the kitchen. There were kids around—shy, dark-eyed little girls, a couple of boys, all looking happy.

They had the kettle on. The bloke told me about his win. He got the daily double up at the greyhounds the previous night, he said, then put it all on a long shot in the last race, which came in at fifty-to-one.

I drank the tea, which was delicious. I settled in a little, started enjoying the company of these decent folk. Myra brought out some cakes, which were also delicious, and after a while a deck of cards was produced, over Myra's protests.

"Don't worry, old girl," Jimmy said. He winked at me.

After a couple of hands of show poker, one of the littlies said why didn't we play for pennies. Jimmy said no, it wouldn't be right. Since he was on a winning streak, it wouldn't be fair.

The oldest, a cheeky young feller of ten or eleven, dared his dad to bet against me at two-to-one. That is, for every penny I put down, he was to bet two.

Somehow we started playing that way, and I cleaned up. Myra started frowning. The kid stopped smiling, looked anxiously from dad to mum. My pile of pennies grew and grew, but Jimmy was like a man possessed. He insisted on changing to silver, then paper money. He kept betting against me two to one. I tried to bail out, but he wouldn't hear of it. After an hour I'd won over a hundred quid.

Then the tide seemed to turn. I started losing a bit. I went back a few quid, then started winning again. At two-to-one, I only had to win every now and again to get back in front. But over half an hour, I seemed to win only the small pots, while Jimmy won all the big ones. Even then, it seemed that I was still doing all right.

Then suddenly I was back to zero. I started dipping into the previous day's rent money, which I still had in my kick. I built my pile up again, but then in a quick succession of losing hands, I did the whole lot.

Jimmy looked at the clock on the mantelpiece, put the money away, looked at me impassively. "How you going there, sport?"

"I'm stoney broke," I said.

He stood up. "Cripes, I've kept you here too long, haven't I? You must have things to do. Myra will hit the roof if I don't fix that dunny door today." He led me to the front of the house. I didn't see any happy family members anywhere now.

At the front door, Jimmy patted me on the back. "Well, we

had a bit of fun, didn't we?" His eyes were bright, and he was still smiling. But there was a kind of sharky look I hadn't noticed before.

"I've done all my dough," I said.

"I told you I was on a winning streak, didn't I?" And the door closed behind me.

I stood there in the street trying to figure out what had just happened. A street sweeper who'd stopped to roll himself a ciggy called out, "They have a lend of you, did they?"

I turned around and stared at him.

He nodded. "You should watch yourself with that mob."

"Who?"

"Them in there. The showies."

I looked at him blankly. "Showies?"

He laughed. "Show people, gypsies. They do card tricks, fortune telling and all that." He waved his arm at the houses on either side of the street. "They're in all these places. The Palmer Street Gypsies." He shook his head. "They'd steal the steam off your shit if you let them."

I went back and banged on the door. There was no answer, but I kept it up until Jimmy opened up, looking suspicious.

"Yeah?"

"How did you do it?"

"Do what?"

"Look," I said, "you did me like a dinner. That's all right, I'm not trying to get it back. But I want to know how you did it."

"Luck." He smiled.

"Luck, eh? Well how about I go and tell that to the sergeant up at Darlo, see if he's convinced of that?"

From inside the house Jimmy's wife called out, high and loud, "Hear that, you *fool* of a man? You'll bring coppers down here on us!"

Jimmy looked at me.

"I want to know how you did it," I said.

"You want me admit to rorting you? What kind of mug do you think I am?"

"I'm not trying to trap you. You've got my money. Keep it. But I want something back."

"What?"

"Show me some card tricks."

He looked at me warily, looked back inside.

Myra was there walking around dusting, banging things down. She looked up and shook her head in disgust.

"Card artistry isn't easy," he said. "To learn *or* teach. It'd take too long."

"I can come back every week. You show me things."

He looked doubtful.

"Or else I'll go to the coppers," I said.

"Then he said quietly, "Let us off the rent and you're on."

"Free rent? Fair go!"

"Each time I give you a lesson, the rent is wiped for that week. That's a pretty good deal, feller. You'll be learning skills which will stand you in good stead for the rest of your life."

I thought for a couple of seconds. "All right," I said.

Jimmy smiled. "Come in, son."

So we sat down at the table again for lesson number one in cheating at cards.

Jimmy shuffled the deck, much more expertly than when we'd been playing for money. "First, the grip!" he said, picking up the deck in his left hand. Then he put it down again. "Pick it up and hold it the way I held it."

When I did, he shook his head and took the deck back.

"Rather than putting all your fingers along the long edge, put your index finger at the leading narrow edge here, and stick your little finger at the back here—like this, see?"

I did it.

He nodded. "That's called the 'mechanic's grip.' It's the basis of nearly all sleight of hand. Get that right and you're on your way. The peek, the bottom deal, the second deal, the false shuffle—they all depend on a good, comfortable mechanic's grip. You have to keep an eye out for other people using it, too."

He showed me how to keep a card on the bottom of the deck while shuffling, and how to deal from the bottom, how to keep a card on top of the deck and deal the second top card instead. Then he demonstrated how to get rid of an unwanted card, and how to introduce a card to the top of the deck.

After an hour and a half he sent me off, saying that was more than enough for this week.

"Carry a deck with you all the time. Every spare minute you've got, practice. And when you start getting the hang of it, then practice in the dark, or with your eyes closed. The cards have to become a part of you. That's the way to get good at it."

That night I was sitting up at the kitchen table, practicing with the deck, when the phone rang.

Mum answered, called out to me.

I went in quickly. "Is it Mick?" I said.

She shook her head.

It was Cyril, Toohey's taxi driver pal.

"Hello there, Bill," he said. "Sorry to bother you at home like this, but something's come up."

"Yeah? What's that?"

"I need to talk to you. In private. As soon as possible."

"Well—"

"It concerns you, Bill. Listen, I'm driving tomorrow. I usually stop into the Hastee Tastee around ten in the morning. Can you meet me there?"

"Yeah, I suppose so. What's going on, Cyril?"

"I'd rather not say over the phone."

The next morning, Cyril was there before me, with a sandwich and a pot of tea in front of him.

"You want a feed?" he said.

"I'll just have a cup of tea. What's up?"

"What are you doing with those cards?" he said.

"Just practicing. What did you want to tell me?"

He looked around the cafe, lowered his voice. "Something funny's going on, Bill. You know the Durban Club burnt down, don't you?"

"Yeah, but that was an accident wasn't it? A bonfire that got out of hand."

"Yeah, except it was the day after the celebrations. Have you heard anything from Mick since then?"

I hesitated. "Well no, I haven't, as a matter of fact. And I'm getting a bit concerned. What about you?"

He shook his head. "Nothing. But I had a visit from some fellers."

"Oh yeah? What sort of fellers."

"A bit like coppers, but not coppers. Sort of military blokes, except they weren't in uniform. One of them had a crook leg. They were waiting for me at the base when I knocked off last Friday. They took me aside. Asked me about Mick, about what had happened on VP Day, where he went and so forth. Are you sure you don't know anything about this?"

"Yeah, bloody sure. What did you tell them?"

"I told them to get fucked. They got a bit rough."

"They belted you up?"

"They pushed me a bit, that's all. Nothing came of it. The reason I called you, Bill, is that they mentioned your name."

"*My* name? Jesus! In connection with what?"

"They asked who you were, where you lived, and whether you were privy to Mick's business doings."

"What did you say?"

"I said all I knew was you were just a young bloke who did an occasional bit of running around on Mick's behalf, that's all, and that I had no idea where you lived. But I thought I should warn you."

"I appreciate it, Cyril."

"There's more," he said. "I've spoken to a few of the blokes, and no one's heard anything from Mick. Not a word. Which is odd. You know Ernest? He told me he was into Mick for sixty quid. They were supposed to square last week, but Mick didn't show, didn't even ring. Now, *that's* bloody unusual."

I thought about it for a second. "Could he be on the nest?"

Cyril looked at me closely. "What makes you say that?"

"Would the name Lil mean anything to you?"

He shook his head slowly. "You know Mick," he said. "He plays his cards close to his chest."

"That's for sure. After all this time, I don't even know where he lives. I mean, apart from his room at the Durban Club. Do you know?"

"Christ, he'd be dark if he knew we were even *talking* about him like this. He's got a house at Double Bay. Manning Road. The number's in the book, even. I know he's not there, though."

"Can I ask you something else?"

"What?"

"Do you know this bloke, the Filthy Blighter?"

"Not really. I've seen him around, of course. Picked him up in the cab a couple of times. Why?"

"Do you know where I could find him?"

"I took him to the Metropole Hotel once. But that was a good six months ago. What's he got to do with this?"

"Nothing. Never mind. Cyril, how long have you known Mick?"

"Over thirty years. Why?"

"You know how . . . well, Mick has his finger in a few different pies?"

Cyril eyed me doubtfully. "What of it?"

"How about blackmail? Would that ever be his go?"

"What makes you say that?"

"I found some . . . well, let's say some bits and pieces. Nothing conclusive, mind. But the only sense I could make of it all was that Mick and someone named Lil were cooking something up."

Cyril, gave me a long, anxious look. "I wouldn't know about that. And I wouldn't *want* to know." He stood up, anxious to get away now. "Listen, Bill, the reason I've stayed a mate of Mick's all this time is because I know how to mind my own business." He went to the counter, paid up, then came back, leaned over.

"I called you up because I thought you should be told about things. You being a young bloke and that, I didn't think you should be dragged into business that's not of your making. But maybe I'm the one who's in the dark. What you said about Mick—personally, I can't see it. Not Mick. If you know different, then all I can say is, watch yourself."

I went to the counter, asked the waitress for the phone book. There was only one Toohey listed in Double Bay, and the initial was D. Mick's middle name was Daniel.

I drove straight there. It was a big house, with gardens front and back. I banged on the door. A large, middle-aged woman opened up. She didn't seem to understand a word I said except for "Mick." The more I questioned her, the more confused and distressed she became.

She shook her head, then said something in a language I couldn't understand. Frustrated, she came back with her purse, opened it, then spread her hands, as if to say, "no money."

I nodded, then spoke slowly. "Where is Toohey?"

"Gone. Long time, long time! No pay." Then she walked away from the door came back with a handful of envelopes—Mick's unopened mail. She picked out a gas company bill, another from the electricity. "Must pay! *You*?" she said.

I didn't know whether she was asking whether I'd been paid, or whether she wanted me to pay her or the bills. Whatever, I shook my head, and turned to leave.

Then she stepped out the door, took my hand and led me to the side of the house. She pointed to a broken window, just out of sight of the street.

"Is bad man robber bastards come."

"When?"

She gestured back over her shoulder, "Two day."

I said, "'Bad man robber bastard,' you say. Who?"

She did a weird mime then, of a limping, fat man. Then she led me inside the house, showed me what must have been Mick's study. She pointed to a filing cabinet with a broken lock, then pointed to the desk and indicated where the drawers had been levered open.

Then she said, "You know?"

I shook my head.

She said, "I go bugger off."

When I got home, I put the cigar box with the love letter and the photo back in Mick's trunk. I put the rent money I hadn't lost into the cashbox, put that in the trunk too. I took a peek around outside, then lugged the trunk to the boot of the car and drove back to the empty residence in Paddo.

I backed the car up to the gate, dragged the trunk into the back bedroom. The room had a fireplace with no grate. I crawled inside it and shone a torch up the chimney. Then I fetched a chisel and chipped away the mortar inside the fireplace until I was able to take two bricks out. I put the cashbox in the cavity and replaced the bricks. The trunk I left in the back room with an old blanket over it.

The next day, around midday, I went to Herb Atkins' flat. His girlfriend Kitty opened the door. She told me Herb was a bit under the weather, but she'd get him anyway. I went into the lounge room and waited.

Herb stumbled in, still wearing pajamas and dressing gown.

"Crikey, you're pissed already?"

"What if I am?"

"Nothing."

"This wowser streak is very fucking unbecoming in you, I must say."

"A thousand pardons. Listen, what's happening with this coupon buyer of yours?"

"Any day now."

"And you still think he's fair dinkum?"

"Of course I do," he said, but I could hear in his voice that he didn't.

"Well it's time to give him a bit of a hurry up. I don't like having them all in my possession."

"All right, all right." He ran his hand through his hair.

"And we should have a backup plan in case your bloke doesn't come through."

"Hmm, maybe."

I got up to leave. "Let me know the minute you hear anything, all right?"

Herb brightened up suddenly. "By the way, did you find the Blighter?"

"No, not yet. Why?"

He went to the couch, picked up a newspaper, thumbed through it, and handed it to me.

"Look at that."

It was Clive Bascomb's column, *Around Sydney*. It began, "I was having a recuperative snifter or two with my bosom pal the Filthy Blighter yesterday when—." I read on quickly. The rest of the piece seemed to be a long, meandering joke about something that happened in the upper house of the state parliament, and had nothing at all to do with the Blighter that I could see.

I looked up at Herb. "What's this mean?"

"I read that and remembered you'd been asking about him. Bascomb does that sometimes, starts his column like that. 'The Blighter and my good self were at the Journalists' Club the other day when blah, blah, blah.' It's a kind of journalistic device."

"Oh, right."

"Anyway, if you're still looking for the Blighter, you might try the Journos' Club. That's one of his watering holes."

"Thanks, Herb, I will. And remember what I said about the coupons. We've got to get them sold."

The doorbell rang just as I put my hand on the doorknob. I could hear a woman laughing outside. I opened the door and came face to face with Lucy Chance, the would-be chanteuse from the Rocket Club, standing next to a fresh-faced, square-head-looking bloke.

Her smile disappeared instantly, but she recovered quickly. She turned to her boyfriend. "Oh Wilfred, this is Mr. Glasheen." She looked around in a stagey way, then whispered, "Mr. Glasheen is a genuine black marketeer. His overcoat is probably stuffed with bacon rashers." The boyfriend looked from her to me to the floor.

Kitty called to them from the kitchen.

Lucy said, "Come on, Wilfred," and they stepped inside, greeted Herb, and disappeared into the kitchen.

When they'd gone I said to Herb, "You know what? That sheila really rubs me up the wrong way."

That night I dreamed about Lucy Chance. She was smiling in that nasty way of hers, but in the dream she was a bit sexy, too. I woke up in a bad mood, and it stayed with me all morning.

After lunch I paid a visit to the Journalists Club. I hung around for a while, got into a yarn with a few blokes at the bar, then casually asked if anyone had seen the Blighter today.

One feller lifted his glass and intoned in a plummy voice, "They seek him here, they seek him there, they seek the Blighter everywhere!"

Another feller said, "The Blighter's out of town. Out of the country, in fact. Something very hush-hush. Malaya, I believe."

The third bloke said *he'd* heard the Blighter had been recalled to the army and was presently in Japan with the Occupation Force. On my way out the barmaid called out to me. "If you're looking for the Blighter, try the Three Bells. He sometimes drinks down there."

The Three Bells at Woolloomooloo was a rough old joint, by any standards. Wharfies, dockers, seamen, and assorted petty crims, prostitutes, standover thugs and lairs. I'd never set foot in the place before, and it was a bit of an eye opener. But in my zoot suit I fitted in well enough. I ordered a beer.

"The Blighter been in yet?" I said to the barmaid when she gave me my change. She shook her head. The blokes to my left stopped talking for a moment and stared at me. I moved away from the bar.

One feller followed me over. "Who did you say you were looking for, mate?"

"The Filthy Blighter."

"What do you want with him?"

"I have a message for him. An important message."

"Oh yeah? What's that?"

"Are you a mate of his?"

"Yeah. What's your message?"

"It's outside in the car. I'll go get it."

I left my beer, went out to the car, drove off and kept going.

I went back home, rang the *Telegraph*, and asked to speak to Clive Bascomb. The phone rang for a while before a gravelly voice answered with a bored, "Mmm?"

"Is that Clive Bascomb?"

"Yeah."

"My name's . . . well, that's not important. I'm trying to contact the Filthy Blighter."

No response.

"It's sort of an urgent matter," I said.

Another silence, then, "Who are you?"

"My name is Glasheen."

Another silence. I could hear voices, typewriters, and laughter in the background.

"Hello, are you there?"

Bascomb's voice came back on. "Sorry, sport, I was called away. Who did you say you were?"

"Glasheen. I need to speak to the Blighter."

"Try the Three Bells," he said, and hung up.

I put the ammo box of tools in the boot of the car when I went to collect the Chippendale rents the following Saturday. Jack Carmody opened the door before I could even knock.

"I've got tools for you," I said. "They're in the car."

"Good on you, son. I got the building materials from Les," he said. "He bought them around this morning. Early, to keep it nice and private."

"That's good. You still reckon you're up to doing the work?"

"Of course I bloody am."

I went out to the car, brought the ammo box inside, put it down in the kitchen.

Carmody took a few pieces out. "There should be more."

"Eh?"

"These are my tools. There should be more here."

"If they're yours, how come they were—"

"I pawned them a year ago. To Misery."

"He took your tools of trade?"

The old feller nodded. "In lieu of the rent. If it was anyone else I'd have been out on my arse long ago." He turned to me. "But they're not all here."

"What's missing?"

"Saws, drills, screwdrivers, all the bits and pieces. They were in a wooden tool chest when I handed them over."

"Jesus, I think it was in Mick's office. Give me a few days, I'll see what I can do."

He nodded.

"So you've known Toohey a good while, then?"

"Since the Great War. He was a young bloke with us at Gallipoli. I was a lance corporal."

"What sort of bloke was he then?"

"Full of sauce and vinegar. Younger than you are now, only sixteen or seventeen. Game, though. *Bloody* game."

"You ever hear of a sheila named Lil?" I said.

Carmody's face went completely blank. "Wouldn't know anything about that," he said finally. "You'd have to ask Misery."

"Yeah, I will. What about the Filthy Blighter? You ever hear of him?"

He nodded. "Yeah, too right. The tipster in the *Telegraph*."

"A tipster?"

Carmody nodded. He went to the kitchen came back with the form guide, handed it to me.

"At the bottom of the page."

A little, two-column box bore the miniscule heading "The Filthy Blighter's Whisper from the Track." There was one convey-ance tipped for Randwick gallops, another for Harold Park trots and a greyhound for Wentworth Park dogs.

"I never noticed this before," I said. "How long have they been running this?"

"A year or so. His tips are no good, though, I can tell you."

I called in at Jimmy Stevenson's place in Palmer Street. He showed me into the kitchen again.

"All right, show me what you've learned."

I did some shuffling for him. I dealt from the bottom of the deck, I disposed of a card from the top and then introduced it back into the deck. I did a bogus shuffle, during which the same card remained at the top of the deck.

"How am I going?" I said.

He called his son and told me to do it all again for little Jimmy's benefit.

I ran through the tricks again, and as I did each one, little Jimmy called out a running commentary, saying which cards were being manipulated and how I was doing it.

Jimmy senior shook his head. "See? An eleven-year-old lad can pick every move you make. You've got a long way to go, feller."

I stayed for nearly an hour while he showed me four different methods of false shuffling, how to "shift the cut," and how to palm a card. Then he sent me away, with instructions to keep practicing.

Next I went to Martin Place and parked near the Durban Club. Planks had been nailed over the windows and doors on the ground floor, and the walls and joinery on two sides of the building were blackened by smoke. I peeked in one of the broken windows. Charred furnishings, blackened timbers, and an acrid smell.

I went around to the back door, which had been smashed in then roughly nailed up again, and tried to pull one of the planks off it. When I got soot on my threads, I brushed it off and re-solved to come back later, more suitably dressed.

5

I got in late that night after the Harold Park trots. Ron was waiting up for me, sitting with Mum at the kitchen table.

"Hello gang," I said cheerily. "G'day, Ronald. How was Katoomba?" I winked at him.

My brother walked quickly over to me. "What in blazes are you mixed up in now?"

"What?"

"You heard me."

My mother looked at me. There were circles under her eyes. "There's been trouble. Some men were here looking for you."

"Who were they?"

"They said they were police, but . . . they were rough fellows. One of them was carrying an axe handle." She pointed to the table top in front of her. "He banged it down on the table here. Left a mark." She started crying.

"What did they say they wanted?" I said as offhandedly as I could manage.

"They said they were investigating the distribution of forged coupons," Mum said.

My guts sank.

"But they didn't even look twice at the coupons on the mantelpiece there," she said.

"Did they say their names?"

"No."

"What did they look like?"

"One had fair hair and a moustache. Sort of round-faced, wore a Homburg. Quietly spoken. With a very bad limp. He did all the talking. He didn't say his name, but I heard one of the other fellows call him Aubrey."

"Aubrey had the axe handle?"

"No, that was one of the others. The one they called Aubrey was quite well spoken. But he was an awful man. They searched your room."

"Did they have a search warrant?"

My brother cut in. "Blind Freddy could see they weren't coppers."

She shook her head. "They didn't, but they said if they had to go away and get one, it wouldn't go well for us when they came back. Then that other one started getting awfully cranky. That's when he hit the table with the axe handle. I let them in to your room after that. I was frightened."

I nodded. "They take anything?"

"I don't think so. But they made a terrible mess. I tidied up after they left."

"Wasn't Dick here?" I said to Mum.

"He left yesterday."

My brother grabbed my shoulder. "What's this about?"

"Get your hands off me."

He stared at me, breathing hard, then exhaled slowly. "I'm sorry," he said quietly, and sat down.

He pushed a chair out. "Take a seat, Bill."

I sat down.

"Look," he said, speaking quietly and slowly. "I know you've had to make your own way in the world as best you could. I should have been here to give you some direction, but I wasn't, and that couldn't be helped. Uncle Dick could have stepped in too, but we both know he's not worth two bob." He glanced sideways. "Sorry Mum, but it's the truth." He turned back to me. "So maybe it's too late now for me to start playing the big brother. But whatever's going on, Bill, you can't bring trouble home with you. Not with Mum here. Understand?"

"Yeah, I know that."

"All right. Now, you don't have to tell me if you don't want to, but are you in over your head?"

I didn't answer straight away. "I don't think so. It's a misunderstanding. Whatever's going on doesn't concern me. I know that much."

He nodded, then stood up and filled the kettle at the tap. "How about a cup of tea, Mum? Go and put your feet up, I'll bring it to you in the lounge room."

When she was gone he said, "Like I said, I don't want to butt in where I'm not needed, Bill, but if you need some back up—" He nodded at me, made a fist. "You know what I mean? I can get a few good fellows together at short notice. We can straighten those bastards out if we have to."

I was so taken aback by this change of attitude, I didn't know whether to laugh at him outright, or . . . something else. When I tried to speak, my voice went a bit croaky on me. I cleared my throat and said, "Yeah, thanks Ron. I'll bear that in mind."

The next morning, after Ron had gone out for the day, I said to Mum, "What's come over Ron? He's turning into a human being all of a sudden."

"It's this girlfriend of his," she said. "She's a good influence on him." She turned around with a sly smile on her face. "What about you, Bill? Any lasses on the horizon?"

As soon as she said that, a picture of Lucy Chance, her black hair and white skin, flashed into my mind, even though I detested everything about her.

"Me? I'm breaking hearts all over Sydney."

That night after dinner I put on an old shirt and one of my hundred pairs of dungarees, which Mum had thoughtfully boiled up in the copper. The dungarees were a bit long, and I had to turn them up at the cuff to keep them from dragging in the dirt.

I put a crowbar in the boot of the Chev and headed into the city, intending to have a quiet poke around the Durban Club. But it was a warm evening and Martin Place was a bit too busy; people were out strolling or listening to the pipe band playing near the Cenotaph. I waited around for a while, till it occurred to me I could kill a little time checking the jukebox at Burt's Milk Bar, which I had been neglecting. Maybe I could get a free milkshake while I was at it.

I parked outside in Macleay Street, ambled in, said hello to the girl behind the counter, and headed for the jukebox. There were a few people in the place, but the machine was idle. I emptied the coin box—less than a quid in it—and went over to the counter.

The girl didn't offer me anything in the way of gratuities, so I ordered myself a milkshake. "I see the jukebox doesn't get much traffic," I said when she handed it to me.

She glanced over at it apathetically. "Nah, not really," She gave me my change and went back to her magazine.

Someone tapped me on the shoulder. I turned around to see a loutish fellow in a corduroy jacket, sporting a Cornel Wilde haircut.

"Howdy, buddy," he said.

I didn't know this bloke, but I knew the type. He was a "Kings Cross Yank"—as Australian as me, probably, but he spoke with a fake American accent. In 1942, Sydney had gone yarra over Americans and all things American, and quite a few blokes had taken to impersonating Yanks for the benefit of Sydney womanhood. And Sydney womanhood had responded in the most obliging way. Once people got used to actual Yanks around the place, the fakes started dropping off, but for some blokes it had become a hard habit to break.

I nodded to him and turned back to my milkshake.

"I was wondering, seeing you wearing those jeans, you know, would you consider selling them to me. Or if any of your pals from the ship have any they want to sell—"

I turned to face him. He wasn't being smart. His face had a hopeful look.

"You want my *jeans*?"

"Oh, cripes, you're an Aussie. Sorry, mate, I thought you were a septic."

"That's all right. What was that about my dungarees?"

"Like I said, I thought you were a Yank. Sometimes they come up here, you know, sell records and that. Those Levis you're wearing, they're the grouse."

"You like jeans like this?"

"Me and my mates. Our girlfriends, too. We're always looking out for them."

"Well now, there's a coincidence," I said. "I can't promise anything, but I might be able to get you a pair."

"Really?"

"They could cost, though."

"Shit, yeah. I know that."

"I'll see what I can do. How can I find you?"

"We're always here," he said. He gestured over his shoulder, to the back of the shop, to a group of loudly dressed boys and girls, my age and younger.

"All right," I said. "But, as I say, they might cost a bit." I watched his face closely. "Maybe as much as ten bob."

He nodded eagerly. Christ, I thought, I started too low. "Possibly more—I'll have to see the bloke."

"Yeah, sure." He nodded some more.

I stayed and drank another milkshake, then at half past nine I drove back to Martin Place. It was quiet. I parked well away from the hotel, then went around to the back door. As carefully and quietly as I could, I pried the bits of wood off the door and let myself in. I flashed my torch around. The walls were black and there were pools of filthy water on the floor. The smell of burnt wood and mildew hurt my nostrils.

The fire damage got worse as I went further inside. The ceiling had collapsed over the hallway, and the main stairway to the first floor was gone. As I flashed the torch around I heard a scuttling sound.

The kitchen door itself was blocked by sodden plaster. I lifted a big piece, but it fell apart in my hands. I kicked the pieces out of the way, cleared room to open the door, and stepped through. The cupboards were burnt, the lino was destroyed, and there were gaps in the floorboards. Pigeons were nesting in the ceiling. The refrigerator was off, of course, and the room stank of rotting food and mold. The rats had evidently been having a good old party.

I stood there for a few moments, taking it all in. The fire damage hadn't been attended to, and even the perishables had been left there to rot. Surely it must be someone's job, I thought, to clean up and secure places like this.

I went down the narrow stairs to Mick's cellar office. The door wasn't locked. The room wasn't as burned out as the main floor, but it was a mess. The safe was open, the desk drawers were out, the contents thrown around, papers all over the floor, chairs overturned. The place smelled of piss. Stiffs must have been dossing here, although I couldn't see any of the usual telltale empties in brown paper bags. I heard a buzzing sound, and flashed my torch around, looking for the toolbox. It was still where it had been on VP Day. I walked forward and was hit by the smell of rotting meat. Then I saw the khaki trousers on the floor under the table. Another step and I saw the rest of the body. I shouted out involuntarily.

I bolted straight out the back door and into the glare of a spotlight. A voice called out for me to stop, but I kept going. Then I was tackled around the knees, and ended up on the deck. I copped a couple of sharp thumps in the kidneys, but I was still shouting.

"Shut up, you big sheila," and another thump. I went quiet.

"So which particular rat did we catch in our trap?" said another voice behind me. It was Ray Waters.

The light was turned on me. "Ah, the bloke who doesn't know anything. Put him in the car."

The one who'd tackled me let go of my legs and stood up. I did likewise. The light was still shining on me.

"There's a dead body in there," I said.

"Is that so?" he said. "Well, don't you worry yourself about it. All right, gents, let's adjourn to Darlo, where we can continue our little chat in private. We'll see what young Mister Glasheen has to tell us."

They were none too careful getting me into the interview room this time. Then they sat me down and left me there.

It was a good two hours before Waters came back, with another bloke I didn't recognize.

"So if I was to ask you what you were doing at the Durban Club, Glasheen, would you tell me the truth, and thereby earn my goodwill, or would you try to piss in my pocket and so earn my extreme displeasure?"

"There was a dead body in there, for Christ's sake," I said.

"You don't miss a trick, do you?" He looked at the other bloke. "Young Glasheen has a sharp eye for detail. Maybe we could use him on the force."

They both laughed.

Waters stopped smiling. "You're in a bit of bother this time, Glasheen. You'd do well to answer the questions I put to you, and not try to get smart with me, understand?"

"Yeah."

"What were you doing at the Durban Club?"

"I went there to collect some tools."

"And what would *you* want with tools?"

"I'm building a chook shed."

"And did you find these tools?"

"I did. But like I said, I came across the, ah, dead body. Is it Mick Toohey?"

Waters shook his head. "It appears to be the remains of one Edwin Worrall."

I knew Eddie Worrall very slightly. He'd been the manager at the Durban Club for a while, then he drifted away and later reappeared in uniform—as an officer, no less. An unfriendly bloke. He'd kept a room upstairs, off and on, and was sometimes around, sometimes not.

"Eddie? How did . . . how did he die?"

"We don't know that yet. What can *you* tell us about that, Glasheen?"

"I don't know anything about it."

"Did you kill Eddie Worrall?"

"Of course not."

"When did you last see Worrall?"

"Months ago. I'd have to think when, exactly."

Waters punched me hard in the face. I went flying.

"Get up."

I got up slowly.

"I don't know what your part is in this, Glasheen. But I don't like it at all, you hear me?"

The other bloke took his jacket off and loosened his tie.

I knew I had to say something, soon, or I'd be in for some serious rough stuff.

"Some blokes came around to my house," I said. "Three of them. They told my mum they were police."

Waters looked interested. "Go on."

"They searched my room."

Waters looked at the other feller, then said, "And why do you think they did that, Glasheen?"

"I don't know. But the other week, you asked me about, what was it, the register? Then these blokes arrived, and went through my things. So, I thought, maybe there's a connection there."

"Do you know who these fellers were?"

I shook my head. "Only that one of them was named Aubrey."

Waters and the other copper exchanged looks, then Waters leaned over.

"Where is it?" he said quietly.

"Beg your pardon?"

He came even closer. I could feel his breath on my face. "The register."

I shook my head.

"Do you know what I'm talking about?"

"No, I don't."

Waters stared at me for a few seconds more, then straightened up.

"That vacant, idiotic look on your face seems real enough. But what I don't understand is why you went to the Durban Club at all. That bullshit about getting tools just doesn't wash."

Then he poked me in the chest and smiled. "You went there to rob the safe, didn't you?"

"I'm not a thief."

Waters turned to the other copper. "Listen to this lair will you? All outraged innocence." Then he turned around and took another swipe at me. It caught me lightly on the forehead, but it was enough to knock me off the chair.

This time I got to my feet fast. I skipped away from Waters and waited until he came for me, then I moved in quick and landed one on him. It didn't do him much harm, but it did me some good. For a moment, anyway. Then there were two of them on me. It was brief. I copped some hard thumps and passed out.

When I came around, I was still lying on the floor of the interview room. Sergeant Jennings was shaking me. My ears were ringing and there was blood in my mouth.

"You awake, son?"

"Yeah, I must have dozed off."

"Go in and clean yourself up. I'm knocking off now. Hurry up and I'll give you a lift home."

"I can go?"

He nodded.

"My car's at Martin Place."

"I'll drop you there, then. Come on, smartly now."

I washed my face and took a look in the mirror. I didn't look too hot. When I walked through the police station, Waters and the other bloke were nowhere to be seen.

Jennings was waiting in the car. I got in and we drove off.

He was silent for a while, then said, "Detective Sergeant Waters said you're to keep in touch. If you hear anything about Mick Toohey, or anything relating to the death of Eddie Worrall, you're to contact him immediately. Understand that?"

"Yeah."

We drove on in silence, then after a minute Jennings said, "You feel angry, do you, son?"

I wasn't sure what I was feeling. I didn't answer.

"Angry. And ashamed," he went on. "Well, there's a lot more of that coming your way. I could say that you'd better get used to it, but the truth is that people don't get used to it."

I kept quiet.

Jennings looked at me, then went on. "You're a bit flash, Glasheen, and you probably think you're a bit smarter than all the mugs around you. But how smart are you, really?"

I just stared out the window.

"Oh, I know, you've had a good run so far, with the war and everything. You've made some easy money, and the police have been too busy to pay any real attention to fellers like you. But I'll tell you something—the easy days are over for you, Glasheen. From here on, it's a downhill run. If you think you're tough enough to deal with people like Ray Waters on a daily basis, tough enough to cop the beatings and go to jail sooner or later, then by all means go for it. If you're prepared to wait for hours in a back lane for a chance to bend an iron bar over some wretch's head, then you're on the right track."

He let his words sink in for a moment, then continued. "And somewhere down the track you'll become a give-up. They nearly all do. You can forget that code of the underworld rubbish—I know all those crims you probably admire talk a big game, but there isn't one who won't give someone up to get out of trouble themselves. And you're still just as likely to end up in a pool of your own blood somewhere, or if you're lucky maybe you'll survive and wind up a miserable drunkard, homeless or living in a one-room flat you wouldn't keep a dog in."

Another pause. I still didn't say anything.

"All that's waiting for you in the not too distant future."

"Mick Toohey doesn't live like that," I said.

"Doesn't he?"

I turned to look at him.

He went on, "Where *is* Toohey, anyway? If he's such a good fellow, how come he left you in the hot seat? Toohey's just another rat, in my book. You see, you actually have a choice,

Glasheen. You can start doing the right thing now, get a proper job, settle down, mix with decent people. Or you can continue the way you're going."

He stopped the car at Martin Place. "Do you drink, Glasheen?"

"I have a beer sometimes. Why?"

"No spirits?"

"No. I promised my dad before he died."

Jennings nodded. "Well, that's a start. Do you smoke?"

I shook my head.

"Don't start. It stunts your growth. Listen, Glasheen, there are a few young chaps who get together down at Marrickville, at the Police Boys' Club. If you want to come down sometime, you can meet some good fellows and learn a bit about scientific boxing. Or have a talk about things. Sometimes it helps to have someone on your side."

I got out and walked towards the Chev. Jennings called me back. "Think about what I said, Glasheen. Ray Waters doesn't take me into his confidence, and I don't know what's going on with this Mick Toohey business. I don't think you know either, although you might think you do. Mr. Waters is the senior man and I can't help you if you get in trouble."

I got home at two in the morning, and stayed in bed most of the next day.

Finally, late in the afternoon, I snuck out of the house and drove over to my Paddington hideaway. I opened Mick Toohey's trunk and took everything out of it. I went through every single page of Mick's account books and checked every key tag. I reread the letter in the cigar box and pored over the photo fragment.

What was going on? My guess was that Toohey and Lil had been running some kind of blackmail rort. Toohey had gone away. Toohey hadn't rung me to check on his properties. Toohey wasn't collecting his debts.

So Toohey was dead. Maybe Lil, too.

The Filthy Blighter, whoever he was, was involved somehow. He wasn't dead, although everyone seemed to agree that he wasn't around at the moment.

Ray Waters was watching, waiting for this register to turn up. Big money was at stake. Three heavies had come to my home; they were also looking for the register—maybe for themselves, maybe on behalf of the people being blackmailed.

I wasn't involved. Not really. I could walk away from it.

I went to the Hole in the Wall for a feed and a think. I went over it all again—Waters, the hooligans, Mick Toohey probably being dead. I was scared. And there was nothing much in this for me.

Then I mulled over Sergeant Jennings' little sermon. I had a choice. I could start doing what I was told: get a normal job, start living like every other squarehead mug, cave in like a gutless wonder. Or I could call to mind the Eureka Stockade and the Wild Colonial Boys, the defiant rebel spirit of Ben Hall, Frank Gardiner and Ned Kelly. I could say, "Come on then, have a go. Do your worst, you bastards. I'll fight, but I'll not surrender." And die fighting.

Big choice.

But maybe there's a third way, I thought. Maybe I could hold on to my own lurks and perks, and keep my head pulled in at the same time. See the business with the counterfeit coupons through. Keep collecting Toohey's rents. Keep looking after the jukebox and the slot machines. Keep putting aside the rent money. If Mick ever turned up, I could present him with the take, and negotiate my commission. And if he didn't show . . . well, then I'd just have to come to a decision about that later. And while I was doing all that I could keep my eyes and ears open for any chances that might appear. The more I thought about it, the more I liked it.

When I finally got home my mother and brother nearly had kittens over my split lip, blackened eye and grazed cheekbone. My mother wanted to dress my wounds. My brother wanted to add to them.

"You should see the other bloke," I said.

My brother calmed down quickly, which surprised me. But then it turned out he had good news. He'd landed a job in the pay office at Leichhardt Council. They were taking on returned men, he said. There might even be a chance of something for me in the future. I was all ready to sneer, but I pulled up.

"Is that right?" I said. "Let me know if anything comes up."

"You fair dinkum?"

"Sure, I am. Working the government stroke at Leichhardt Council might not be the worst way to end up."

Ron beamed. "Good on you, Billy. That's the right attitude." He waited until Mum had left the room, then said quietly, "That offer I made the other day still stands, Bill. I could get a few good tough blokes together at short notice. Whoever did this to you," pointing to my battered face, "we could repay the debt—with interest."

"Thanks, but don't worry about it. It's over, Ron. It really is."

One afternoon the following week, I collected the coupons from the Oxford Street hideout and took Max over to Herb's flat to get matters settled once and for all.

Kitty opened the door. Herb was still asleep, she said, clearly none too happy about it. We waited in the lounge room while she shouted at Herb. Then Herb appeared, grumpy and disheveled. He poured himself a nip of rum, and slowly started to come good. Max took a drink as well.

"So what do you want at this bloody hour?" he said.

"We've got to get those coupons moving," I said. "Your buyer has shot through, right?"

97

"Well, I haven't heard from him for a while, it's true. The bastard. But I've been too busy to go looking for him."

"Bugger that," I said. "I've got a better idea anyway. We can sell those coupons ourselves. No middleman. They cost us nothing, so if we sell them direct, we'll make a motza on them."

"It'll take us twenty years."

"So what?" I handed him that week's edition of *The Truth*. "See what Ben Chifley is saying—rationing is here to stay, for at least another two years, maybe more."

Max shook his head. "Man, I'll tell you, I'm sick to death of all this austerity bullshit. What is it with this Chifley bloke, anyway? The friggin' war's over, but that miserable bastard doesn't want anyone enjoying anything."

"It's for the national good, Max. Like he says, if we're not careful, the Depression will come back—and then where would we be? Old Ben's right. I'm a Chifley man, and you should be too."

"Selling the coupons direct will be slow going," Herb said.

"We can set up a network. We sell them wholesale to anyone with a bit of savvy. There are some bodgie Yanks up at Burt's who might be in it. And there are people you know around the nightclubs and pubs—let them do the footwork. What do you reckon?"

"Yeah, I guess so."

"All right. The coupons are in the car. We can do a whack up right now."

Max and I went straight to Burt's Milk Bar, to see the louts.

The girl behind the counter told me the jukebox was on the blink. The needle was shot, so I went out to the car to get a replacement. When I came back Max was holding a pile of records he'd taken out of the rack.

"You making any money with this stuff?" he said.

"Not a lot."

He started flipping through them. "No wonder. 'Dugout Ditties' by the Jolly Old Fellows; 'Chin Up, Cheerio, and Carry On'; 'Painting the Clouds With Sunshine'—God help us, what a crock." He walked over to the counter. "Hey love, put these in the rubbish bin for me will you?"

"You can't do that, Max. Mick—"

Max broke a couple of discs over his knee.

"—paid a lot of money for them."

"Then he's a goose." He handed the broken pieces of shellac to the girl and walked back to the jukebox.

Max's little demonstration had attracted the attention of the milk-bar cowboys up the back. A few of them came up to the jukebox.

Max picked up more discs. "'Underneath the Arches,' 'Tiptoe Through the Tulips,' and what's this? 'McNamara's Band.' Suffering Jesus on the cross, I ask you!"

I tried to grab them out of his hand, but he spun around and sent one record sailing out the door, then another. I got hold of another one, but by then the louts were following Max's lead. They threw the records to each other over my head, and started smashing them, or throwing them out the front door. The more I ran around trying to stop them, the better fun they had. In less than three minutes Mick's record collection lay shattered on the floor, and outside on the roadway cars were driving over their broken remains.

Then everyone suddenly stopped dead. The girl came out from behind the counter and began sweeping up the mess.

"You fucking bastards," I said. "You smashed every one of them."

The hooligans looked shame-faced.

"Bull," Max said. "Look, I saved this one." He held up an unbroken disc.

I stared at him.

He smiled. "Bunny Berrigan, 'I Can't Get Started.' You wouldn't break that one. But the rest of them"—he looked around the floor—"they were all shit." He turned to the louts, "Weren't they?"

"Well, yeah, they weren't much chop, pal, it's true."

"You bastards, you had no right." I sat down and groaned.

Max came over and said, "Listen, Bill, if you're going to be like that about it, I'll give you a few from my personal collection."

"Fucking great."

"Better than that lot, Bill. We can go and get them right now."

"You got enough to fill the whole jukebox?"

"Yeah. We can even rotate them every couple of weeks if you like. Of course, I'd expect a cut."

"Let's go get them, then."

The bodgie Yank spoke up. "And don't forget, you were, ah, going to see about those jeans."

"What?"

"The dungarees. The American strides. Remember?"

"Oh yeah. I'll see what I can do."

Two hours later I'd brought back a sack of dungarees and Max had restocked the jukebox with his own jazz and hillbilly records. Spike Jones, Louis Jordan, Lionel Hampton, Lucky Millinder, T-Bone Walker, Ella Mae Morse, Spade Cooley, the Delmore Brothers, Gene Autry . . .

As we were closing the lid I said, "But this is no good. There are no Benny Goodman records here, or Artie Shaw. What about Glenn Miller? And Bing Crosby, for Christ's sake?"

"Strictly for unhep squares, dad. Get hep to the rebop, pop." He put a zack in the machine and punched in a selection.

The needle dropped. A boogie piano, with a tenor sax blasting over the top, then a blues shouter with a voice like Tarzan's yodel:

Up jumped the devil, he was driving a Chevrolet,
Well, up jumped the devil in a big old Chevrolet
He said, "You've had your fun, now it's time for you to pay."

"Who's that?" I said.
"No one you'd know. But it's the duck's guts."
The mob in the milk bar seemed to like it too: a couple started jiving.

Up jumped the devil playing a mellow saxophone,
Yes, up jumped the devil playing a mellow saxophone
He said, "Follow me children, I've come to take you home."

Another couple started dancing, really going for it. The bloke's jacket and tie flew all over the place and the girl's skirt fanned out, showing a sweet pair of legs and a flash of underwear. A middle-aged bloke stood up from one of the booths, put his hat on and ushered his missus and two little kids out of the place, muttering "Disgraceful" as he passed.

The fox and the rabbit were doing the bumpity bump,
Monkey and the ba-boon were goin' all bumpity bump
All the hepcats were boppin' at the Devil's jump.

By the time it finished there were a dozen kids dancing in the aisle between the booths.
"What's the name of that song?" I said to Max.
"'The Devil's Jump'."
"What does that mean?"

"I don't know. It's a dance step, I guess."

Someone put another sixpence in and played the song again. The kids played it another three times before they started on the others—Nat Cole doing "Straighten Up and Fly Right" and Lionel Hampton playing "Flying Home."

I sat there and watched, not doing a thing, as sixpence after sixpence went into the jukebox, and pretty girls kept dancing up a storm. Was this what virtuous god-fearing enterprise looked like? Maybe not quite, but at least it was legal. More or less. And watching those zacks dropping into the slot, I knew there was something in this, something big.

I sold four pairs of dungarees, too, at fifteen shillings each, with an arrangement to unload another half dozen pairs as soon as I could get back there with them.

Before we left I said to Danny, the bodgie Yank, "You blokes ever get over Newtown way?"

"Oh yeah, sometimes. Why?"

"You know the Hi Society?"

He shook his head. "We don't go there too often. The Abercrombie Mob hang around that place. They'll turn on a blue as soon as look you."

"So I've heard. Well, I don't want to get you into trouble, but if you and your mates were to just pay a quick visit to Newtown—not to get involved in a blue, you understand—but if you could at least let the Abercrombie mob see you, wearing your dungarees, then maybe I could get hold of some more for you at a special rate. Maybe you could do all right for yourself."

He gave me a shrewd look. "Oh yeah? I'll see what we can do. And listen pal, don't get the wrong idea. We're not *scared* of those sheilas over at Newtown, or anything."

"Yeah, I know that. Listen, while we're talking business, can you use any ration coupons?"

6

The inquest into the death of Eddie Worrall was held in mid-December. There were questions as to why Worrall's uniform was undamaged by fire, and the fire brigade feller said that Worrall had apparently been caught in a section of the building where there was more smoke than actual fire, and had succumbed before he could escape.

The coroner had harsh words for the authorities about the body having remained in the ruins for so long; neither the police, the city council nor the fire brigade was able to explain how it happened, except to say they had been so chronically under-manned that they'd been unable to follow up on all accident and fire scenes. He returned a finding that Eddie Worrall had died by asphyxiation.

I wasn't called on to give evidence.

I went back to the Durban Club one more time to try and find the toolbox in the cellar office, but everything had been cleared out. So I got a list from Carmody of what tools he needed and hit the second-hand merchants in Newtown.

The weeks passed. I kept out of trouble, sticking to the path of righteousness, or at least my version of it. Things fell nicely into place on the commercial side. The coupons did a steady trade and so did the dungarees. Even the jukebox at Burt's started to produce a handsome return. I kept collecting Toohey's rents, and over the months the combined take from the various enterprises built into a very attractive bundle, safely put away in the fireplace of my Paddington hideout.

I saw nothing more of Ray Waters; Aubrey and his pals didn't reappear, either. I kept myself amused by going to the races. I did some penciling for a couple of different bookmakers, and in my spare time I practiced my card tricks.

Jimmy Stevenson kept showing me moves and maneuvers, but I could tell he was getting bored with it. One week he had me show him everything I'd learned so far. When I'd finished, he shook his head and said, "I'm sorry feller, but I have to tell you—you're never going to make a good card man."

"But it's only been a few months," I said. "It would take years to get any good at these, I know that. I'm willing to put in the time."

He shook his head. "It's getting to be hard going. For *me*. I think I'd rather go back to paying rent." Jimmy called his son into the room and handed him the deck. "Show Bill what you can do," he said.

The kid looked nervously from his dad to me.

"It's all right, son," he said. "Just go for it."

The kid shuffled the deck, flicked the cards from hand to hand, fanned them out, cut and then dealt me, his father and himself each a card. "Jack of diamonds," he said, tapping mine. He pointed at his father's card. "Eight of hearts," and as he picked up his own said, "Ace of clubs."

We turned our cards over. He had it right.

He held the deck out to me. "Take the top card, look at it."

I did. It was a seven of diamonds.

"Put it back on top."

I did, and the kid then shuffled the deck—thoroughly and

fairly, as far as I could tell.

"Take the top card," he said.

It was the seven of diamonds.

"How the hell did you do that?" I said.

The kid smiled. "That card never moved."

"You see," said Jimmy. "If you really had the knack it'd be showing by now."

I shook my head and sighed.

"But I'll give you one more lesson—maybe the most important one of all. You won't make it as a shark, but I can show you some things that'll make it hard for a shark to put anything past you. Close your eyes and listen to this. Son, do a legitimate deal."

Little Jimmy dealt the cards.

"Hear that? There's a kind of clicking sound. Now son, I want you to bottom deal."

Jimmy dealt again.

"Good. Now hear that sort of swish-click, Bill? That's the sound that second dealing and bottom dealing make. It's a sure sign, even if the movement looks all right, and young Jimmy's deal looks so good that even *I'm* hard pressed to spot the chicanery!

"Now, let me and young Jimmy here show you a thing or two about collusion . . . "

So ended my dream of becoming a card shark.

I started dropping in at the Police Boys Club. Sergeant Jennings didn't quite treat me like the lost sheep returning to the fold, but the first time I walked in, it was close. "A brand snatched from the burning," he called me. After introducing me around, he put me in a pair of boxing gloves and sent me into the ring with a bloke from Sydenham named Ernie.

Ernie had a broken nose, skinny arms, round shoulders, and a sunken chest, so I didn't think he'd present too many problems.

In fact, he wasn't too bad, and knocked me on my arse twice in the first round. Jennings intervened to give me some tips, and I was able to make Ernie lose his balance once or twice in the next round.

That pretty much remained the pattern on all my visits to Marrickville Police Boys Club. When it came to the manly art of scientific pugilism, I ranked around the middle.

The fellers didn't let on much about what they got up to away from the club. But breaking and entering figured in it, I discovered, as did a certain amount of standover. I was invited to participate in some of the group's extra-curricular activities. I said thanks, but no. But I was able to interest Ernie and some of the brighter lads in coupon distribution, which worked out well for all concerned.

Jennings was a lay preacher, something of a bible-basher, and took his work among wayward youth very seriously. The way to a decent life, he said, was to develop inner strength, live cleanly, do your bit, and be content with what you got in return. Drinking, gambling, fornicating, swearing, jitterbugging—all these things drove you down the slippery road to perdition, while a clean mind and a healthy body were stepping stones on the golden path of virtue. And so on.

Sometimes he'd tell us stories supposedly drawn from his experiences as a copper. He reckoned every villain he'd ever known had come to a bad end and that lurks and rorts and petty crime were for weak individuals who couldn't or wouldn't knuckle down to honest work and do their duty. This didn't entirely square with my own experience—every time I'd ever made a sly quid it made me feel good; smarter, quicker, stronger and luckier than the vast mob of squareheads—but I kept that opinion to myself out of respect for Jennings' feelings, just as the Marrickville boys didn't let on about their break-ins and standover activities.

Mum and Ron smiled upon my new approach, though Ron

was of the opinion that my future welfare might depend on more than just good intentions.

"Get yourself a ticket," he said.

"What, you mean a trade?"

"Yeah."

"Like a fitter and turner or a boilermaker or a pastry cook or something?"

"It doesn't have to be just that. Before I was demobbed the army sent around a booklet saying we should give some serious thought to our futures. This booklet said how if you weren't sure what to do, then try to think about what you like doing, and then try to find an occupation that included that in it. If you liked mucking around with motors, you could become a mechanic. If you were good with tools, you could be a carpenter. So what do you like doing?"

"Nothing you get paid for."

"When you were at school, you used to draw all over your school books—the Phantom and Boofhead, and racehorses and tanks, stuff like that. You weren't too bad, as I remember."

"Well—"

"I've got it. Commercial Art! You don't even have to get dirty."

So I enrolled in a commercial drawing course at East Sydney Tech. The first day the teacher propped his push-bike up in the middle of the room and told us to us to do as exact a drawing of it as we could. A couple of the fellers in the class were pretty good at it. My own effort was so-so.

I didn't get much better as the days passed, but I did a nice little trade in coupons with one or two sharpies in the class. At the end of the second week a few of the fellers started talking about job prospects.

"A mate of mine got a start working for Althouse and Geiger, designing the big billboards."

"Oh yeah?"

"Yeah. They're paying him over three pounds a week."

"Three quid!" I said.

"Too right. Lucky bastard."

I'd made double that on my very first day driving for Toohey, and I'd been only sixteen at the time! After that, I found it hard to maintain my enthusiasm for educational self-improvement, and my attendance at tech became patchy.

As the first summer of the peace wore itself out, I wasn't feeling too bad about things in general. And then came the capper—my virtue was rewarded.

One Saturday in late March I was at Randwick races. It was a bright sunny day, and there was a big crowd. There were plenty of good nags running around the track, and plenty of good money chasing the nags. Mid afternoon I ran into Lucy Chance in the leger with one of her silvertail boyfriends. We had established a habit of trading insults each time we crossed paths, but I was sort of glad to see her anyway.

She was wearing a light-colored dress with a pattern of big dark red roses. Her skin was still pale, her hair blue-black. We greeted each other coolly, as usual, chatted briefly about our selections for the next race, and went our separate ways.

I saw her again at four o'clock, but she was alone this time.

"What's happened to your mate?"

She made a face, but didn't look at me. "Gone," she said. Then she muttered quietly, with an edge in her voice that was pure Botany, "Friggin' goose that he is."

I stood and stared. Was this really Lucy Chance, who always spoke with such carefully rounded vowels, who carried herself like a great lady and dressed like a fashion model?

She turned to me. "Have you got a cigarette?"

I wished I had. "I'll go and get you one."

"Don't bother."

Just then the breeze picked up, carrying a hint of autumn chill. Goose bumps appeared on her bare arms, and she rubbed her shoulders.

"Do you want to go somewhere?" I said.

She looked at me for a few seconds. "Yeah, all right."

We spent the rest of that day together—a meal at King's Cross, then dancing at the California. Afterwards we sat talking for a long time in the Chev outside her flat at Darling Point. There was no hanky panky, but we parted with an arrangement to meet again the following week.

Next morning I woke up thinking about her. She was so different to what I'd always thought. She seemed warm and soft. She told funny stories, too. I wanted to touch her, talk to her, listen to her speak.

We met the next week, went to see *The Grapes of Wrath* with Henry Fonda. Afterwards I dropped her home. This time I was invited in. As soon as we got in the door I put my arms around her shoulders. Lucy leaned against me and let all her muscles go soft, so her body molded itself to the shape of mine. We went to her bedroom.

There was a power blackout that night, so we did it mostly by touch. Even in the dark Lucy's white skin glowed. I wasn't exactly a novice, but this was something new. Every inch of her skin felt good. Wherever it touched mine I got an electric charge. When we were naked, with her dark hair rolling around, her arms around my neck, every touch, every sound and smell was better than anything I'd ever experienced. I spent hours discovering her, and at the end felt like I hadn't even begun.

I went home just before dawn, and thought about her all the next day. For the first time I could remember, I thought: I'm glad to be alive. I was glad I was drawing breath, glad I would be seeing Lucy again soon, glad I would be sleeping with her again.

Then I started worrying that maybe I wouldn't see her again, that it had just been a brief fling for her. The more I thought about that, the worse I felt.

I rang her at five o'clock on Sunday night.

"This is Billy," I said when she answered.

"Billy who?" she said.

I stuttered, then was lost for words.

Lucy laughed. "Take it easy, lover boy. I'm just stirring you." We talked on the phone for an hour, and I felt good again.

When I hung up, I knew I loved Lucy Chance. I loved everything about her.

I started seeing her, once or twice a week. For a while there, I was the happiest bloke in Sydney. We went dancing, to the pictures, to nightclubs. We went away for a long weekend, camping down at Port Hacking. I caught some flathead and she filleted them perfectly—something very few people can do.

"Here was I thinking you were too posh for such things," I said.

"I used to do this for my dad," she said.

That whole time we were there, she got around in one of my cotton shirts, tied at the waist, nothing underneath.

On more than one occasion we talked all through the night. We told each other everything. Or nearly everything—we both skirted around our shadier activities. I only referred in passing to Mick Toohey and related matters, and she didn't go into any details about the commercial side of her life.

But I kind of understood anyway. She'd grown up in bad circumstances in Botany, with a no-hoper father and a mob of useless brothers and sisters. Her mother was sure her youngest, prettiest daughter was meant for better things, and so with a few elocution lessons, some careful introductions, and a lot of inborn talents, Lucy had made it to Darling Point, to a flat she was currently sharing with Molly Price.

At first it didn't bother me too much. Lucy and Molly were only doing what plenty of girls had done during the war years, when entertaining Americans and boosting morale was considered an honorable part of the war effort. If she was still doing it now, after most girls had got out of the game, how awful was that, really?

But over time an idea started to grow in my mind—that maybe I could marry Lucy, that we could set ourselves up, and that she wouldn't have to hawk it any more, that we could live together all the time. I kept the idea to myself, waiting for the right time. To tell the truth, I was a bit scared of putting it to her directly, or too soon. I was just a young feller, after all—with plenty of promise, maybe, but not a lot of runs on the board yet.

I wasn't completely without assets, though. There were two tidy and steadily growing bundles of cash in the cavity behind the fireplace at 36 Oxford Street—the proceeds of the coupon racket and Mick Toohey's rent money. It was a moot point just how much of the money in the fireplace was rightfully mine. Mick was always one to put a headlock on a quid, and if he was around to argue the toss, he'd probably say five per cent was a reasonable commission, perhaps less. I was thinking more like ten, even twenty per cent.

Lurking in the back of my mind, of course, was another thought. If Toohey really was dead, was there any good reason why, with a bit of luck and a bit of cunning, I couldn't keep all the rent money?

It wasn't enough for me to live the rest of my life in ease, but it was plenty to get started somewhere. Enough maybe for a love nest for me and Lucy. But sooner or later I'd have to get a job. That was the fly in the ointment.

Then my brother stepped in. He came home from work one day, smiling broadly.

"I might just have a surprise for you, William," he said.

"And what might that be?"

"George Mooney at the depot says they'll be needing a young bloke in the Parks and Gardens Department in May. Your name was mentioned. He says if things work out, you could start in a couple of weeks."

For some reason, I got an awful, dead feeling.

"In the office?" I said.

"No—in the ranks, so to speak."

"Sweeping the flaming streets?"

Ron laughed. "Keep your hat on. You wouldn't be sweeping the streets. Get this—they need an apprentice signwriter. Right up your alley."

"Well . . . ah, thanks, Ron."

"They're a tremendous bunch of blokes down there at the council. Returned men, most of them."

"Copacetic."

"You get two weeks paid annual leave, it's a forty-four hour week, and they'll even give you time off to go to tech. And later there'll be paid sick leave, and superannuation."

Ron stood there grinning. I tried to be thrilled to bits, but I couldn't manage it.

Ron's face darkened. "What's the matter? You don't seem too pleased."

"No, I'm knocked out solid, Ron, really."

"I know you have your doubts, but it's the right thing for you, Bill, I know it."

And as I thought more about it that night, I figured maybe it wouldn't be too bad. I certainly hadn't seen too many council blokes working themselves into an early grave. And a bit of regular money wouldn't hurt. I guessed this was what *not* being a lurk merchant entailed.

The next day Ron got me to drive him out to Padstow, a sleepy little stop on the East Hills line. He directed me down a new dirt road which cut through the bush about half a mile from the station, and then told me to stop at a bend, where a "for sale" sign was nailed to a gum tree.

Ron got out of the car. "What do you reckon?" he said.

"Breathtaking."

"I've bought this land. A quarter acre. This is where me and Glenys are going to build our house."

He walked over into the scrub. "We'll put the house here." He paced it out. "And the garage over here. A chook shed out the back there, a swing for the little ones, all that." He turned around, smiling. "What do you say? Pretty good, eh?"

"Yeah, tremendous."

"I know it's not much now. But when they get the sewer in and the roads are sealed, this will be a good place. Quiet and clean. Decent people. Good fishing—the Georges River is just over the hill. There are flathead down there that'd take your arm off."

I nodded.

Ron walked back over to where I was standing. "There are other blocks for sale around here."

He paused, waiting for a response, but I didn't oblige.

"Bill, it might not be the main thing on your mind right now, but you should think seriously about getting yourself some land, for later on. Not in the rotten shithole city, but out here, in the fresh air. It'll cost you a bit, mind. Two or three hundred quid for something reasonable. But I can help you out with money if necessary."

I just looked at him.

"Sooner or later you're going to want to settle down." He was grinning.

I looked down the length of grey scrub, tried to picture a bungalow, a garden in front, a veggie patch out the back, a car parked in the garage. I could *almost* see it. I pictured myself inside, sitting by the fire in my smoking jacket after a hard day's work, a pipe stuck in my dial, the evening paper on my knee, a faithful hound at my feet. Lucy bringing in two snifters of brandy. Then to bed for a night of passionate lovemaking, a pair of blissful love birds in our cabin built for two. Or maybe three, come to think of it. After all, if Lucy did marry me, sooner or later she'd probably want to have a sprout or two running around the place.

As I stood there thinking, it began to seem like it might not be the end of the world. Maybe it could be all right. I could teach the little feller to kick a football, catch a fish, forge a ration coupon . . . No, that wouldn't do. If there were to be love nests for two, kiddies and veggie patches, then it would have to be the squarehead life for William Glasheen, Esq. Which I suppose I was prepared for. Yes, I was definitely prepared for it. Pretty definitely.

"Well, what do you reckon? Ron said. "Can you picture it?"

"Nearly."

By the time April 1946 rolled around, things were going swimmingly on the property-management front. The gypsies were paying up all right, and even most of the chronic defaulters were more or less up to date. True, the Abercrombie Boys were touching me for ten bob a week, but each time I saw them wearing blue jeans they'd bought indirectly from me, I felt a little less bad about it.

Old Carmody in Chippendale was something of a nagger, though. Once he started talking it was hard to get away, so I tended to avoid him. He'd been at me for months to come in and have a squiz at the work he'd done, but I really didn't care that much, and kept putting him off. Finally, when I ran out of excuses, I went inside for the grand tour.

The holes in the walls had been patched up, and he'd run the plumbing in to the kitchen. Overall the place looked clean and sound. Almost comfortable.

"You've done a lot. Cripes, it's come up good."

"I still haven't dug the trench to run the kitchen waste water into the sewer out the back, so the kitchen tap's just for show," he said. "But my back's too crook for any real digging. I started, but I had to pull up again."

"Can you get one of the kids around here to dig it, if I give you a few bob?"

"Not likely. But I've got a mattock and shovel here."

"You want *me* to dig it?" I said.

"Then I could lay the terra-cotta pipes this afternoon, do the backfilling myself tomorrow. Of course if you think you're too good to get your hands dirty—."

"Give me that bloody mattock."

"That's the way. Take the Devil's jump!"

I stopped and looked at him.

"What?"

"Have a go! I've got some work togs here. You wouldn't want to ruin your clothes."

I thought I'd knock it over in an hour, but the back yard was full of buried refuse—bits of rusted iron, bones, broken house bricks, even an old gas stove. I dug up endless pieces of junk, all pressed hard into the compacted dirt. Carmody cleaned up as I went, but he wasn't up to any heavy work.

By mid-afternoon I was halfway through the job, and Carmody made a pot of tea, which I was more than ready for. We sat down in the shade. He rolled a smoke.

"How you holding out there?" Jack said.

"Fine. Good to get it done."

"Misery was a bit slow getting around to things like that."

"Yeah he was," I said. "Can I ask you a question?"

His face took on the guarded look. "You can ask me. I might not be able to tell you."

"That expression you used earlier on. You said I should take the Devil's jump. I was wondering what you meant by that."

"Why do you ask?"

"Misery—Toohey, I mean—used that expression once. He said he was for the Devil's jump."

"Why don't you ask him what he meant?"

"Well, Mick hasn't been seen around for a while. I suppose you knew that?"

"I might have heard something to that effect, but you hear all sorts of things, don't you?"

"Yeah, you do. So, the Devil's jump. I was wondering, you know—"

Carmody's expression became serious and then sort of far-away. He was silent for a couple of minutes. I kept my mouth shut.

When he turned back to me, he was smiling, but his brow was creased.

"The Devil's jump . . . it was Gallipoli slang."

He looked away again. Another minute passed. Just when I thought he'd said all he was going to say, he started up again.

"We were stuck in these shitty trenches—and I mean *shitty*—for weeks on end. We were all young blokes, but Misery was the baby of the mob. The Turks were only a couple of hundred yards away. Nothing was happening. Days would go by and not a shot was fired, but the moment you stuck your head up, some Turk arsehole would take a pot shot at it. Blokes were doing their business right there in the trench. So one night a few of the blokes crawled out and dug a bog behind a little rise, about thirty yards from our trench. They did a good job, too—it was wide and deep, even had a bit of tin for a roof. Next day we resolved there was to be no more shitting in our own nest. It was

116

all a bit of a joke, you see."

"Yeah."

"We treated everything as a joke. Not that we weren't scared. We were scared all the time. But you didn't show it. Or tried not to, at any rate. We all acted up, game as Ned Kelly. Anyway, we decided that we would all make use of the long drop from now on. The problem was, you had to run a bit of a gauntlet each time you wanted to use it. The snipers were a long way off, but the odd bullet would go whizzing past your head . . . it sort of put the wind up you."

"I can imagine it would."

"We used to act like we couldn't care less, though. You'd go to the bog, hands in your pockets, whistling, like you were strolling down to the thunder box in your own back yard on a Sunday morning. Then the Turks would start shooting at you. You'd do your best to ignore it, which really gave the Turks the shits. Of course, you were walking as smartly as you decently could, but without *seeming* to be in any hurry. Once you got there, you were safe—the seat was out of the firing line. It was getting there that was risky.

"The bog got to be called the Devil's jump. You put off going as long as you could, but the time would come when you couldn't wait any longer. So if a bloke was off to the bog, he'd say, 'Oh well, nothing else for it. It's time for the Devil's jump.' After a while, it came to mean taking a risk of any sort. But not just any risk—it meant that you were risking your life, everything, but you were blowed if you'd let on that you were worried about it."

"And Toohey was in on it?"

"Come to think of it, it might have been him who came up with the term in the first place."

Carmody went off into memory land again for a moment.

"Then one day Clarrie Nolan *did* cop a bullet on his way to the bog. It sent him into convulsions—he was lying there, twitching and jerking. Like a fish out of water. He died after a couple of minutes. Then one of us said, 'the Devil's jump'. So it came to mean that, as well, from then on."

"Dying, you mean?"

"Yeah. You'd say, so and so took the Devil's jump."

"So, if Mick Toohey told me he was for the Devil's jump, what do you reckon he meant?"

Carmody looked at me closely. "When did he say that to you?"

"A while ago. The last time I saw him. At the end of the day the war ended."

He looked away and nodded slowly. "Could've meant a lot of things. Could've meant anything, really." Subject closed.

It was nearly dark before I'd finished the eight or ten yards of trench.

"Good job," Carmody said. "I'll do the sewer tomorrow." He turned to me and said, "Thanks son. You're a good feller."

"Forget it, uncle. A bit of digging never hurt anyone," I said, even though my palms were blistered and my back was sore.

As I was leaving he said, "Sprague's electrics are all stuffed up."

"Yeah I know. She's been at me for weeks."

"I can do a bit of electrics."

"Go ahead then, do what you can. But if you're going to do that, you may as well forget about paying rent for the time being. See you later."

Carmody wasn't at home the following weekend, but when I got to the Spragues, the old girl told me he'd fixed the wiring. I gave her the address of another of Toohey's properties, down the road at Ultimo, where they were having plumbing problems, and asked her to sound Jack out about having a look at it if she saw him in the next few days,.

"I'll do that," she said. "It does him good, you know, doing these odd jobs."

By the following weekend Carmody had sorted out the plumbing at the Ultimo place, and fixed the guttering on another house.

Soon he was more than working off his rent, so I'd started paying him cash money on top. He was reluctant at first, said he liked to be useful, but I pressed it on him. He wasn't a bad old bloke, really, but he still buttonholed me every time I came around, wanting me to inspect his handiwork. I'd given him the go-ahead to patch up a section of ceiling and fix the leaky roof on his own place, and he dragged me upstairs to show me the patch, as well as a new manhole he'd installed.

"I'll get the ladder, you can get up there and have a look inside."

"That's all right, Jack," I said, "I can see from down here that you've done a beaut job. Toohey will be pleased."

Carmody nodded, but said nothing.

In May I started at the Council depot. They put me to work writing signs like *LADIES; GENTS;* or *DO NOT LOITER – By Order, Town Clerk*; or a list of the opening hours for the Baby Health Center, or a warning that Bill Posters would be prosecuted.

The job paid one hundred and twenty-five pounds a year and the working day started at seven-thirty in the morning. But at least it wasn't hard work. Somebody else would pencil in the letters, then I colored them in. Mid-morning I'd make the pot of tea for smoko, then do the same thing again mid-arvo.

On the afternoon of the second day the supervisor said I was doing all right, and in a few weeks time he would give me a crack at something more interesting. I told him that'd be really tremendous. He looked at me for a few seconds, not sure whether I was being smart or not.

After work on my third day I dropped into the Toxteth, just for the one. As I sat at the bar thumbing through the afternoon paper, a bloke sidled up to me and said quietly, "How you going there, sport?"

It was the same hard-faced returned man who was forever threatening to get together with his mates, whoever they were, and give the commos a good kick in the arse.

"Real good."

He pointed at my newspaper. "How well do you think things are going in the country right now?"

As usual the newspaper was plastered with news of strikes and dissension and hardship. There was the Bunnerong Power workers' strike, the wharfies' ongoing work-to-rule, and the coal miners *never* seemed to do a full day's yakka. Then there was all the talk about a return to the Depression years. Chifley seemed to be doing his best, but no one knew where things really stood. Everything was still in short supply. Returned soldiers were sleeping in air-raid shelters and public toilets; there was a rat plague in the Horseshoe; and I had to get up to go to work the next morning.

So what could I say to the feller but, "I think things are up to shit."

He nodded. "Tell me this, then. Do you want to do something about it?"

"Such as what?"

He looked right and left, leaned in closer and whispered, "Tomorrow night. Leichhardt Scout Hall. A meeting of the Patriotic League. Good, decent fellows. You're welcome to come. But you'll need to be vouched for by someone . . . your former commanding officer, or someone in the police."

"Thanks for the invitation, pal. I'll give it some thought."

He grabbed my sleeve. "Civilization is at the crossroads. The commos are poised to take over. Those unpatriotic swine in the unions take their orders directly from Joe Stalin, and the Labor Party is dancing to their tune. Did you know that? I'm telling you, the commos are a bigger threat now than the Japs were in '42. Look at what's happening to the north, in Indonesia, Malaya, China. Look at the darkie rabble in India. It's all the work of the reds. The signs are all there. The Allies should have given Hitler a free hand to clear the riff-raff out and then stepped in afterwards to clean him up." He let go of my sleeve. "Think about it," he said.

"I certainly will, old cob."

"The Chifley socialists are planning to flood the country with filthy Eyeties and Greeks and Slavs, and Christ only knows who else. What do you think of that?"

"Crikey, look at the time! I've got to shoot through, uncle."

7

As I neared home, something seemed wrong. Unlike the others on the street, our house was dark, even though it was getting late and Mum rarely went out in the evenings. Then I saw that the front window was smashed. I parked the car and walked carefully around the back. The kitchen door was open.

I called out, "Mum, Ron? Anyone home?"

"I'm here," Ron answered from the darkness of the kitchen.

The light came on. Ron was holding an axe handle. The kitchen was a mess, tins of flour, sugar, golden syrup upended on the floor.

Ron put the axe handle down. "The rest of the house is worse than this."

"What happened?"

"I was hoping you could tell me."

I walked through to the lounge. More broken windows, the couch turned over, the drawers of the sideboard pulled out and their contents tipped onto the floor. My room was even worse, and someone had pissed on the carpet.

I went back to the kitchen.

"Where's Mum?"

"She's in hospital."

"Who? Did they . . . ?"

Ron shook his head. "She called the doctor. She's been having dizzy spells, and she fainted three times this morning. They've put her into Marrickville Hospital for tests."

"Is she all right?"

"The quack said it's probably a woman's problem. He just wanted to be sure."

"What happened here?"

"You reckon you don't know?"

"Well, no."

Just then a car door slammed outside. Male voices came up the side passage. Ron looked at me and picked up the axe handle.

A voice called from outside, "Ron? You there?"

"In here, Charlie," he said.

Four blokes came in, carrying iron bars and wooden clubs. His old Army mates. They shook hands with Ron. He didn't exactly introduce us, just gestured dismissively in my direction, saying, "this is Bill."

They had a sugar bag full of beer bottles with them. Ron righted a few chairs and they sat down. Silence for a moment while they all took a long drink.

"So what happens next?" one of them said.

Ron fixed me with a hard look. "Brother William here tells us who did this and what's going on. Then we go and get quits."

"Don't look at me," I said. "It could have been anyone, maybe a house breaker."

Ron shook his head. "I thought—that is, I *hoped*—you'd separated yourself from the riff-raff and profiteers and started to wake up. But I was wrong."

"Get rooted. How do you know this concerns me?"

He reached into his top pocket, took out a piece of crumpled paper, and threw it across to me.

"That's how."

I picked it up and straightened it out.

B. GLASHEIN — THERES MORE OF THIS FOR YOU
IF YOU DONT HAND OVER THE REGISTER.
WE ARE WAITING FOR YOU AT ZIEGFELDS.
IF WE HAVE TO COME LOOKING FOR YOU
AGAIN IT WILL JUST BE WORSE FOR YOU.
BRING THE REGISTER IMEDIATELY OR YOUR IN
FOR IT. COME TO THE CAFE TONIGHT OR
TOMORROW AND ASK FOR HARRY, OTHERWISE
WE WILL BE BACK AND IT WONT GO WELL FOR
YOU, YOU CAN BE SURE OF THAT

I looked up.

Ron said, "Well? What's it about? What's the register?"

"I don't know, I really don't. I thought this business was all over. It just doesn't make sense."

"What about these, do these make sense?" He threw a bundle of coupons at me.

I didn't answer.

"Mum found them in the wash."

Ron's mates were staring hard at me.

"Listen," I said, "there's no need to get shitty. I'll cut you blokes in, too. A special rate, as mates of Ronny."

One of them stood up, went outside, shaking his head. Another looked from me to Ron, back at me again.

Ron's mouth was set, and he was breathing noisily through his nose. "I got you a job," he said quietly, "a job with a future. You *said* you were on side. You *looked* like you were on side. But all along you were rorting and running lurks. And running around with tarts from the Eastern suburbs."

I was on my feet and half way to him, but his mates held me back.

"What do you mean by that?" I said.

124

"I hear things, don't you worry. I know where you go and who you see. And I know you're mixing with the wrong type of people. Or that's what I thought. But now I'm starting to think you're mixing with exactly the right sort of people—because you're one of them. You haven't got the gumption to stick with this job and settle down."

I stopped straining against the two blokes holding me, and they released me. I sat down again. "Ron," I said, "I'm sorry to have to tell you, but you're an idiot. You wouldn't understand what I do, and you wouldn't understand the people I see, so I'm not going to try to explain myself—or them—to you. As for the job? Well let me tell you, writing *Please Flush After Use* twenty times a day wasn't quite what I had in mind for my life's work, thanks all the same."

"Go for your life," Ron said. "All I care about is that you've brought your trouble home—again. And now it's up to me to sort it out, because you obviously can't. Those mongrels who came around last year. Are they the same people as this lot?" He held up the note.

"Buggered if I know."

Ron stood up. "Well we better go and find out then."

"What?"

"We're going to pay these bludgers a visit, let them know that if they pick a blue with the Glasheens, they might just get more than they bargained for."

"Oh come on, Ron, don't be stupid."

Ron's mates were on their feet, too, eager to go the thump, as though their crankiness with me had now been redirected to all enemies of the Glasheen clan. Cripes, I thought.

Ron said, "We didn't fight the Japs back over the Kokoda Track, yard by yard, mile by bloody mile, only to come home and be pushed around by a bunch of gutless ratbags and lurk merchants."

His mates voiced their agreement.

"All right," he said to them, "Let's go then."

"Where are you going?"

"To this Ziegfeld's place."

"Oh, beaut. I'll call the hospital in advance then, will I? Tell them to be ready for you?"

"On your feet, Bill. You're coming with us."

"Forget it."

Twenty minutes later we pulled up outside Ziegfeld's. I'd never set foot inside, but I knew the place. It was an after-hours spot in King Street, in the city. It had a little band; there was dancing and indifferent food. The place maintained a generally tolerant and welcoming attitude to the more disreputable elements of Sydney society. One night Jack Davey and his socialite crew might be there for some after hours grogging on, the next night someone would be knifed. Shootings were not unknown, nor was it unheard of for a beer glass to be applied forcefully to someone's face.

We got out of the car. Ron and his mates were grim-faced, clutching their makeshift weapons. Hoochie-coochie music leaked out of the club, then came a peal of female laughter.

Ron said, "You can wait here, Bill. This is a job for men."

"Oh, really?"

"Just mind the car and be ready to shoot through when the time comes."

He faced his mates. "All right, fellers. Let's show these pricks they've bitten off more than they can chew"

Grunts of affirmation.

Miraculously, there was no bouncer on the door right then, and the five of them trooped in unchallenged. Nothing happened for a few moments. I walked nearer to the door.

There was a crash and the music stopped. Then I heard Ron's

voice. "My name's Ronny Glasheen, and I'm looking for a bloke named Harry."

Then there was a scream and another crash. Two couples came out the door smartly, then another bloke, while sounds of general mayhem intensified inside.

More people emerged and hurried away. By now there was a jam of people at the door. Then a couple of rough-looking types pushed their way out, looked around, and headed straight towards me. There was no preamble, just a wild straight-arm swing from the bloke nearest me. I put my scone down, leaned in, and got clocked on the side of the head. I came out of it and gave him an uppercut to the face, which slowed him up a bit. The other bloke started bouncing around, jabbing at me, pretending he knew what he was doing. He was no Vic Patrick, but he was able to annoy me nonetheless.

I kept trading punches with the main bloke, who was about my size, a bit older and a bit thicker set. I was getting hurt, but one of the things they'd drummed into me at the University of Marrickville was to ignore the pain and box on. Which I did, but then I got knocked down, and the second bloke was right there putting the boot in, hard. I knew these blokes would kick me to death if I let them, but I was too busy keeping myself rolled up in a ball to get out of their way. Then somebody tripped over me. It gave me a chance to roll away into the road and get back to my feet.

There was more fighting going on by the door. Patrons were streaming out of the cafe, and the stampede had put my main opponent off his stroke.

I grabbed the offsider and half ran, half dragged him into the middle of King Street. Then I swung him around by his coat and pushed him into the path of a truck coming up the other side of the street. There were screams. The truck braked hard and pulled up a foot from his head. When I turned around the other bloke was backing off, wide-eyed.

The bloke in the roadway got up and ran off along King Street in the opposite direction.

I went back to the car, breathing hard, my head ringing. One of Ron's mates was sitting in the gutter, spitting out blood and teeth. Another was leaning against the car, his right eye closed. Ron was helping one of the others into the backseat.

"Where the hell did you get to?" he said. "We've got to piss off. Quick, help me with these blokes."

We got them into the car. As we pulled away, a half brick thudded onto the boot, and cracked the back window.

I kept going. There was no talk, just a lot of hard puffing, groaning, and dry-retching.

We got to Newtown and stopped while one of the blokes in the front got out to spew. I looked at the sorry-looking crew packed into the backseat. One feller was mopping his nose with a bloody hanky. When he took it away, I saw there was a ragged crescent of teeth marks across the end of his nose. The cut immediately filled with blood again, which dripped off the tip of his nose.

"Looks like they bit off more than they could chew," I said.

We left two of them at Marrickville Hospital Casualty to get stitched up and went home.

The remaining survivors sat around the kitchen table. Ron gave them each a glass of rum.

They were pretty quiet. I was sore, too. My ribs were bruised, maybe cracked, one middle finger was swollen and sore, and I had a bloody graze on my cheekbone.

"So what happened inside?" I asked.

No one answered. Ron looked at the floor.

One of the others said, "We went in. The band was playing. People were dancing. Ron here walked straight to the middle of the floor, called out that he was Ron Glasheen, and he wanted to talk to the mongrel called Harry."

"I heard that much from outside."

Charlie was half smiling now. "It was a pretty good start. But it went downhill from there. No preliminaries, just straight into it. I was jumped from behind. Somebody hit Jacko with a bottle. There were seven or eight of them against us, maybe more." He shook his head, took a long sip of his rum.

Ron shook his head, still looking at the floor. "We were completely outclassed," he said quietly.

No one contradicted him.

"How about you?" Charlie said to me, "I saw you sorting a couple of blokes out."

"Only one of them was worth worrying about," I said.

I turned to Ron. "After all that, did you find out who they are and what they want?"

He stood up, went to the sink and spat into it. "They're a bad bunch, I found out that much. It was a bad day when you decided to get mixed up with them."

"Well, then. That was really worth it, wasn't it?"

He turned to me. "You watch your tone. I'm still finding it hard to believe that you really don't know what all this is about. What about that rent collecting you do? Is it tied up with that?"

I shook my head.

"And what's happened to that bloke Toohey? Is he part of this?"

"Who knows?"

He looked at me for a moment then turned away shaking his head. "If you won't tell the truth, I can't bloody help you. There's no honesty in you. We've done what we can, but you won't do your bit. From here on in, you're on your own."

Next morning we cleaned the place up. Ron scarcely spoke a word to me. In the afternoon I went down to the hospital to see Mum.

She smiled when I walked into the ward, then looked alarmed. "What happened to you?"

I touched my bruised face. "This? It's nothing, Mum, really."

She nodded, looked absently away, and didn't ask any more about it. We chatted for a few minutes. She said she'd be home in a few days, maybe a week, but somehow she didn't seem to care much one way or another. I went and got her a newspaper and some oranges, stayed for another half an hour, and then shot through.

I went home and told Ron I'd be moving out for a while. He said he didn't give a shit what I did. I asked if he wanted an address in case he needed to get in touch. He said he didn't think he would. So I packed up some clothes, got a saucepan, a kettle, and some washing things together, and drove to the Paddington hideout.

I parked outside the back fence and walked up the pathway to the house. The door was open.

I rushed inside. A woman was nursing a baby in the kitchen, while a tall, lean bloke in a khaki army shirt hammered in a piece of wood above the kitchen fireplace.

They looked at me, mouths open. Angry, scared, I couldn't tell.

"Who the hell are you?" I said.

The woman looked nervously from me to the bloke. The baby started bawling.

The bloke put the hammer down and stood up straight. "My name's Cecil Greenwood," he said. "Call me Cec. And this is my wife, Mavis. May."

She smiled nervously at me. She was slightly plump, in a nice-looking way, with curly brown hair.

The bloke seemed ready to shake hands, or maybe throw a punch, I couldn't tell.

"What are you doing here?" I said.

"You'd better tell me who you are first, sport."

"My name's Bill Glasheen. I look after this property on behalf of the owner. How did you get in?"

He pointed at the door. "That lock wasn't much chop. I'd be having a look at that if I was you."

"This is private property."

"Me and May had nowhere to stay. This place was empty."

"That's trespassing."

He nodded agreeably. "We've been dossing down wherever we can. We camped over behind the racetrack one night last week, then stayed in someone's back shed a couple more. We couldn't keep that up for too long. So I had a bit of a look around. This place seemed empty. We let ourselves in three days ago. Once we got inside, we saw your stuff out the back there, the trunk and that, and we weren't sure what to do. We decided to wait until somebody turned up in person."

I walked straight out back. The coupon cupboard was still padlocked. I went through to the back room and closed the door. I reached up inside the fireplace, took out the loose bricks, and grabbed the tin box. The money seemed to be all there.

I put it back then went out to the kitchen.

Cec Greenwood looked at me. "We put our things in the other bedroom. I bodgied up the electricity and the gas—we'll have to undo it before the official connection blokes get here." He was grinning slightly.

"You're talking as though you'll be staying," I said. "Don't you think that's a little, well, presumptuous?"

He shrugged his shoulders.

His wife said. "We're perfectly prepared to pay rent, aren't we Cec?"

"A fair rent," he said.

I sat down on one of the packing cases at the table.

"I'll put a cup of tea on, will I?" said Cec.

I shook my head. "Christ, I feel like I've woken up in the middle of *The Grapes of Wrath*. Now listen. I'm sorry, but you can't stay. It's impossible. I'm moving in here myself."

"Well you move right on in. We'll keep out of your way. All we need is that one room out there to sleep in, and a fair go in the kitchen and the bathroom. You'll hardly notice we're here."

The baby started crying again and the wife took it out of its blanket. It had dark brown skin and curly black hair. Something must have shown on my face.

"I see you've spotted something unusual about the little feller," said Cec Greenwood.

I looked from him to her. She was smiling calmly.

"You've no doubt noticed that although he's a boy, he's wrapped in a pink blanket. But that was all we could get hold of, you see."

I stared at him.

He was grinning. "I'm just pulling your leg, son. I'm not the little feller's dad, obviously. May and me have only been married for three weeks."

Mavis said quickly, "Don't get the wrong idea. I *was* married, but the baby's father was killed. At Iwo Jima."

"An American?" I said.

She nodded.

"I'm sorry," I said.

"When he died, I was in real bother, pregnant, friendless. My family didn't approve of me hooking up with a Yank, let alone a Negro. I couldn't go home. I had the baby with the nuns. They wanted me to adopt him out, but I thought, if I did that, I wouldn't have anyone, would I?"

"I suppose not."

"Then I met Cec. Or re-met. We used to know each other before. He was just back from Japan." She looked at Cec, smiling.

Cec Greenwood said, "Cute little feller, isn't he? I'm not sure

132

whether we should call him Nat King Cole Greenwood or plain Cecil. What do you think, Bill?"

"I think you can't stay here. You must have your service pay-out. Go to a hotel, or the government hostel at Herne Bay."

"Slight problem on the finance front, I'm afraid," he said.

"Cec is a bit of a soft touch," the woman said. "He was swindled out of his back pay on the train back from Brisbane by a professional con man. What do you think of that? What sort of person would cheat a returned soldier?"

"I really can't imagine. But the fact remains, you two, three, just can't stay here. That's that."

Cec Greenwood nodded. "All right. You just go and get the coppers and have us thrown out."

"What?"

"If you want us out, you'll have to get us charged with trespass. Have us up before a magistrate."

There were stories in the paper every week about squatters—usually returned men and their wives—appearing in court for trespass. There was a big backlog of cases, and when a squatting case did get heard, the magistrates were loathe to impose anything more than a five- or ten-shilling fine. As Cec Greenwood seemed to be well aware.

I sighed deeply. "I could do it the quick way. Get a few blokes together and just throw you out."

He smiled, shook his head. "You may be a landlord's agent, but I can tell you're not *that* sort of grub. Look at the positive side, Bill. Mavis here is a pretty good cook—all we need is a few bob for some mutton and spuds and I bet we can persuade her to cook up a you-beaut stew for us all."

"What about the rent you just minutes ago offered to pay?"

"Well, of course, that'd be when I start earning something."

"Great."

"But rest assured, Bill, my prospects are terrific."

The wife nodded enthusiastically. "They are, too. Cec is awfully handy. And resourceful."

He came over and patted me on the back. "You're a good feller, Bill, I can tell. We're all going to get on famously."

I snuck back home the next night to get a few more things, and discovered there'd been more trouble. The front door and part of the jamb were blackened, and now the front windows were broken. I found Ron inside, packing clothes into an overnight bag.

"Now what's going on?"

"They tried to burn us down last night. Next door's heard the windows smash. They came over and put out the fire."

"Who did it?"

"You're asking me? Your mate Harry and his mob, I suppose."

"Where are you going?"

"I'm staying over at Charlie's for a while."

After that I drove over to the Police Boys Club, but not for a workout. Jennings was a squarehead through and through, but he was a tough piece of work, and he'd told me all those months ago that I could come to him in confidence if I ever needed help in extricating myself from the snares of Satan. The business at Ziegfeld's probably wasn't quite what he had in mind, but he was starting to look like my best and only chance of an ally.

There were a dozen or so fellers in the gym, including Jennings. He came straight over and nodded for me to follow him into the corner, away from the others.

When we were out of earshot, he said, "I trusted you, Glasheen. I thought we were getting somewhere. But I was wrong."

"What?"

"Not content to be on the wrong side yourself, you set about corrupting innocents. Evil seeks company."

"I don't understand."

"You've been recruiting these young fellers to do your bidding."

I looked over his shoulder. Ernie shook his head behind Jennings' back, as if to say, this is none of my doing.

"What are you talking about?"

"I'm going to do something I shouldn't do. But it's to protect these young fellers here. Much as I'd like to see you get your just desserts, I've decided not to report *these*," he pulled a bunch of coupons out of his pocket, "to the Rationing Commission. It's more than you deserve, but I don't feel it would be fair to these fellers."

Jennings looked at the floor. "But they're not to blame. I am. I allowed them to be led astray. I should have been more alert."

Ernie made a gesture of helplessness over Jennings' shoulder.

Jennings turned to me again. "But you can clear out, Glasheen. If you ever come back here promoting your rotten enterprises, I'll see you prosecuted, understand?"

In the morning I bought an army mattress from a disposal store at Paddo, salvaged some bed linen from home, and set myself up in the back room of the Paddo hideout.

Then I rang up the council depot and told the foreman I wouldn't be back. He said that was too bad—he'd been planning to give me a go at the venereal disease warning signs next week.

Despite all the trouble and Mum being sick, it felt good somehow to be out from home and to be shot of the council job and the God-bothering copper. No one had caught on about Toohey's properties yet, let alone the rent money, so that was still safe. Maybe it was mine. As for that register, I knew for sure that I didn't have it, so I felt in the clear on that score too, although I'd certainly have to watch my step, for a while at least.

In fact, as I thought about it further, I came to the conclusion that maybe this wasn't all bad. Maybe I was being shown which way to go. Things had suddenly gotten a lot simpler. I had money, and I wanted Lucy with me. What was I waiting for?

The usual arrangement with Lucy was that I didn't pop in unannounced. At first I hadn't minded. Not too much. It saved awkwardness all round. But that day I just went straight there, at seven in the evening.

She answered the door, and I knew straight away that the timing was all wrong. She was dressed up in a dark-blue, low-cut evening dress, and looked shocked to see me.

"What are you—? Bill, you should have rung." Her voice was low.

Inside I could hear voices. Male and female. Laughing.

"Who's here?"

"Bill, this is the wrong time. I'm just on my way out."

A voice called from inside, "Lucy, sweetheart, tell them to piss off, we don't want any." More laughter.

I pushed the door open. There was a feller dressed in a dinner suit, standing by the sideboard pouring drinks. Round-faced, with wavy oiled hair plastered to his skull, he was smoking a cigarette in a holder. Molly Price was sitting on another bloke's lap in the armchair.

Molly stood up quickly. Lucy tried to push the door closed again, but I wouldn't let her.

The bloke by the sideboard looked at me and smiled amiably. "Sorry, old chap, thought you were an encyclopedia salesman." He looked from me to Lucy. Maybe he guessed what was going on, but if so, he didn't let on. He picked up a glass of whisky and walked over to where I was standing.

"Eric's my name," he said. His voice was well-modulated, resonant, reassuring. "We're just on our way out, but there's certainly time for a quick snort before we go." He held the drink out to me.

I smacked it out of his hand. Molly gasped. It scarcely fazed

136

the bloke. "I really don't think that was necessary, friend."

I turned to Lucy. "Are you going to tell him to shoot through or will I throw him down the stairs?"

Lucy spoke through her teeth. "Shut up and go away, Bill. You don't know anything."

"You don't need this bloke around. If you can't get rid of him, I will."

Lucy closed her eyes, shook her head slightly, then whispered, "Don't."

The bloke looked at me hard. "Who *is* this fellow, Lucy?" he said.

She grabbed my coat sleeve, trying to get me to leave.

I took her hand from my sleeve, stepped up to the bloke, and said, "Bill Glasheen's the name." Then I punched him in his pudgy face.

The other bloke was on his feet now, but he didn't look too ready to mix it.

The fat-faced bloke staggered back, his hands over his nose. Blood trickled out from between his fingers. He stood still for a few moments, then looked at his bloody hands, took out a hanky and started mopping his nose.

I was still shaping up, but the bloke simply straightened himself, picked up his hat from the couch and walked past me and out the door.

I ran after him and caught him on the first landing. I would have hit him again, but Lucy was right behind me and somehow tripped me up before I got in position. All I managed to do was knock the bloke's hat off.

When I got back to my feet he was gone. The other bloke ran past me and out the front door. Neighbors' doors were opening, heads peeking out at us.

Lucy said, quietly but fiercely, "For Christ's sake, get back inside before one of these gigs calls the police."

She was angry, although I didn't quite see what *she* had to be angry about.

Molly went out and left us there alone. I made a pot of tea, and we sat on the couch. I told her I was sorry I'd hit the fat bloke, but not for his sake—he got what was coming to him—but for hers.

Lucy's mood shifted from anger to a sort of weary resignation. She kept repeating that I shouldn't have interfered. "You know nothing, Bill," she said. "You don't even know who he is. And now you've spoiled everything."

"Look Lucy," I told her, "If I *did* stuff things up for you, then I did you a favor. That life isn't for you."

"You think you're in a position to start lecturing me on how to live?"

"I know, I'm not all the way there yet, but I'm getting there. I'm making arrangements."

"Like what?"

"I'm looking into the idea of a normal job."

"Oh, Bill, spare me please."

"And I've got a bit saved up."

She looked away, shaking her head, and reached for a cigarette.

"No, listen to me, Lucy. My arrangements include you. I've got enough to buy a piece of land, or put a deposit on a house. We wouldn't have to stay here, either, if you didn't want to. We could go to Melbourne or Brisbane. Set ourselves up somewhere decent. We could get married or we could shack up."

At least she was looking at me now. "What would you do?"

"I'll go back to learning to be a commercial artist, or start a business or something. There are a thousand things I could do. You could open a florist's shop if you felt like it. Something like that. We'll make a running start."

She started crying again. I put my arm around her, patted her, hugged her.

"It's not realistic," she said.

"I know you've had some bad experiences," I said, "But just keep an open mind. Things will turn out." I kissed her. "Don't decide now. I'll give you a few hundred quid to tide you over if you want, so that you don't have to have those parasites around here. Meanwhile, just kind of let the idea grow a bit. Will you do that?"

She wiped her eyes with her balled-up hanky. "All right, Bill."

"There you go!"

She looked directly at me. "But it's only fair to tell you where I stand. If we're to hook up, you'll need a *real* bank. Enough for us to get set up and stay that way. I don't want this boom and bust business, up one week, down the next, Bill. I do have feelings for you, but deep down I worry that you're the same type as my father."

"I've never run short of zoot suits," I said.

"That's what I mean, Bill. Everything you've said today—ask me again when you're really fixed." Then she clasped my hand a little tighter, leaned a little closer. "You think I'm hard-hearted, don't you?"

"No, I understand. You've had a tough life, and that makes you see things that way. Some time with me will fix all that." I kissed her. "You deserve a good run, and I'm just the bloke to give it to you."

We went to bed, and I stayed over. We had a slow breakfast, and went back to bed afterwards. Late in the morning Lucy went into the city to do some shopping. I hung around.

Molly came back at midday. She didn't seem surprised that I was still there, and asked if I wanted some lunch.

Molly was quiet, sort of watchful, as we ate our bacon and eggs. Over a pot of tea she said, "You and Lucy sorted things out after last night's . . . upsets?"

"Yeah. I asked her to hook up with me. In earnest, not this sneaking in and out stuff."

"What did she say?"

"She said she'd think about it."

She gave me a long look, then smiled, reached over and gave my hand a squeeze. "I hope it works out for you both."

"Oh, it'll work out."

She took a sip of tea, lit a smoke, and said, "You didn't pull up too lame after your rumpus the other night?"

"Rumpus?"

"At the Ziegfeld Club."

I stared at her. "How do you know about that?"

"I was there."

"Fair dinkum? Who with?"

She shook her head. "No one you know. I heard the leader of your little war party declare to all and sundry that his name was Glasheen. Was that your brother?"

"Yeah. He's no great shakes as a diplomat. Listen, Molly, you get down to that place a bit, do you?"

"I've been there once or twice with different fellows."

"Would you by any chance know the blokes who jumped us?"

"You're asking if I know them?"

"I mean, do you know who they are?"

"Yes and no. There's a bunch of them who hang around the place. Riff-raff. Thickheads. I avoid them. But they provide that rough-hewn underworld color that makes Ziegfeld's so popular with the squareheads."

"Do you know who Harry is?"

"That'd be Harry Strettles. He's pretty rough."

"Can I tell you something in confidence, Molly?"

"Go ahead."

"These blokes came around to my place looking for trouble.

No one was home. They messed the place up, left a threatening note. The thing is though, I don't really know what the bloody hell they want from me. There's been a mistake, and I need to straighten it out."

"That's too bad. But what can you do about it?"

"Well, I can't just waltz in there and say, 'Good day there Harry, old cock, what's all this nonsense about, then?' Not now, anyway. But—"

"You want *me* to tell him what you just told me?"

"No, not that. But I'd like to have a little get together with him. A calm pow-wow, no rough stuff. I was thinking maybe you could help me arrange a meeting with him. On neutral ground."

She thought about it a moment. "Are you sure about this, Bill? Even the really tough blokes are wary of Harry. They say he's killed at least one man."

"Oh, great. But what else can I do? Yeah, I'm sure, Molly."

8

A week later, I was sitting in the General Gordon Hotel at Sydenham, waiting to meet Harry Strettles. Molly had very carefully let him know that she knew me, and told him I wanted to meet him to try and straighten things out. But we'd need to meet in a public place, and he'd have to come alone—and if he tried to thump me, he'd get no result at all.

He'd agreed to the pow wow, just the two of us. But to be on the safe side, I had Max and Herb sitting across the other side of the bar, in case Strettles did the dirty on me. I hadn't told them what it was all about, just that I might need some back up and it was unlikely they'd be called upon. We'd driven out there in my car—I was thinking of it as my car by then. Max had been sniffing inhalers all arvo, and was jumping around and shadow-boxing on the street when we arrived, all ready to go the knuckle. I told him to take it easy.

I went inside and bought a beer, sat down and waited. Max and Herb came in a minute or two later and went to the bar.

I picked Strettles the moment he walked in. Not tall, but broad-shouldered. Olive skin, thick dark eyebrows, and a hard, square face. His grey woolen suit was well tailored, his shoes were new, and he was wearing a silk tie and gold cufflinks. He wore his hat down low.

The barman and the few tradesmen having their after-work drink glanced nervously over, but no one looked at him directly.

Strettles walked straight to the bar, ordered a beer, and had a look around. He glanced at Max and Herb, then spotted me and came over, smiling.

"You'd be Glasheen then, would you?"

"Yeah." I said. "Is this going to be all right? If we can talk about this business reasonably, then we're on, but if there's to be any heavy stuff I'll shoot through now."

He sat down smiling. "No, she'll be sweet, unless those tigers over there want to start something." He nodded in the direction of Max and Herb, who were looking our way.

"Who do you mean?" I said.

"Those two clowns over at the bar. Your mates. Who look even more piss-weak than the mob you sent into Ziegfeld's the other day."

"That wasn't my idea, believe me. Don't worry about those blokes over there, I just want to talk. Are we on?"

"I'm not in any way worried about those two blokes. But yeah, you'll be all right, son," he said. "What have you got for me?"

"Well, that's just the thing, er, Harry. I don't actually know what it is that you want. And whatever it is, I'm certain I don't have it."

He just looked at me.

"So, I'm asking you, what's going on?"

"Fucked if I know."

"Come again?"

"I don't know. The boss asked me to get a few fellers together, go around to your place, and collect the register from you. Or at least put a bit of a scare into you. There was to be an earn in it for me."

"This doesn't add up. *Who* told you?"

"Well, I couldn't go telling you *that* now, could I?"

"I want to clear this up, but you have to help me. I told you, I don't even know what it is you—they, whoever—want. If you won't tell me who wants it, then I'm completely stuffed."

He looked at me a while then said, "I can't tell you any names, but the way I heard it, my bloke is acting for a number of separate parties who are interested in getting hold of this register thing."

"Well who the hell are they?"

"Settle down and hear me out. I'm not going to tell you who they are, so get that straight. But as I understand it, some kind of offer was made to this feller that I know, and he was going to go middle-man in selling the register on to the highest bidder."

"But where do I come in?"

"You're Billy Glasheen of 3 Hilltop Avenue, Marrickville?"

"Yeah, that's me. So?"

"That's who the original offer came from."

"*What*?"

"My principal got a message from Billy Glasheen—"

"Bullshit! I'm Billy Glasheen, and I never—" I stopped. Blokes were looking at us.

Strettles said, "Do you want me to tell you what I know or not?"

"Yeah, go on."

He nodded. "He got a message, like I said, from Billy Glasheen, saying that he, Glasheen, was in possession of this register, which he understood to be of considerable value to certain people. He—*you*, that is—was asking my bloke to broker it for him."

"So why the rough stuff then?"

Harry Strettles laughed. "Why *not* the rough stuff? If you'd wanted Chamber of Commerce behavior, you wouldn't have gone asking my boss to run things for you. He doesn't operate that way."

"But I didn't, for Christ's sake!"

Strettles drew back.

I took a deep breath. "All right, Harry. I appreciate you being straight with me. But I'm telling you, I don't know anything about this. I don't even know what this register is, let alone where it is. I just want to get my head out of the noose. Can you tell your boss that?"

He watched me as I talked, smiling, obviously not believing a word of it. "Listen sport, I'm just the help. If the boss knew I'd been talking to you on the sly, he'd think I was trying to cut him out. Now, Molly said you were all right, and I know *she's* all right, so that was good enough for me. So I've come out here and told you what I know."

"Yeah I appreciate it, fair dinkum."

"Well that's good, because, now that you've dragged me all the way out here, my question to you is, what have you got for *me*?" The smile was gone. His eyes were narrow and hard.

"But I haven't. That's what I'm trying to say, Harry, there isn't—."

He reached out, put his big hand on the back of my neck and gave it a lazy shake. "Well you better make it your business to find that bloody register. Understand? And when you do, there's no need to go talking to the boss this time. Just speak to me. Got it?"

I didn't answer. The bar had gone strangely quiet.

Strettles let go of my neck. He laughed and stood up. "I'll be off now. You can leave a message for me at Ziegfeld's. I'll be waiting for it. See ya." He walked over to Max and threw a fake punch. Max looked to nearly shit himself. Strettles laughed, patted Max on the cheek and went out.

When I did the rent round that week Mrs Sprague told me that Jack Carmody had died the previous Monday.

"How?"

"He was crossing King Street, got hit by a bread van. His eye-

145

sight wasn't too great. He went instantly, for what that's worth. They said he wouldn't even have known what hit him."

"I wish I'd known," I said.

"I tried to reach you, but I didn't know how. I don't even know your second name. The hospital people didn't want to wait on the off chance someone might come forward and take care of the arrangements, so they gave him a pauper's burial."

"I could've paid."

"Well it's too late now. And Jack's past caring."

I nodded. "Poor feller. It was a hard life for him, I suppose. He wasn't such a bad old bloke."

"He liked you," she said. "He liked doing the odd jobs. I don't think he was too miserable towards the end. What are you going to do with his place?"

"I don't know."

"My brother's just back from the army. Working. I know he could pay the rent. He's just married, and his wife has one on the way."

I hesitated, but I really couldn't see any reason why not.

"He'll pay what Jack was paying," she said. "It'd be good to have some family in the street."

"Yeah, all right then. Tell him he's on. I'll get you the key."

I kept my head pulled in all the next week. On Friday I nipped in to Burt's Milk Bar to check out the jukebox, maybe flog some coupons. The coin box was nearly full, but among the sixpences was a disappointingly large number of slugs. I didn't hang about any longer than I had to, and as soon as I'd unloaded a few quid's worth of coupons, I took off. On my way out the door, the girl behind the counter called me over.

She leaned close so that no one would overhear. "A chap was in here asking about you a little while ago."

"Oh yeah? Anyone you know?"

She looked around, then said very quietly, "No, but I can tell you that he didn't have a Cornel Wilde haircut, he wasn't wearing jeans, and he wasn't jiving to 'The Devil's Jump.'"

"A government man?"

"I don't know. He was sort of unusual, if you know what I mean."

"A rough sort of cove?" I said.

She smiled, shook her head. "Oh, no. He had lovely manners."

"What did he want?"

"Well, he seemed to know that you usually pop by here of a Friday—"

"Christ, how did he know that?"

"I don't know. But he said if was to see you today, could I give you a message."

"What was it?"

"He said he'd be at Toohey's house, and that he wanted ever so much to have a little chat with you."

"Did he tell you his name?"

She shook her head.

As soon as I stepped outside, I had the feeling I was being watched. I looked around, but couldn't spot anyone paying any special attention to me. Suddenly I was breathing fast. I felt very strongly that I was on my own in the big city, that everyone else knew something I didn't—and that what they knew was to my disadvantage. I hurried to the car and took off.

The feeling stayed with me. When I came to a stop in traffic at the corner of Bayswater Road, a big black Wolseley pulled up on my right. Two blokes were in it. The grey-haired feller in the passenger seat held a camera with a flash attachment. The moment I turned to face him, he took a picture, then they drove off quickly down Darlinghurst Road towards St Vincent's Hospital.

The traffic in my lane was still stationary, but when it got moving again I sped after them down Darlinghurst Road, drove over the rise and stopped, not sure what to do. I got out of the car and looked around. A dago in a corner shop looked at me. Was he one of them?

I walked over to him. He smiled, then frowned.

"What are you looking at?" I said.

"You look at me, I look at you."

"Oh, yeah. Sorry."

I got back in the car, thinking—jeez, too much more of this and I'll be completely yarra. I wanted to bolt to my Paddington hideout and pull the shades, but I drove on towards Oxford Street. And there at the corner was the Wolseley, stuck in a line of cars, held up by something across the intersection.

I pulled over to the side of the road and ran forward alongside the line of stationary cars. The grey-haired bloke in the passenger seat was smoking a pipe, with the window open, and still holding the camera. I made a grab for the camera before he saw me and pulled it out the window, but his right hand held onto it. When he tried to yank it back from me, it popped out of my hand and banged against the side of the car, then fell to the roadway and burst open. I looked at it for half a second, thought, "That'll do," and took off back to my car.

They were still trapped in the traffic, so I did a U-turn, raced back along Darlinghurst Road, turned right into Liverpool Street, then pulled into a side street and waited for a minute or two while my breathing slowed down. The blokes in the car hadn't looked like thugs, nor did they look much like shiny arses from the Rationing Commission. The photographer's bushy moustache, the impression of quality tailoring, a good car—it all added up to something rather different. Intelligence men.

I drove to Mick Toohey's place in Manning Road. The house was semi-derelict now. One room looked as if it had been burned out, fence pickets were missing, and the guttering and downpipe had been pilfered.

I parked the car and walked around the house. The back door was wide open. The kitchen was a mess. There was a radio on somewhere inside; Mildred Bailey was singing "Penthouse Serenade." I followed the music.

In the lounge room a bloke in a suit sat in an armchair, drinking from a crystal glass.

"Incredible isn't it?" he said as I entered the room. "All this time and the electricity still hasn't been disconnected." He walked over with his hand extended. Tall, thin, longish hair, good suit. "Mr. Glasheen, I presume."

"Who are you?" I said.

"Well, old chap, the actual name is Beaufoy Edward Hawley-White. Lieutenant, if you want to be formal. But they call me the Filthy Blighter."

"I can see why."

"Quite." He held up a bottle of Johnny Walker with a couple of inches left in it. "Can I offer you a drink from what remains of Michael Toohey's private stock? We have quite a bit to do, but it wouldn't do to forego the civilities, would it?"

"Stick the drink. What do you want with me?"

He looked at the bottle, poured the rest of it in his glass, said, "Bottoms up," and drank it down. "Quite a bit, I'm afraid, old chap."

"Who are you?"

"I assume you're not asking me to recite my name and title again. Who am I?" He looked at the empty glass in his hand, and then at me. "It sounds awfully stuffy, but I suppose I represent the Commonwealth."

"*You*? You don't look it. Which mob are you with—the Rationing Commission? Manpower?"

He sighed deeply. "I'm on the cloak-and-dagger side of things.

I was in Army Intelligence during the war, and now I'm working for the Commonwealth Investigation Service, in a sort of advisory capacity."

"Is that right?" I said. "Then how about this? Why don't you just advise your mates to leave me alone, forget whatever it is you think you want from me, forget I ever existed, and while you're about it, how about you go and get fucked."

"Bravo! Well said! But not really possible at this stage, old chap. You're very much the man of the hour, and I fear that if you're not with us, you'll be rather on your own."

"That's all right, I'll get by. See you." I started for the door.

"Not a good idea, old chap. Unless you intend to go into permanent hiding."

I stopped and turned around. "What *do* you want?"

"Well, if you could see your way clear to handing over the register, then we can hopefully put this whole wretched business to rest."

"I haven't got it. I don't know anything about it. I don't even know what the hell it is."

The Blighter looked at me for a few moments. "Yes, that's rather as we suspected."

"So will you go back and tell your mates that there's been a mistake?"

"Not really possible, I'm afraid."

I stepped up to him and gave him my best combination. The first caught him in the throat. His hand went up and then I got him in the gut. He buckled over, then fell to his knees, coughing and retching.

His face went a greenish-white and then he spewed some weird colored fluid on the floor.

"Christ almighty," I said.

He stayed there, still retching. I crouched down, gave his shoulder a shake. "Hey, are you all right?"

He didn't answer.

"Do you want something? Water?"

He shook his head, waved the idea away.

After a couple of minutes the retching stopped. He got off the floor and settled in a dusty armchair, puffing.

"Christ. I'm sorry, sport."

He shook his head, with his eyes closed. "I think there's still an inch of scotch in the decanter over there. Be a good chap, would you?"

"Scotch? Are you sure?"

He nodded emphatically.

I poured it into a glass and brought it over to him. He drank it down, and his breathing steadied.

"Shit, pal. I didn't mean—"

He shook his head again. "Probably our fault, really." He felt in his pocket, brought out a pack of Senior Service and lit up. He looked at me. "You truly don't realize just how involved you are, do you?"

I sat down on one of the other chairs. "I know next to nothing."

He nodded. "Well, like it or not, you seem to be at the center of it. So much so that you can't just walk away from it. Not now."

"So what's to be done?"

"You could consider going on the government payroll for a while."

"I only just chucked in what was supposed to be a good job with Leichhardt Council."

"We'll pay you considerably more than the council."

"To do what?"

"Ostensibly you'll be a driver. My driver."

"But in fact . . . ?"

"You'll be assisting me in locating the register."

I didn't respond.

The Blighter watched me for a few seconds then said, "Of course, if you have other, ah, private interests you'd rather keep quiet about, I quite understand. They shouldn't conflict."

I nodded. "I suppose you'd better tell me more then."

The Blighter stood up. "Much to tell, too little time I'm afraid." He went over to a gladstone bag sitting on the floor and brought out a hammer, a chisel and a large screwdriver. "If I may assume you're on the team, then let's begin by searching this place. I'm not optimistic, frankly, but it'd be remiss of us not to rule it out."

He walked over to the wall, crouched down, hammered the chisel in behind the skirting board, and began prizing it off. He said over his shoulder. "More tools in the bag. You might start over the other side there, if you don't mind. I'll tell you what I can while we work."

I got the tools and we started tearing Mick Toohey's house apart. The Filthy Blighter worked methodically, talking the whole time.

"All this began, for me at least, around the middle of 1945," he said. "I was just back in Australia. I'd been in London, attached to Army Intelligence. It was no secret. Everyone knew I was in Intelligence, including Michael Daniel Toohey, with whom I had run up a fairly hefty debt."

"How?"

"Slow horses, fast companions—the usual sort of thing, I'm afraid. Anyway, despite the debt, or perhaps because of it, I got on rather well with Toohey. Then one day in July he told me he had come into certain information that might be of interest to me and my superiors. More to the point, he said this information might enable both him and me to earn a few much needed pounds."

"The register?"

"Indeed. This goes back. I don't expect you've ever heard of the Patriotic League . . . ?"

"Well, if you mean a bunch of ex-army clowns who meet out at Leichhardt Scout Hall . . . "

The Blighter smiled. "You are a continual surprise. May I ask how you know them?"

"A couple of them drink at a pub I sometimes go to. I hope you're not trying to tell me that anyone, anywhere seriously gives a rat's arse about what those fellers get up to?"

"Alas, secret armies, new guards, patriotic alliances, and what have you don't seem to excite intelligence chaps to even a fraction of the extent that reds, trade unionists, and left-leaning Labor people do. But the Patriotic League is of great concern to the government, and for good reason. Incidentally, Bill, how do you stand in relation to the present government, if you don't mind me asking?"

"I'm a Chifley man," I said.

"Good show. Well, let me assure you, the Patriotic League extends well beyond a few duffers at Leichhardt Scout Hall. For a while we in Intelligence have been aware that all kinds of rabid anti-Labor elements were organizing independently for the impending peace. There were the leftovers from the New Guard, a pre-war group you may have heard of, plus a whole range of newer organizations—independent groups of old service chums, strike-breakers, right-wing Catholics, Freemasons, RSL fellows, and more. These various bunches were just, you know, around. No great threat, really, and most of them hated each other nearly as much as they did their political opponents. Which was good, as far as the Commonwealth Police were concerned.

"But then, somehow, in 1945 they all started coming together. However unlikely it seemed, they suddenly started looking like a real secret paramilitary."

"Let me tell you," I said. "If it's that Leichhardt mob we're up against, we can stop worrying right now."

"Actually old chap, there are rather a lot of them. No one's quite sure exactly, but there appear to be at least a hundred thousand of the wretches throughout the country. Armed, well-organized, supported, and protected by many powerful people. But I'm getting ahead of myself. This room seems to be clean. I suggest we move on to the next."

We went to the dining room and began pulling down the fittings there.

The Blighter continued, "The leaders of the League were well aware of the need for maximum secrecy. So when they set up the structure, they instituted a rather clever "need to know" information control system. No one in the organization, except for a few chaps at the top, knows anyone else. The independent groups have remained largely independent. Each local cell is only in contact with its own commander, and the commander in turn only knows his direct superior. No one knows the full extent of it. So it's damned hard for us to keep tabs on them—impossible, in fact. We send in a few men here and there to infiltrate, but what do they find out? That Killara branch has two hundred members, almost none of whose last names we know, and that Killara branch has links with St Ives branch, but we don't know the last names of its members, either."

He put down his hammer and lit a cig. "They're frightfully anti-democratic, and probably criminally seditious. They're convinced the communists are about to take over, and are prepared to move in as a provisional government-cum-police force."

I shook my head. "I can see that a bunch of blokes might want to get together and toast the king and relive past glories and all that bullshit, but take over the government?"

"Hmm. Did you know that Mr. Chifley, of whom you are so fond—as indeed am I—rather has his heart set on nationalizing the banks?"

I shrugged. "So long as he leaves my money alone, he can do whatever he wants with the banks."

"Our friends in the Patriotic League do not share your relaxed attitude. For them, such a move would be a sign that communists are indeed in control. But I see you're yawning, Bill. Let's go back to last year. In the early days of the League, when the confederation of these individual groups was being established, an almost complete list of the groups and their leaders did exist on paper. It itemized every district commander, every second-in-command, and quite a few rank-and-file members as well. It was, in effect, a plan of the command structure. It was referred to as the Patriotic Register—and Mick Toohey managed to get hold of a copy."

I thought for a minute. "This copy . . . would it have been a photographic print, by any chance?"

The Blighter's eyes widened. "So you've seen it, then?"

"I found a fragment among Mick's stuff. It had your name written on the back of it."

"The full document runs to many pages. Toohey contacted me when he first got wind of it. He thought that together we might be able to sell it—either back to the League, or to the government—and split the proceeds. I was to make the appropriate overtures to the government fellows and to the League."

"So what happened?"

"I made use of the cloak-and-dagger network—they're mostly old-school-tie chaps, you know—and told them the register existed. As a former Army Intelligence person with nothing much to do, I was immediately put on the Commonwealth payroll, to help them with the investigation—and hopefully take part in the eventual disbandment of the League.

"Did you ever get to see the register?"

He shook his head. "Toohey rang me a few days before VP Day to say he expected to have it in a day or two. When he got it he'd let me know. I let it be known to the League that there was a copy of the register in existence. The League had long since destroyed the original, of course, but that one copy could still hang them. I told them that if they wanted to keep it from the Commonwealth Police, then it might be available, for the right price. Then I made a similar offer to the cloak-and-dagger chaps. We planned to sell it to the highest bidder."

"The government was going to pay to get it?"

"At that time there was still plenty of money available for national security matters, and the story I took to my people was that there was an informer in the League who might be bought out for the right price. I didn't let on that I had a financial stake in the affair, of course. As far as they were concerned, I was only passing on information."

"You were double dealing, selling everyone out."

"We Intelligence chaps tend to be quixotic fellows. Anyone who's any good is, at any rate. But that doesn't mean I'd sell *anyone* out. Not the same thing at all."

"What went wrong?"

"Toohey was to contact me the moment he took possession of the register."

"Right. You were waiting in room fifteen at the Mansions Hotel," I said.

The Filthy Blighter looked at me and said slowly, "Yes. That's right."

"I was supposed to deliver the message," I said. "But I couldn't get through that night because of the celebrations. When I went back the next day, you were gone."

"What was the message?"

"That Mick had the register and for you to ring him."

He nodded. "The word from Toohey didn't come. I was forced to leave the Mansions the next day because of a . . . financial misunderstanding. Suddenly I was left high and dry. I'd egged everyone on, urging them to buy the register and hang the cost.

Now suddenly Mick Toohey was gone and I was in the hot seat. I quickly became persona non grata with the League chaps, and I had to do some rather fast talking with the Intelligence boys."

"Do you know where Toohey went?"

"He covered his tracks remarkably well. His natural distrust of everyone would have made him a natural for intelligence work. All I've been able to find out is that he had a place in the country somewhere, to which he retired every now and again. I've never spoken to anyone who's been there, or even has the least notion where it is."

"All right," I said, "so Toohey disappeared and the register went with him. Everything went quiet. Why is it back on now?"

The Blighter gave me a searching look.

"I know, I know. Some joker has put the word out that I have the register. I worked for Toohey, all right, but I haven't got it. Can't you understand that?"

"I understand that you don't consciously have it. But perhaps you are unwittingly holding it."

"Nope. I've checked and double-checked. I definitely haven't got it. Blighter, do you have any idea at all who started this Billy-Glasheen-has-the-register story?"

"Afraid not."

"What if it was Toohey," I said. "Maybe he's still alive hiding somewhere, pulling the strings. Had you thought of that?"

"Of course. But that raises more questions than it answers. Where is he? Where has be been? Why would he wait until now to make a move? You don't have any reason to think he's alive, do you?"

"No, I think he's gone. But what about the copper, Ray Waters?" I said. "He questioned me back then, asked me if I knew anything about the register."

"What did you say to him?"

"I played dumb. I didn't know anything anyway. How's he

involved?"

"He's a most unscrupulous character. I believe he got wind of it—quite a few people did back then. He rather hoped to intercept the list and sell it on his own behalf."

"So who burned down the Durban Castle?"

"Perhaps Waters. Perhaps the uglies from the League."

"The uglies?"

"Yes. As you have rightly observed, the vast majority of the Patriotic League's membership is made up of rather harmless suburban chaps—of arch-right-wing inclination, to be sure, but basically respectable bourgeois types. But one of the more criminally inclined groups, under the leadership of a certain Brisbane chap, took over the role of internal security within the League. And they're quite bloodthirsty types, given to turning up at strike meetings and leftist gatherings to heckle, bully, and what have you. The League's leadership apparently wanted to pay up and hush things up as best they could, but the leader of the renegade uglies was all for taking matters into his own hands."

"Aubrey someone? Feller with a crook leg?"

"You confound me yet again. Yes, Aubrey Edwin Munce. You've met him, then?"

"Not in person. He came to my place with a couple of blokes and heavied my Mum. So what about Harry Strettles and the Ziegfeld's mob? Where do they fit in?"

"Opportunists on the sidelines. Ever heard of a Mr. Joe Grimshaw?"

"Runs a baccarat school?"

The Blighter nodded, reached into his jacket pocket, and handed me a photograph. It showed a large, gruff-looking feller, looking defiantly straight into the camera.

"As I understand it, Strettles and co were acting at Grimshaw's behest. He was approached, recently one assumes, to broker the list. Although apparently he had no idea what it was."

"So who was it went to Grimshaw then?"

"Everybody seems to think you did."

"But I didn't."

"Then we don't know."

"Can't we just bloody well ask Grimshaw?"

"Too late. The poor fellow was shot dead a few nights ago in Darlinghurst. Unrelated matter, apparently."

"Well, that's something, at least. I mean, rest in peace and all that, but it takes him out of the game, doesn't it?"

"Not really. Strettles is now apparently keener than ever to hijack the register and sell it himself. Grimshaw was a restraining influence. I strongly suggest that if you happen to cross paths with Strettles you absent yourself with maximum haste."

I didn't say anything to that, but thought for a while. "It's got to be the woman."

"Who?"

"Lil. She's orchestrating it all. Find her, and you've got it."

"What do you know about Lil?"

"She was Mick Toohey's woman. He kept her bloody quiet. She got hold of the register in the first place, delivered it on VP Day. She was hiding in the saloon bar at the Durban Club when I went back that night. Christ knows why she's brought me into it, though. Anyway, find her, and it's solved. It's clear cut," I said.

"I'm afraid not. Lil is dead. Forget her. But really, Bill, we need to finish our work here."

We searched the whole house, moving from room to room. We prized out skirting boards, lifted rugs, looked under loose floorboards, removed moldings. We found nothing. In fact, we found absolutely nothing—no letters, no records, no papers of any kind, apart from a few old gas bills and water rates notices.

By four o'clock we'd done the whole house. I said to the Blighter, "The list isn't here. There's bugger all here."

"Yes. Evidently, Toohey conducted his business from else-

159

where."

"What about his office at the Durban Club?"

"That's been gone over. Many times, in fact. By me and by the police, and also by the uglies. Nothing of consequence there."

"So what happens next?"

"That rather depends. Can I take it that you're on our team?"

"Well, Blighter, it's like this: you haven't told me enough to convince me of anything. And you admit that you're out for yourself."

"Not quite so simple, old pal," he said. "I work for the elected government of Australia. It just so happens that I wish to look after my own wellbeing along the way."

"However you want to put it, I can't trust you."

"Wouldn't expect it, old chum."

"So, there's the League of Righteousness on one side and the Commonwealth Investigation Service on the other as rival buyers, with Harry Strettles and maybe Ray Waters hovering separately around the edges, hoping to hijack whatever they can. Is the auction still considered to be on?"

"We shouldn't get too far ahead of ourselves, old chum. Let's leave that question open for the moment. For now, I represent the Commonwealth, and I'm asking you whether you're prepared to cooperate with us. For wages, of course. Quite good wages at that."

"Cooperate in what way?"

"Assist in bringing the matter to a suitable conclusion."

I thought for a few moments. The whole business stank.

"All right, Blighter, I'll tag along with you for the time being. I don't really have that much choice. But be warned: if things don't work out, or if I don't like what's happening, I'm taking off. Understand?"

His face broke into a broad smile. "Wonderful! I'm awfully

glad, Bill. You know, this government work can be rather fun."

"I'm a-quiver with expectation. What do we do next?"

"Well firstly, allow me to give you your wages in advance. The back room boys felt that if we paid you up front, it might help to win you over to the cause." He reached in his pocket and handed me an envelope. "Four weeks pay, at the special rate."

I opened it up. Crisp new pound notes. About four months at the council rate. I nodded and slipped the envelope into my jacket pocket.

"That helps, no doubt about it," I said.

"Most damnable thing, though, Bill," the Blighter said. "I had my hopes pinned on a horse at Randwick last Saturday which let me down rather badly. I hate to ask, but could you possibly see your way clear to advancing a few of those back to me? I'd be ever so grateful."

"You're putting the bite on me? I don't believe it. How much?"

"I owe my bookie twenty-three pounds, and on top of that I made a rather rash promise to my current landlord. Would thirty-five quid be straining the friendship too much?"

He had an open, untroubled look on his face.

"You're bloody serious, aren't you?" I said.

"I'm afraid so."

"I don't know why you even gave me the money in the first place. Here, take it."

He put the money in his wallet. "I suggest we retire to the Golden Sheaf for drinks. I think we're going to get on splendidly, Bill, don't you?"

"Yeah, absolutely spiffingly."

9

At five in the afternoon, the Sheaf was filled with men single-mindedly getting as many drinks into them as they could before closing time at six. The Blighter was warmly greeted by the regulars leaning against the bar.

We got our drinks and retired to a quiet corner.

"So tell me about this Lil," I said. "Who was she? And how do you know she's dead?"

"How do *you* know about Lil?"

"There was a letter from her to Mick with that bit of the register. They were in a box of cigars I lifted from Mick's office."

The Blighter looked at me a long time, then looked away.

"You'd make a good spy, Bill. You've done remarkably well," the Blighter said quietly. "Except for the quite understandable mistake of assuming Lil is a she."

"Eh?"

"I'm sure you heard me, Bill."

"What are you saying?"

"Lil was a chap."

"But the letter was full of lovey-dovey stuff ... Hugs and kisses even."

"Yes, quite."

"Are you trying to tell me Mick Toohey was strange?"

"Queer as a corkscrew."

"Bullshit."

"I'm sorry, but it's the truth. Mick Toohey was as camp as Chloe."

I didn't say anything. Jack Carmody's silence on the Lil question, the fact that Misery never remarried. It fitted.

"But he was an athlete, a man's man! He even chased after my mum at one stage." I said.

"Perhaps he tried rather too hard, don't you think? Sorry to tell you, Bill, but I'm absolutely right about this. He kept it quiet, though. No one much knows."

"Well listen, Blighter—to be honest, I have more doubts about *you*. Maybe you're just saying this because you're one of them."

"Sorry again, Bill. Despite my accent, I'm not of the persuasion, unless you count the odd trifling incident at boarding school. An English accent doesn't automatically make one a sodomite, you know."

I thought for a moment.

"All right then. So Lil's a bloke, and Mick Toohey was a pervert, you say. I'll accept that for now, for argument's sake. But how do you know Lil's dead?"

"The body you found in the ruins of the Durban Club."

"Eddie Worrall was Lil? Eddie Worrall and Mick Toohey—a pair of horses?"

I took a drink and thought about that one for a minute.

"So what are we doing, then, really?"

"We're going to keep an eye on you, and see what happens. As far as the League and Strettles are concerned, we'll let them go on thinking that you do have the list. Meanwhile we'll be doing our best to locate it."

"So I'm the bait."

"You do rather seem to be the key to it all."

"Tell me something," I said. "Why do they call you the "Filthy

Blighter"? Apart from the fact that you've got a shit of a real name, I mean."

"Because I'm an absolutely unprincipled scoundrel, old chap."

"I see." I finished my beer and stood up. "I'll shoot through now. What happens tomorrow?"

"Where are you going?" he said.

"Never you mind."

"Sorry, old chap, but the terms of the arrangement are that we stick together."

"Yeah, sure. Give me a phone number and I'll ring you in the morning."

"Oh dear. You're not going to be tedious are you, William?"

"Look. I don't know you, I've got no reason to trust you, and I don't particularly care for your poofy pommy ways. I'm going to piss off. If you want to set your bloodhounds on my tail again, then go ahead. But I'm going."

He sighed deeply and stared into his glass. "Oh, very well. But the bloodhounds are dreadfully inept, I'm afraid, so don't assume they'll be there keeping an eye on you. Today they were just lucky. Under normal circumstances they couldn't find their own dicks with a map and a flashlight. So if you should get into trouble, you'll be on your own." He looked up at me. "Unless, of course, you want to tell me where you're staying."

"No, I don't. What's on for tomorrow, boss?"

"I think Canterbury."

"Canterbury? What, the races?"

"Yes. Why not? Why don't you pick me up from my room at the Metropole." He took a pad out of his pocket, wrote a number on a sheet, tore it off and gave it to me. "Ring me if anything happens in the meantime."

It was half past six when I got to the Paddo house. The squatters had made themselves pretty much at home. Cec had scrounged some pieces of broken furniture and fixed the place up a bit, and his wife had put the kitchen in order. I'd given her a few quid to buy food with and she was keen to make the most of it. Cec was sitting at the kitchen table, bouncing the baby on his knee, while May attended to the evening meal.

"Just in time for tea," he said.

"Yeah, right. Terrific." But I went straight out the back, got my torch from the trunk and started looking around the house. One thing I *had* got from the afternoon's labors was a crash course in concealment techniques. And the idea had dawned on me half-way through that the rear of number 36 Oxford Street might just be Mick Toohey's little hidey-hole. I'd have to wait until Cec and May went out to search the whole house thoroughly, but I could make a start on the back room at least.

I went around carefully tapping the skirting-boards, looking for signs of recent interference, then closely checked the flooring. I found a section of loose floorboards in the corner of the room. I got a screwdriver under a corner and the boards came up in a single section about a foot and a half square. I shined the torch into the hole, poked my head in. There was a pile of old sherry and port bottles directly below, some broken house bricks, pipes, and what looked like the remains of a rat's nest. A serious search would mean getting into overalls and crawling around underneath. But it didn't look promising.

I lifted my head from the hole and turned to see Cec walking down the passage way.

"Dinner's ready," he said. Then he took in the scene. Floorboards up, tools out. He looked at me curiously.

"There've been rats down there," I said.

"Uh huh," he said. "Well, if you're doing any work around the place, give me a yell. I'm a fair hand at building work and odd jobs."

165

"I'll remember that," I said. I put the boards back and stood up. "Dinner, you say?"

"Yeah, mate. Come and get it while it's hot."

After dinner I bought a bag of oranges and drove out to see my mother, who despite her earlier predictions that she'd be out in a few days, was still in hospital, supposedly for tests. She was thin, and suddenly looked quite old. Uncle Dick was sitting by the bed.

Mum got in first. "You look thin, Bill. Are you eating all right?"

"Yeah, sure."

"You getting on with your brother?"

"Like a house on fire. How long are you staying in this place?"

"I'm not sure, Bill. I might be out soon. I thought I might go down to Gert's for a while." Gertrude was her sister in Nowra.

"What do you want to go down there for?"

"I'd like to see her. Have a rest."

"Are you all right, really?"

"Of course I am. I'll be on deck in no time."

In the morning I picked up the Filthy Blighter and we drove out to the mid-week meeting at Canterbury Racetrack.

The old bloke on the turnstile said "G'day, Blighter. Fancy anything today?"

The Blighter tipped him Timely Miss in the fourth. Later on a woman working on the Tote thanked him for his tip at the dogs the previous week. It was like that all day: jockeys, trainers, and assorted silvertails all said hello, as did lurkmen and urgers, bookie's runners, and loiterers.

I merged into the crowd as best I could, but the Blighter made a point of seeking me out each time I tried to melt away. "Billy, old sport," he'd call out loudly, "what's your fancy for the next?"

Later in the day I became aware of a couple of blokes watching us—me in particular. One was short and thickset, with spiky fair hair, a bushy mo, and a limp; the other was lean, with a long scar down his face, and a not-quite-well, slightly-around-the-twist look about him.

By four o'clock I'd spotted a third character, another grim-looking gent whose eyes darted away every time I looked at him. If the Blighter had noticed them he didn't let on, and I didn't get a chance to talk to him one to one for the last twenty minutes of the meeting. I was glad when it all ended.

As we walked out to where the car was parked, the Blighter kept up a continual chatter about the afternoon's events—he'd won for the day, and had already paid me back the thirty-five quid.

I looked behind us and saw the scar-faced goon thirty or forty yards back, dodging behind a group of punters, his head down.

The Blighter was saying, "Of course, they should have rubbed out the blasted jockey on Timely Miss for the way he rode that race, but considering I had twenty quid on Receiver, I can only applaud his run, eh?"

"Blighter, cut out your blathering for a minute and listen to me," I whispered. "There are some heavies who've been watching us for the last hour. One of them's behind us now!"

"Keep up appearances, old boy," he said quietly. "Had noticed them, you know. Just play along."

He resumed his prattle, talking about the reasoning that had gone into each of his selections for the afternoon.

When we got to the car park the crowd had thinned out. The scar-faced bloke was still behind us, and as we approached the car I spotted the two others up ahead.

"Oh shit," I said. "We'll have to make a run for it, Blighter. I could take one of these blokes, maybe two on a good day, but they're right out of your league *any* day. Are you up to a sprint?"

The Blighter looked at me, his face calm and untroubled.

"A *sprint*? Really, Bill."

The blokes closed in quickly.

The Blighter said to me quietly, "I'll talk," and then hailed them. "Good afternoon, fellows. Have a good day?"

The one with the mo said in a surprisingly friendly, educated voice, "Now, none of that nonsense, Blighter. You know why we're here."

"Well, old chap, if you have the required money then perhaps we can proceed. But otherwise, you're rather wasting your time, I'm afraid. As you well know."

The three moved in a little closer. The Chev was just thirty yards in front of us.

The bloke with the mo pointed at me and said, "This would be Glasheen, then?"

Enough, I thought. I ran at him and threw a wide wild right at his head which got him around the ear somewhere. He staggered back, but his eyes didn't close, and he didn't go down.

"Come on Blighter!" I said, "The car!"

I took off, fumbled the key out of my pocket, dropped it, picked it up again and kept running.

I got nearly all the way to the car, then realized I was on my own. I looked back. The scar-faced feller was on the ground holding his side, and the other had backed right off. The Blighter was shaping up—if you could call it that—to the bloke with the mo, who was reaching inside his jacket. He made a high fast kick and something flew out of the bloke's hand. The Blighter kicked again and got him square in the chest, so the bloke fell awkwardly backwards. Half crouched in some sort of jujitsu pose, the Blighter did a quick circle. One of the trio was fifty yards away now, melting into the gathering crowd; the other two were on the deck. The Blighter straightened up, looked over towards me and smiled sheepishly.

I walked back to where they were. The bloke with the mo was on the ground retching, the other was bleeding from the mouth and holding the side of his head.

"What happened? How did you—?"

The Blighter signaled me to keep quiet. He walked past the bloke with the mo and stooped to pick up a pistol. He removed the bullets from the chamber, then went back to the bloke with the mo, crouched down and shook his shoulder gently.

"Sorry, Aubrey. Let's leave the rough house out next time, shall we? Now, to business. Are you paying attention?" he said, and gave his shoulder another shake. "All right then. The terms are the same as before: ten thousand for the return of the register. There is no other way it can be done. Tell the chaps that, would you?"

The Blighter straightened up. Twenty or thirty people had gathered to watch, standing back at a discreet distance. "You'd better pull yourself together and clear out before the coppers come."

"Just a tick," I said. I walked past the Blighter, up to the bloke named Aubrey. "Terrorize my mother, will you, you grub. Cop this then." With that I laid in the slipper with all the force I could muster. There was a hollow sound, like a cricket bat hitting a ball and I felt an immediate shooting pain in my foot.

"Suffering Jesus Christ on the cross!" I said.

"I believe you kicked his *wooden* leg, Bill." the Blighter said. "Come on, quickly now."

He tapped me on the shoulder and we walked—I hopped—over to the car and drove away. A few hundred yards down the road the Blighter threw the bullets out the window.

We didn't say anything for a few minutes, until I said, "How'd you learn to fight like that?"

"Oh, during the war. They were frightfully insistent that we become well versed in that advanced hand to hand stuff. In fact, I've hardly ever used it."

"So when I belted you yesterday," I said, "you could have cleaned me up."

"Wouldn't really have been cricket, old chap."

"You let me win. At cost to yourself, too, unless that vomiting was faked too."

"No, that was perfectly authentic."

I looked at him.

"You must think I'm a prize mug," I said.

"Look, Bill, I'm sorry, but this cloak-and-dagger stuff can be a ghastly, deceitful business. But sometimes deceit's the only way to get the result. Don't let it spoil things between us. I know we can be great chums."

"The three stooges back there—Aub Munce and his cronies, I take it?"

"Quite so."

"How did they know we'd be at Canterbury today?" I said.

"Oh, I told them. Last night. A phone call."

"Why did you do that?"

"To draw them out. See what they'd do."

"Oh really? Yesterday you said you were representing the Commonwealth, and all that bullshit. But that doesn't square, does it?"

"How so, Bill?"

"You said to that bloke back there it was ten thousand pounds for the register."

"Mmm."

"So you're still running this auction lurk?"

"Well, Bill, why ever would one *not*, for God's sake?"

"You didn't say anything about that yesterday."

"Yesterday would have been altogether too soon to start talking about such things."

"So where do I fit in?"

"I was rather hoping we could be partners. Equal partners, of course."

"Where'd you get the idea I'd nod my head to a blackmail lurk?"

The Blighter exploded in laughter, spraying the windscreen with droplets of spit. "Oh, Bill, really. You're a villain down to the marrow of your bones."

"Thanks a lot."

"I don't mean like those uglies back there. Or Joe Grimshaw or Harry Strettles. Or Mick Toohey, for that matter. But Bill, you know who you are. Zoot suits, counterfeit coupons, slot machines, and whatever else you do—"

"How did you know about that?"

"The cloak-and-dagger brigade. All that stuff, Bill, you know, it rather marks you out as, well, not a run of the mill citizen, don't you think? You may not be able to see it, but—"

"Everybody else can?"

"Rather, old chap. But one shouldn't feel *bad* about it. Quite the reverse. Personal destiny and all that."

"It's funny you should say that. I did have a crack at being a solid citizen."

"Really? And?"

"I couldn't get the hang of it."

"No."

We drove on. Neither of us spoke for a few minutes.

"Ten thousand pounds for the register," I said. "Will the Legion of the Whispering Skull really pay that much?"

"I believe they will."

"What about your mates in the government? Would they be able to pay as well?"

The Blighter looked at me. "What have you in mind?"

"Is there anything really which says we can only sell the register *once*?"

"No-o-o-o, not really. My, but you do learn fast, William."

"Yeah, like you say, I was born to it. So, would the government also spring for the whole ten thousand, do you think?"

"Ten thousand might be stretching things a bit, given the current climate. Maybe half that, though, if the back-room boys believe it's sufficiently important."

"Could you convince them that it is?"

"Perhaps."

"All right Blighter, this is where I stand: I could use some money right now, and I'm prepared to have a go at getting it. If these Masked Avenger blokes are the mongrels you reckon they are, then fuck them, they're fair game. And if the government people want to pay for any information that *we* might be able to turn up as a result of our own efforts, that's fair enough too—due reward for risks taken and all that rot. Try it on with the government for the whole ten grand, but settle for five if that's the best we can do."

"Good show!"

"So, we split fifty-fifty. Even if we only sell the register once, back to the Knights of the Scarlet Arsehole, that's still five thousand each." As soon as I said it, my heart sped up a bit. "Agreed?"

"But of course old fellow. I wouldn't think of doing it any other way."

"Now before we go any further, this business of my supposed approach to Joe Grimshaw—is there anything about that you haven't told me?"

"No, I'm completely in the dark on that one."

"So at some stage we're going to have to deal with whoever it was who first approached Grimshaw using my name, aren't we?"

"In all likelihood, yes."

"So maybe they—whoever *they* are—maybe they're holding the register? We find them, take the register from them—and bingo, we're in business. Or maybe a three way split."

"That too is a possibility."

"What's the next step then?"

"It's time for you, Mr. Glasheen, to think long and hard about the evening of VP Day."

"Yeah? Why so?"

"Because as it stands, you are apparently the last person still alive to have had any contact with Michael Daniel Toohey."

We got back to the city at five thirty and retired to the back bar of the Metropole. The Blighter had me tell him all I could remember about VP Day. I gave him what I could—the gathering of the faithful in Toohey's pub, the bottles of scotch all round, Mick telling them all that he was going to late Mass at St Mary's. I told him about Cyril, how he'd said that none of the others who'd been present at the last supper knew anything.

I didn't tell the Blighter about the rent-collecting stuff, though. Somehow, despite all that had happened, that particular cat had managed to remain in the bag, and I saw no good reason to let it out now.

"How about this, Blighter—"the Devil's jump." Does that mean anything to you?"

"Hmm. In what sense?"

"It was the last thing Toohey said to me. He told me he was for the Devil's jump."

"Means absolutely nothing at all to me, old chap." He finished off his scotch and ordered another. I shot through.

That night I rang Lucy, told her to get dressed for a slap-up feed. I picked her up at seven thirty and we motored down town to Romano's. A year before I'd got hold of a drape suit for the bloke who worked on the door—at a pretty good price, considering there was a war on—and when he saw me, he ushered us to a quiet little corner with a good view of the band.

I was doing my best not to give too much away, but halfway through our dinner Lucy said, "You're looking rather pleased with yourself tonight. Care to let me in on it?"

I put my cutlery down. "I don't want to say too much yet. But let me just tell you that things are moving along nicely. *Very* nicely, if you get my drift."

"Yeah? And?"

"I've got something on. If it comes good we'll be set. I mean really set."

She looked at me intently, trying to figure out if I was dinkum or not. She nodded slightly and smiled a little. "All right, Bill. But don't gee me up. Don't involve me in your plans. I don't want to hear about things that should've got up, but didn't. I've had a lifetime of near things. Just get the results. Understand me?"

I reached over and took her hand. "I want to look after you, Lucy. I'd do anything for you."

"I know you would," she said. She didn't say anything for a moment, just kept looking at me, squeezing my hand.

Then she retrieved her hand and said, "Keep the night of Thursday the twentieth of June free."

"Yeah?"

"I want you to come and see me sing. All this time, and you've never had the pleasure."

"Not that pleasure, anyway. What's the occasion?"

"Herb's band is playing at the Colony Club. I'm doing a guest appearance. Supposedly in front of all the important radio people."

"Great. I'll be there."

I slept at Lucy's flat that night. I had a dream in which I was fishing. I'd hooked a huge, silvery fish, but the line I was using

174

was so fine that I couldn't haul it in, and had to let the fish run every time it took a mind to. I'd wind in a few turns when I got the chance, but then the fish would run and I'd have to let it out again. This happened over and over. The fish couldn't quite get away, but I couldn't quite land it either.

Over the next week the Blighter and I made the rounds. Stadium fights, baccarat and two-up schools, a rugby league game at the Sports Ground. In between sporting fixtures it was bars, pubs, and clubs. The Catholic Club, the Masonic Club, the Imperial Services Club, Double Bay Sail, and on it went. Wherever we went, he was recognized. Men and women both, he knew their names, they knew his. There was back-slapping, hand-shaking, and much swapping of race tips, jokes, and general gossip.

We were mostly hitting water holes where I wasn't known, so more than once I was asked by doormen to give them proof of my age before they would allow me inside. More often than not a few words from the Blighter would smooth the way. But when that didn't work, I'd take a leaf out of brother Ron's book. I'd set a grim expression on my dial and say to the doorman, "Proof of age? The Jap snipers on the Kokoda Track never asked me for proof of age." It worked every time.

There were no more incidents like the one at Canterbury, but the whole time I was with the Blighter I sensed a kind of hum, a sort of guarded attention. Nothing was said, but I detected a knowing watchfulness in the people we met, the people we drank with and bet with and caroused with.

After a week of it, I mentioned it to the Blighter. "Are those cloak-and-dagger mates of yours shadowing us? I keep getting this funny feeling—it's hard to explain—that the people I meet, talk to or whatever … it's like they know something that I don't."

"Hmm. My people are keeping a respectful distance, by and

large. But that feeling goes with intelligence work, William. Thank God you have the wit to notice. Have to be careful, though. It quite gets to some chaps."

"Yeah, well I don't bloody care for it much, I can tell you. I'm looking at everyone, wondering, 'Are *you* part of it?' Strike me, some days it seems like everyone in Sydney's part of it."

"You're close."

As we cruised around town each day, the Blighter kept up a steady chatter, telling me about his life. He was born into a grazing family somewhere in the north west of New South Wales, sent to boarding school in England, then went on to Cambridge. He said he'd climbed mountains in Switzerland, driven racing cars in France, and gone to Spain during the Civil War, but after a month had given it away as a bad joke. Just before the war he'd been disinherited, but he wouldn't tell me what for.

He'd first got mixed up with "the cloak-and-dagger boys" when he was at Cambridge. His history tutor asked him, in an offhanded way, if he was a member of any of the left-wing clubs, and hinted it might be a good idea if he signed up forthwith. The tutor would then pick his brains, subtly, about what had gone on at their meetings.

"You were acting as a give-up!" I said.

"Oh, yes, I suppose I was. I thought I was acting for the higher good and all that rot. King and country, you know."

"So you were just playing along with the commos?"

"Oddly enough, I believed in many of the same things they did. When I was with them, anyway."

The Blighter was on the turps the whole time. He always had a bottle of spirits in his room, and before we set out each morning, he'd fill a hip flask, and sip from it throughout the day. But I never saw him affected much by alcohol. He was always in a good mood, chatting amiably the whole time.

Until one cool, rainy Monday I called for the Blighter at the Metropole, as per usual, at ten in the morning. I went straight up to his room and knocked, but there was no answer. It was unlocked, though, so I let myself in. The Blighter was sitting at the little table next to the window, still in his dressing gown, staring out at the rain falling in the back lane behind the hotel.

When he turned around, I saw that his eyes were like a dead man's. He turned back to the window.

"G'day Blighter. Come on, son. The day's getting away from us."

He didn't answer.

I went over to him. "Hey, Blighter."

He just kept staring out the window.

I gave his shoulder a shake. "You all right there, Blighter?"

He made a vague gesture with his hand and shook his head slightly, sort of waving me away.

"Do you want me to come back later?"

But he gave no answer at all. After a minute I shrugged my shoulders and shot through.

I went back the next morning and the door was locked. There was no answer when I knocked, although somehow I felt that the room was not empty.

I found the manager and asked if anything had happened to the Blighter. He said no, not that he knew of. He'd been getting meals sent up to his room, and apparently hadn't been out for a few days.

Mum finally came out of hospital that week, and I drove her down to her sister's place in Nowra. If she wondered why I wasn't living at home any more, she didn't ask. My brother had married his girlfriend Glenys two weeks before, she said. They were renting a flat in Ashfield and Ron was spending his week-ends building their house at Padstow.

"Married? Crikey, I didn't even know."

"I wish you and Ronny were closer," she said.

"He doesn't approve of me."

"You get on each other's wrong side, I know. You always have. And in fairness, you don't lose too many chances to stir him up."

"But he's such a humorless piece of work. He asks for it."

"Ronny said you gave up your council job."

"Yeah. It wasn't really me."

"And Tech too?"

"Well, yeah. I've let that slip a bit, I suppose."

Mum looked out the window, her brow creased.

"But don't go worrying about it, Mum. I'm doing some government work now."

"Really? What is it?"

"Hush-hush stuff. I can't really talk about it."

She looked at me anxiously, trying to work out if I was pulling her leg.

When I got back to town I called in at the Metropole, but the Blighter was still not answering. I decided to track down Uncle Dick. He was in the parlor of the boarding house where he stayed, a big old mansion on Dutruc Street in Randwick, reading the afternoon papers. He seemed surprised to see me, but he quickly smiled, shook hands, and asked how I was. I told him things were fine, but I wanted to ask him a few questions.

"Oh yeah," he said. "Concerning what?"

"Mick Toohey."

He put a finger to his lips, gestured for me to move through the big double doors back outside, looked at his watch.

"Come for a walk with me, Bill, while I get a packet of cigs up the corner."

But we adjourned instead to the Coach and Horses, got ourselves fixed up with drinks, and settled in as far away from the mob as we could.

"What's on your mind, Bill?"

"Well, there's this question has come up. About Mick Toohey, like I said. I thought you might be able to help."

"Go ahead, feller."

"I'm not sure how to put it.

"Just spit it out."

"Have you ever heard anything about Toohey being a bit, ah, strange."

"How do you mean?"

"Strange *that* way, you know. A bit queer."

Uncle Dick drew back, horrified. "Mick Toohey a poof? Who on earth told you that?"

"Never mind. Did you ever hear anything along those lines?"

He pointed at me angrily. "You're badly misinformed, feller. Mick Toohey's a hundred per cent. No risk."

"All right, I get it. It was just, you know, someone said something, and I wanted to make sure."

Dick relaxed and leaned back in his chair. "You know how Toohey got that face of his?"

"No."

"It was during the Twenties. Mick was a young bloke then, of course. He was running an SP book at the Bondi Hotel. There was a feller who owed him—owed him a real pile, nearly a thousand quid. Alf Mealey was his name. A rough piece of work, a real glass-in-the-face man. Anyway, the way I heard it, Mick had to start reminding this bloke that time to pay up had come, long since. Mealey laughed at him, said sure, no worries, but then he started getting around town telling people that there was no way he was *ever* going to pay off that young Mick Toohey. Mick went to collect—he was game, you know—but all he copped was a

179

bashing. The bloke had been waiting for him, with a half dozen of his mates. Gave Mick a horrible kicking.

"Mick ended up in St Vincent's. He came good after a while but he was left with that paralysis of the face. He'd been a good-looking lad, too, as your mother told you. It hit him hard. Anyway, Mealey let it be known that he intended to finish the job he'd started on Toohey, first chance he got. When Mick recovered enough to leave hospital, he disappeared—to hide out, lick his wounds, whatever. People assumed he'd shot through for good, that Mealey and his cronies had scared him off.

"Nothing was heard or seen of Toohey for a few months. Then one day he turned up, just like that. He had a drink at the Tea Gardens, then the Bondi, and other places, too. His face had that half-dead look, but he was in good spirits.

"Now this Mealey bloke was a mad rock fisherman. Used to get around the rocks at Ben Buckler, Tamarama, the Gap—all those spots the fishos like. Anyway, the very next day the rozzers fished Mealey's body out of Diamond Bay at Vaucluse. You know the place?"

"Heard of it."

"It's sheer cliffs right down to deep water—no beach or anything. The only way in is to climb down a ravine, then cross some fallen rocks at the bottom, scurry across in between the waves. To get to the fishing spots, you then have to follow a slippery ledge about a foot wide halfway back up the cliff face. You get up there and, I'll tell you what, it's a long way down. The waves are roaring in, hitting the wall below you. It'd scare the shit out of you. They say there's good fishing there, though. It was Alf Mealey's favorite spot."

"So what had happened?"

"No one ever knew. Maybe Alf slipped and fell in the drink. It's happened to quite a few fishos around there. But it happened the day after Mick returned to town, so you can imagine what people thought."

"That Mick had got quits?"

"Yeah. He let them think it, too. The coppers talked to him, but they had nothing."

"What do you reckon happened?"

"Me? I wouldn't know. To take on Alf Mealey on that ledge, on his home ground, you'd have to be pretty sure of yourself. Or pretty game. But yeah, Toohey was capable of it. He's tough, as hard as they come. He proved it plenty of times after that. And I'll tell you something else: I could give you the names of two dozen women around this town who'd vouch for Mick Toohey being a man in every sense of the word. Whoever told you those stories is having a lend of you."

"Yeah, I get it. When Toohey left hospital, way back then, you reckon he went bush to recuperate?"

"Yeah."

"Would you know where he went?"

"Not *exactly*."

"You mean, you might know *roughly*?"

"I might have an idea. But it'd be a guess."

I didn't say anything more for a moment. Dick was looking unconcerned. *Very* unconcerned.

"Dick, tell me, have you been hearing anything around town recently?"

"About what, Bill?"

"About Mick. About other people. About me?"

"Yeah, it so happens I *have* heard a whisper here and there."

"And what would you be hearing?"

Dick looked at me. "That you and your mates are taking on some pretty rough types."

"Look Dick. I'd like to know where Toohey used to get away to. Can you help me find out?"

"It's important to you, is it?"

I stopped. "Oh maybe it is, maybe it isn't. I won't know until . . . well, I just don't know yet."

"All right Bill. I'll see what I can find out."

"Thanks Dick. It's got to be discreet, though. I don't want anyone to know. I mean, anyone at all."

"I get the picture. The only thing, Bill . . . If you're going to play junior detective, you should realize that sometimes it takes a few bob to grease the wheels, if you get me."

"Yeah, that's all right. Get me that information and I'll do the right thing."

"How do I contact you?"

"I'm keeping my head pulled in at the moment," I said. "And I've got no phone where I'm staying. But there's a barber in Oxford Street at Paddo. You can ring him on this number"—I scribbled it onto the back of a coaster—"He'll pass on any message."

"Good-o."

I stood up. "Let me know the moment you find out anything."

He looked at the number on the coaster, then shrewdly at me. "I will, feller, don't worry about that."

I phoned Cyril that night. We chatted for a few minutes, then I asked him, did he ever have any reason to suspect that Mick might be an each-way bettor. Cyril went off his head. He said that was a rotten thing to say about someone who's not even here to defend his own good name. He said Mick Toohey was an honorable man, he was staunch and a man of his word in every way. I mentioned Eddie Worrall's name. Cyril said he wouldn't know anything about that, and hung up.

10

I stayed at Lucy's that night, then went to the Metropole the next morning. When I knocked on the Blighter's door, he called out cheerfully to come in. He was dressed, spruced, and smiling broadly.

"William, old son, wonderful to see you. I was rather hoping you'd be here today. There's much to do."

"You all right, are you?"

"Wonderful, thank you."

"I see."

The Blighter said quietly, "Bill, awfully sorry for the lost time last week. An attack of the blue devils, I'm afraid."

I didn't say anything.

"Happens sometimes. Can't do much about it, except wait for it to pass. Not much good to anyone while it's on."

"You remember I came around here? You were like a zombie."

"Yes, I was aware of it. Hard to explain, Bill. Terribly oppressive thing."

"It's passed?"

"Yes, and oddly enough it's left me in a rather sanguine frame of mind."

"Has it just?"

"Indeed. And we have much to do. Beginning with lunch at the Royal Automobile Club. Top drawer affair. One o'clock. Have to dress up for it, I'm afraid."

I was wearing a sports coat and open-necked shirt.

"You're telling me I have to go and change?"

"Frightful bore, I know. But yes, if you don't mind, old man."

"How important is this, Blighter? I mean, if this is just another day of glad-handing and pissing in pockets, then, with respect, I don't know how badly I want to tag along."

"I understand, Bill, and you're perfectly right to be a little bit ticked off with the old Blighter. But yes, this is important. Things are beginning to happen."

"Oh, really? That's ever so splendid. Weeks of farting around, and now things are beginning to happen. Blighter—is any of this real at all?"

"Whatever do you mean?"

"Oh, I know Strettles and Aubrey Munce and Ray Waters are real enough. And I know *something* is going on with Mick Toohey. But this other stuff. The Patriotic League and the ten thousand pounds and the secret agents and the supposed register and the rest of it—has that all just been cooked up in your imagination? Like the idea of Mick Toohey being a queer?"

"I beg your pardon?"

"I've done some checking of my own."

"Really?"

"Yeah. There's not the least suggestion from anyone that Toohey was that way."

The Blighter shrugged his shoulders. "That's what he told me."

"Toohey *told* you?"

The Blighter nodded.

"Oh, right. Here's a bloke who never let anything slip in his whole life. But he let it out to you."

"Getting secrets out of people is one of the things I'm supposed to be good at. I suspected Toohey was queer right from the start, so I put it to him, in an indirect way. He didn't deny it."

The Blighter looked perfectly calm and assured.

"Look Bill," he said. "You can believe it or not. It doesn't really matter. But as for the rest of it, things are moving along. I received a message last night from a chap, a neutral party, who says he's been asked to talk to us. The League people want to deal. I truly think the payoff is close. Of course I can't stop you walking away from it all now, if you choose to, but that won't decrease the risk to you one jot. Quite the reverse, in fact. Persist for a few more days, on the other hand, and there's every chance of a most handsome collect. And a complete resolution to this affair, of course. But the choice is yours."

I sighed. "I'll give it another day. If there's no result, then I'm going to bolt, sort things out on my own."

"Good show!"

"And I'm supposed to go and get threaded up for this turn today?"

"If you don't mind. Why don't we meet at the First and Last, twelve o'clock?"

I went back to Paddo to get changed. Cec and Mavis were in the kitchen, playing with the baby.

I stepped inside the door and Cec said, "Hello, here he is, the man they couldn't root, shoot or electrocute! How are you, Billy?"

"Good."

There were four plump bream on a sheet of newspaper on the kitchen table.

"Caught them this morning," Cec said.

May said, "Will you have a cup of tea? It's just made."

"No, I'm just on my way through." I turned to Cec. "Hey,

185

listen. I don't mean to be rude, but you know, it's been a while now that you've been camped here, and although you keep telling me your prospects are good, there's not a lot of money coming in, is there? I'm starting to wonder when you're going to do something about your situation."

Cec looked at me blankly for a moment, then said, "Of course, you're quite right, old son. It'll be any day now." He smiled.

I went to my room and changed into a light gray drape suit. The jacket had a single button, way down low, and the strides were full but pegged at the bottom. My best suit. I brushed my hair and headed off.

The Blighter was propping up the bar of the First and Last.

"Oh Christ, Bill. I didn't mean a *zoot* suit!"

For the first time, the Blighter was a little under the weather. He was glassy-eyed, and slurring slightly.

"Get fucked. It's my best suit. You're telling me it's not good enough for the Royal Auto Club?"

"But this is a terribly, terribly top-drawer affair, old chap—a fund-raising lunch for the Liberal Party. Not exactly a jive, reefer, and zoot suit affair."

He tipped the last of his shot glass down.

"It's too late to change now ... Oh well, dressed like that you'll shake them up a bit. I suppose it might do the old cunts some good."

He was talking loudly and slowly. A couple of drinkers looked around at us, but the Blighter didn't seem to notice.

"Let us be off then, William."

We walked a hundred yards up the hill to the club. It was a cold, gray, windy day. The doorman at the club ticked our names off the list and we were shown in to the dining room.

It was noisy, full of well-dressed men, quite a few of them in uniform, and a smaller number of women. I copped a few looks—for the zoot suit, I guessed. We were led to a table, thankfully over to the side and out of the way. Most of the seats were empty except for an ancient couple with walking sticks and hearing aids. The codger was wearing a tam-o'-shanter, and had military decorations on his coat. They nodded stiffly to us as we sat down.

"I wonder if the old feller is holding any reefers," I said to the Blighter.

There were maybe two or three hundred people in the room, talking enthusiastically, getting stuck into the grog. One table was filled with markedly less well-dressed types. They were drinking the hardest.

"The gentlemen of the press," said the Blighter.

A waiter came over and asked what we wanted to drink. The Blighter went for scotch. I had a beer.

"So, who are these gigs?" I said.

"Major financial contributors. A gallery of rogues, Bill, a gallery of rogues!"

The old folks looked our way.

"See that fellow over there, with the moustache. He's a grazier. A New Guard member before the war. Advocated a deal with Japan—*after* Pearl Harbor. Came within a whisker of being had up for treason."

"Is he one of the Patriotic Riders of the Whistling Skull?"

"Probably. Plenty of secret army men here. See that chap over there next to the woman in the big hat?"

A little, harmless looking feller.

"What about him?"

"He *still* thinks Hitler was the most misunderstood man of the century."

"Are we dealing with *him*?"

"Hardly."

I continued looking around the room and saw a familiar face.

A few tables away sharing a private joke with the lady next to him, was the round-faced, brilliantined toad I'd belted at Lucy's flat. He was wearing an army uniform with plenty of braid on it.

"Blighter," I said, "Do you happen to know that bloke over there?"

He followed the direction of my gaze, then gave me a long look, as though he suspected I might be having a lend of him. "That's Eric Prisk. The radio chap. Soon to be Liberal Party candidate for a safe federal seat on the North Shore, rumor would have it."

I should have recognized the voice. He was an announcer on 2GB, second in popularity only to Jack Davey. A big king and empire type, but always smooth and affable. Every time he suggested they lock up the commos or bring back the lash or whatever, he did it in such a quiet, friendly tone that it sounded like the most reasonable thing in the world. His pet topic was the dire threat that commos in the trade unions posed to the Australian way of life.

"I didn't know he was army."

"Oh, it's a bullshit commission. Influence, friends, all that. Prisk pulled strings with the army brass—General Blamey himself is supposed to be a great mate of his—made a nuisance of himself until he got the uniform. Quite unseemly, really."

I moved my chair a foot sideways, out of Eric Prisk's line of sight. "Listen Blighter, I'm not so sure about this place and these people."

"Don't worry about it, William. All you need to do is sit tight, keep your wits about you and enjoy the food—which, I might add, is excellent here. Leave the rest to me."

"Blighter, we haven't even got the bloody register!"

The old folks along the table looked around. The Blighter smiled at them, nodded graciously, then turned back and said in a whisper, "But they *think* we have it, and that's good enough for now."

"No it's bloody well not. It'll just put us—put *me*—deeper in the shit. I'm all for selling the register, of course. When we have it to sell. I don't see the need for the big hurry, Blighter?"

"There is no hurry."

But his eyelids flickered as he said it.

"Are you broke again, Blighter?"

"Well, just the tiniest spot of financial bother, nothing really. But I must confess, I am rather keen to finish this all off."

"We're just making trouble, if—"

But the Blighter was up and off. The old folks further down the table gave me a worried look. I smiled, raised my glass to them.

I sat there, feeling uncomfortable and way out of place. A waiter carrying a bottle of wine asked if I would care for a glass. I nodded.

I took a long drink. It was better than anything I'd ever tasted before, so I had another.

Then I was presented with a bowl of oyster soup. It was delicious. I finished it, then had another glass of wine. I started to feel nicely warmed. Then they brought a main course of roast beef, which was also excellent. I ate my fill, washed it down with another glass of wine. By the time I'd finished the apple and rhubarb pie, I was feeling quite at ease.

The Blighter was still off doing the rounds. His meal sat untouched on the table. I spotted him talking to a bloke, who had his head down, listening and nodding. He looked up at the Blighter, then across to me. I nodded at him, raised my glass. I watched the Blighter go from table to table. He'd have a few words with the blokes, then they'd start laughing, nudging one another in the ribs, and slapping backs like great old mates. Or he'd have little chats with the old ducks, who'd quickly turn girlish.

The waitresses brought out coffee and brandy. Steering clear of spirits had become a habit with me by now, but this time, I thought, why not? The brandy was fragrant and set the coffee off nicely. I leaned back in my chair, thinking, Gee, this isn't too bad. A bloody sight better than the counter lunch at the Bunch of Cunts.

I looked around. Blokes were lighting up cigars, leaning back like me, well satisfied with the meal and with everything else, by the look of it. A bloke at the next table smiled companionably, lifted his brandy glass in greeting. I did the same. I asked the waiter for another brandy.

Then a feller stood up and called everyone to attention. He burbled on for a while, thanking various individuals who had made the day possible. Then he talked a bit about why we were all here, about the greatness of the British Empire and about Australia's sacred role in maintaining British values in this part of the world, where free enterprise and other sacred institutions were currently under dire threat. Then he said it was his happy duty to present the guest of honor, the leader of their great party, the once and undoubtedly the future prime minister of the Commonwealth of Australia, the Honorable Robert Menzies.

I knew who Bob Menzies was, of course. When I was still a kid, before the war, I'd heard the adults talking about "Pig Iron Bob," after he'd had the clever idea of selling iron to the Japs. They, of course, were tooling up for war against us at the time, and it didn't take a genius to see it. Menzies was prime minister when war broke out, but he quickly scurried off to Britain, where he stayed for months on end, and that hadn't impressed anyone much, not even his supporters. Finally he came back home, saying all would be well if we trusted Britain and Churchill to look after us. Which was a mug's bet, because Churchill was quite prepared to let the Japs have Australia if necessary.

Anyway, Menzies' party sacked him, and then the Labor boys

got in. They made friends with the Yanks—groveled to them, some said—brought Australian troops back from the northern theatres of war, over Churchill's bitter objections, and on it went from there. Everyone thought that was the end of Bob Menzies, but now he'd resurfaced as the leader of the spanking new Liberal Party of Australia.

The applause went on for a good thirty seconds. Menzies, smiling, looked around the room, turning his whole body as he did so. He raised his hand to stop the applause.

"Thank you, Mr. Chairman, for your very kind remarks," he said, turning to the bloke next to him. "And thank you, ladies and gentlemen, for your warm welcome on this uncharacteristically cold Sydney day, a day that reminds me rather of a winter's day in the rolling wheat country of Western Victoria, from where I hail."

There was something about the voice. Deep and lazy, but soothing in a way. Not too plummy, but not too broad Aussie either. He started talking about the Labor Party, how misguided they were, how perilous for Australia it was to be led by such a suspicious and divisive bunch as Chifley, Evatt, and the rest.

I didn't pay much attention. The food and drink were percolating nicely through my system, and the warmth of the dining room made me feel wonderfully relaxed. That voice, too, was kind of hypnotic. I sort of switched off, as bits and pieces of what he was saying wafted through my head.

"The great vice of democracy is that people have been busy getting themselves onto the list of beneficiaries and removing themselves from the list of contributors, looking to somebody else's wealth and somebody else's efforts on which they might thrive . . . "

You're dead right there, I thought. All those bludgers forever trying to slip out of paying the rent. Christ, and what about Cec and May Greenwood—Cec out fishing every morning, while I hadn't even had a chance to wet a line for months?

Menzies went on about how Labor reckoned there were two classes in Australia, workers and capitalists, but they had it all arse up, or words to that effect. He said the industrious middle classes were carrying an unfair share of the burden, while all the Labor blokes were doing was encouraging a lot of whingeing bludgers to expect something for nothing.

I leaned back in my padded chair, arms crossed, and let my eyes close, the better to enjoy the comfortable sensations.

"Let us be clear. The Liberal Party is not anti-worker. But we deplore direct action and industrial lawlessness, and we call upon Australian workers to repudiate anarchy, secure in the knowledge that the Liberal Party will forever stand behind arbitration and conciliation in industrial matters . . ."

Sounds pretty reasonable, I thought.

"And today I want you to consider another group of Australians—the forgotten Australians, hard-working and decent Australians who have been largely unrepresented and sadly un-sung until now. I refer to the salary-earners, shopkeepers, skilled artisans, professional men and women, farmers and so on—the very backbone of the nation . . . "

Good show.

He talked about the rough trot this mob had been having under Labor, how they had to pay for everything and everyone else.

". . . To say that the industrious and intelligent son of self-sacrificing and saving and forward-looking parents has the same social deserts and even material needs as the dull offspring of stupid and improvident parents is absurd . . . "

I couldn't argue with that.

"The votes of the thriftless have been used to defeat the thrifty. Under Labor, the unskilled and unthinking class, those who dis-courage ambition, who distrust independent thought, who sneer at and impute false motives to public service—those very same people, ladies and gentlemen, would be the very helmsmen of society."

I drifted away for a moment.

". . . Under a Liberal Government, lower taxes will brighten the future, and bring more contented work and more goods and services . . . happy, prosperous families . . . "

Yeah, I thought, that'll be Lucy and me. I saw that picture again in my mind's eye, the love nest built for two, or maybe three.

". . . instead of Labor's bitter, divisive, hate-filled view, an outlook which encourages weakness, resentment and self-pity, which promotes a lack of independence in the face of adversity, and which ultimately can lead only to the conniving mentality of the safe-breaker, the lout, the lurk merchant, the black marketeer . . ."

I stirred a little. Had he really said that, or was I imagining it? The voice continued its warm, lulling song, and I sank back in with it.

"Chifley and the Labor Party bear a hatred for bold enterprise, they are suspicious of profit, and they resent men of vision. When a Liberal government is elected, we will promptly remove all socialistic impediments to free and legitimate enterprise—first and foremost the ridiculous rationing laws which Chifley has maintained for far too long."

I started to stir as I pictured my store of counterfeit rationing coupons—suddenly worthless. I saw my bank disappearing, and everything else with it. But the voice went on, and again I went along, as if I was lying on a raft floating easily down a shady stream on a sunny day.

"They would have us dismiss and condemn the things of timeless value, the immortal words of the Bard, the priceless gems of English art and literature and learning, the very political values represented by the Crown and the Empire, leaving us with nothing but the tawdry lures of mass culture—those baubles fabricated to appeal to the very lowest, most degraded sections of society. Take for example the idiocies of the zoot suit, the animalistic and mindless dancing of the so-called 'jitterbugs'—their foolish music, their brutal exhibitions and vulgar displays. Let us not yield to such mindlessness . . ."

I must have drifted right off for a while, I don't know how long, but I was brought back by gales of laughter around me. There was something strange sounding about it.

With my eyes still closed I tuned back in to Menzies' voice.

"And so in conclusion, ladies and gentlemen, if I may again use our somnolent zoot-suited friend on my right here as an object lesson, may we doze no longer, blissfully yet foolishly unaware. I call on you as I call on the great Commonwealth of Australia! Awaken!"

I opened my eyes. Menzies was looking right at me, a little smile on his face, his eyes lazily contemptuous.

I looked around. The whole room was looking at me.

As I straightened up in my seat, the entire room exploded in laughter, even the geriatrics at my table. I rubbed my eyes and cleared my throat. I felt my face turning red.

I stood up to leave with as much dignity as I could manage, but the brandy hit me and I swayed a little. Another wave of laughter swept the room. Menzies was looking at me.

"Go on," I said, "have your laugh. But you won't ever get *my* vote. I'm a Chifley man."

Menzies smiled. "And he's entirely welcome to you, sir."

An even bigger laugh.

"Yeah, well how about you go and get stuffed."

I started walking. Menzies waved his arm lazily to summon the attendants. "See this young guttersnipe off the premises, would you?"

194

I stopped. "I was already going," I said. I changed direction, and lurched towards Menzies. He looked quickly around. The attendants, who might have been flash fellers during the Boer War, were still over by the door.

I got to within a few feet of him. "You're a pretty smart talker, pal," I said. "But how would you feel like having a real go?"

I shaped up. There was a rapid intake of breath around the room, and a look of panic flitted across Menzies' face, then I copped a punch in the kidneys which nearly floored me. My arm was twisted up hard behind my back and I found myself being frog-marched towards the door. I kicked and bucked a bit, but I had no real choice but to move in the direction I was being pushed.

Behind me I heard Menzies' say, "Well done, fellows," followed by a round of applause.

I was marched past Eric Prisk's table. He was looking at me, smirking. I called out to the middle aged woman next to him, "And you'd do well to keep this grub here"—I nodded at Prisk—"on a shorter leash. Tell him to stop sniffing around my girlfriend."

My arm was forced even further up my back. Behind me someone said, "Come on. Out you go." I kicked and squirmed, but they kept pushing me nearer the door.

"And for the benefit of all you Patriotic League boy scouts here," I shouted, "you'd better make it snappy with the readies, hear me? Or we'll sell the register to the government."

At that a puzzled murmur went around the room.

We got to the door. The last thing I took in was the Blighter, sitting opposite Eric Prisk, his eyes closed, his head in his hands.

I was given a solid push out the door and another quick punch to the kidneys. One of the old attendants called out to the posse who were holding me, should he call the police. A voice behind me said, "He's not worth the trouble."

195

They chucked me out the back door and locked it after me. I picked myself up and went back to the car.

Twenty minutes passed and my head cleared a bit. I started thinking maybe I shouldn't have said what I did. And maybe I shouldn't have left the Blighter in there. I walked back towards the club.

When I was fifty yards away, a car pulled up in front and Aubrey Munce and his pals got out. A second car pulled up behind them and another four men got out. They huddled for a moment, then split into two groups; one went in the front door, the other disappeared up the side lane.

I found a public telephone, looked up Central Street Police Station's number, and put through a call. A gruff voice asked what I wanted. I put on a foreign accent, told him there was a bomb in the Royal Automobile Club set to go off in ten minutes time. He asked who was calling. I said, "Workers of the world unite!" and hung up.

I got the Chev and drove back down Macquarie Street. The parking spaces directly outside the club were all occupied by big shiny cars. The chauffeurs were gathered in a laneway out of the wind, smoking and chatting. I pulled up short of the club, and waited.

Nothing happened for three or four minutes, then I heard sirens approaching. A paddy wagon and three police cars came screaming down the street. They stopped outside the club, right in the middle of Macquarie Street. The coppers poured into the joint, and a minute later the worthy guests started filing out, very smartly.

The chauffeurs trotted back to their cars, and there was a general scramble. Since the guests' cars were blocked in by the police cars, the drivers started leaning on their horns, urged on by their panicked employers. Meanwhile there was a big squeeze at the main entrance, with quite a bit of unseemly pushing and shoving.

I started the Chev and cruised slowly down the street, stopping just before I got to the tangle of cars and people. A crowd of onlookers had begun to gather, and the whole scene was degenerating into chaos.

The car door opened and the Blighter quickly got in. "Let's go, Bill. Not too fast, but without the least delay, if you don't mind."

I caught a glimpse of Munce's scar-faced crony and a couple of other men running towards us, so I reversed, turned the car around, and headed up Macquarie Street. The Blighter kept watching out of the back window until we were over the hill and out of sight.

"So, how did the negotiations go?" I said.

"Well old chap, they were going fine until your bit of improvisation. After that they took a rather spectacular turn for the worse."

The Blighter took a long envelope out of his pocket and handed it to me. I lifted the flap and peeked in. A wad of ten-pound notes, maybe an inch thick. I handed it back to him.

"A thousand pounds," he said.

"Who gave you that?"

"Eric Prisk."

"He's in on the joke?"

"The League fellows didn't want to be directly involved, so they approached Prisk to go middle man. He's considered to be good at sweet talking, bringing opposing sides together and all that. They briefed him to buy back the register, and generally make sure that everything goes off without further incident, and"—he looked at me meaningfully—"without scandal."

"So everything's on track then?"

"Your little piece of theatre shifted things somewhat. The League chaps have doubts as to your rationality. They now believe it would be a grave mistake to even try and deal with us."

"But they have to. We have the register. Or that's what they think."

The Blighter looked out the back window of the car for a moment, then turned around and said, "As I understand it, there's a line of thought among the League leaders that the easiest solution would simply be to kill us. They wouldn't get the register back, but it would effectively solve their problem just the same."

"Oh shit. How do you know all this?"

"Prisk told me. There was a certain amount of milling around over the port and cigars. Prisk kept running between me and them. Meanwhile one of the League chaps must have summoned Munce and the boys. Was the bomb scare your doing?"

"Yeah. I saw Munce outside, knew something had gone wrong."

"I'm grateful for that. What really upset the League fellows was your mentioning the League in front of Menzies."

"He's one of them?"

"Hardly. He loathes them. He's not your army type at all. He thinks he's sure to win power in time, and any interference by the League can only harm his chances. He knows about it of course, but he daren't do anything to draw attention to it. He would never even admit to its existence. Which suits the League, too. It will be interesting to see if the press report your little outburst today. Did any of the reporters follow you outside?"

"Not a one. Jesus . . . I'm sorry, Blighter. I stuffed everything right up."

"Perhaps not. Prisk is still arguing for a peaceful solution."

"What are we to do?"

"Well, it would certainly help if we could find the register. Until we do, it'd be best to keep out of the way of Munce and co."

"Your room at the Metropole. Do the they know about that?"

"They would, yes."

I glanced in the rearview mirror, thinking, they know the Chev too. I dropped a left into Devonshire Street and headed up the hill towards Paddo. I drove straight around the back of Taylor Square to Boundary Street, and parked in the dead-end alleyway.

"This is the temporary residence. As far as I know, no one knows about it. You can stay here for now."

"Your hideout. How absolutely thrilling!"

"Let me have that envelope."

He passed it across to me. I counted out half the money and gave the rest back to him.

"All right, now you better come in and meet my faithful retainers."

I made the introductions and left the Blighter sitting at the kitchen table, pouring brandies for Cec and May, while I went out the back to my room.

May followed me out. "Bill, the barber bloke from around the front popped in earlier with a message for you."

"Oh yeah?"

"He said you're to ring your uncle."

"Beaut. Thanks, May."

I waited till she'd gone, then reached into the fireplace, prized out the loose bricks and took down the tin money box. I put the five hundred quid along with the not inconsiderable piles of rent and coupon money in a large envelope and slipped it in my jacket pocket.

In the kitchen, Cec, May, and the Blighter were tucking into their brandies, talking like great old mates. I kept going, out into the back lane and down the street to the public phone.

Dick's landlady fetched him to the phone.

"G'day. It's me."

I didn't say my name, and Dick seemed to understand.

"Young feller! I'm glad you rang. I have an address for you."

"Good on you, Dick."

"It's in Kensington."

"*Kensington*? But I wanted Misery's shack in the sticks!"

"Settle down. You'll have to speak to a feller named Formica. Tell him I sent you."

That was a bit of a surprise. "You mean, *Les* Formica?"

"Yeah, that's him." Dick sounded disappointed.

"I know Les. What's he got to do with it?"

"He did some building work for Toohey once. A place out of town. Approach him the right way and he might tell you where."

11

I drove straight over to Les Formica's house, stopping on the way for a bottle of plonko. We had a drink and a yarn. He talked about the building trade, about how hard—and how illegal—it was during the war to trade in building supplies. And about how he and Misery had known each other for a long, long time.

I left Les's place an hour later with a spring in my step, and not just because I was lighter in the pocket by sixty quid. I went to the newsagent on Anzac Parade and bought a couple of maps of inland New South Wales.

Late that afternoon, I tapped on Lucy's door. Molly Price opened up and stood aside to let me in. I could hear Lucy in the kitchen, singing. I put my arms around her and kissed her neck. She squirmed, in a nice way, then turned around, smiling.

She looked up at my face and leaned back a little. "Something's happened?"

"Plenty. Things are shaping up. Let's sit down."

We sat at the kitchen table, facing one another. I held her two small hands in mine.

"The stuff I talked about is about to come good. I think it is. I *hope* it is. I've got to go away for a couple of days. After that, I—we . . . both of us, with a bit of luck, we'll be set. We can go away somewhere. A holiday. Take our time to think about where we'll settle, what we'll do. We'll have plenty of breathing space. We can go anywhere, do anything."

Lucy looked at me, her eyes bright and sharp and said, "Remember what I told you. No geeing up."

"Yeah, I know, just the results. But it's getting close. That's all I mean."

She nodded, "So where is it you're going? Should I be jealous that I'm not going along for the ride?"

"I don't think it's your sort of place. Just leave it with me."

She didn't say anything for a second. "All right. But what about tomorrow night?"

"Tomorrow night?"

"Oh, Bill, I *told* you. I'm singing at the Colony Club. You're escorting me, supposedly."

"Ah, yeah, of course. No problem. What time do you want to be picked up?"

"Make it early. Six o'clock. Herb wants a lift, too."

"All right."

I thought about leaving the Blighter back at the Paddo address, sniffing around while I wasn't there, and added, "There might be a mate of mine tagging along too."

It was dark when I got back to Paddo. As I came in the back gate, I could hear laughter from inside. They were all well away. I sat down with them, had a feed and a drink or two. At midnight May made up a bed for the Blighter in the empty bedroom. I waited in the kitchen until everyone had settled down, then went out into the yard, quietly dug a hole under the oleander bush, put my roll of money in a jar and buried it. I pressed the dirt down and kicked the dead leaves back over the spot.

Next morning I got up early and had a good look at my maps. The Blighter slept till after midday. When he got up May served him some breakfast. The Blighter politely asked her if she was going out to the shops, and if so would she mind terribly getting him a newspaper and a half bottle of brandy.

Later he set himself up at the kitchen table with the form guide, the radio tuned in to the race broadcast.

Mid afternoon, May and Cec took the bub out for a stroll. As soon as they'd gone, I turned the radio off and said to the Blighter.

"I think I may be on to it," I said.

He sat up straight, smiling. "The register?"

"'Fraid not. But the next best thing. Toohey's getaway."

"You've *been* there?"

I shook my head. "I know where it is. Roughly. About half a day's drive from here, to buggery up in the hills."

The Blighter was silent for a moment. "How did you find this out?"

"From a feller who trades in building materials. He took a big truckload of stuff up there, years ago, before the war. For Mick Toohey."

"Ah!"

"Remember when we tore Mick's Double Bay place apart, there was bugger all in the way of personal papers?"

"Of course."

"Well this bloke took enough building materials to fix up an old place pretty well, apparently. He also took along a brand new, top of the line Mosler wall safe."

The Blighter nodded. "But you only know *roughly* where the place is."

"Toohey had this bloke deliver the stuff to a feller in the town nearby, rather than all the way to the cabin. Mick apparently did all the building work himself. There's no guarantee, of course, but if that is Mick's hideaway, then there'd have to be a chance, at least, that the membership register of the Phantom Riders of the Empire is sitting in that bloody safe right now."

"But you don't know where the cabin is?"

"I know how to find the town—it's sort of hidden away, apparently—and I know the name of the feller there who took delivery of the goods. He's a local sharpie, and my informant was pretty certain that he'd have a fair idea where Mick's cabin is, even if he's never actually been there. We can offer him a few bob and if that doesn't work you can beat it out of him. "

"Really, Bill!"

"Hey, you're the expert, aren't you?"

"Who is this fellow? Where is this place?"

"I'll keep that to myself for the moment. No offence, Blighter."

The Blighter shrugged.

"The way I figure it," I said, "we can go there tonight. Later on. It might be better to drive by night anyway. And we've got something on earlier this evening."

"And what would that be?"

"My girlfriend—you haven't met her yet, but you'll love her, she's terrific—she's a singer and she has an engagement at the Colony Club. It's a bit of a nuisance, I know, but it means a lot to her. There's a few of us going together in my car. You're invited too. We can leave right after it's finished."

The Blighter leaned back, smiling. "I'm entirely in your hands, William."

"I don't know how good a night it'll be, but I can guarantee that it'll be at least as much fun as a speech by Bob Menzies."

We pulled up outside Lucy's flat at seven thirty. I'd already collected the mob: Herb Atkins, zooted up and nursing his saxophone; Max, sniffing inhalers and smoking loco weed, and dressed in cowboy gear ready for his guest spot as "Tex Perkal, the Singing and Swinging Boundary Rider"; and the Blighter, passing around a bottle of brandy.

Lucy came out wearing a sparkly blue-black dress, bare at the shoulders and revealing deep cleavage at the front.

She did a twirl for me. "You like?"

I shook my head slowly. "You're going to fair dinkum kill them. Let's go."

Molly came too. There were cheery greetings all around, and much swapping of loco weed and brandy. We took off in a jolly old mood, except for a certain tension between Lucy and the Blighter, who'd seemed to take an instant dislike to each other.

After ten minutes driving and some more weed, Max said, "Hey Herb, are you tooled up tonight?"

"Yeah, as a matter of fact, I am."

"What is it, a Colt?" As if he really knew anything about guns.

Herb gave him a funny look. "A Colt 45. US Army issue."

"Loan it to me for a while, will you."

"Why?"

"For the act."

"What's a singing and swinging boundary rider need a roscoe for?"

"Varmints."

Herb shrugged his shoulders, reached into his sax case and brought it out. "Be my guest. Just don't shoot anyone."

"Mighty neighborly of you, pardner."

We drove south out of town along the Princes Highway. After thirty minutes we swung around a big corner and the Colony Club's neon sign came into view—"DANCE, DIVE, DINE." The nightclub sat among four others clustered on the peninsula on the George's River, known as Tom Ugly's Point.

On the outside, the place was done up like a huge undersea grotto. The same underwater motif continued inside. There were plaster fish stuck around the place, and a wall mural depicting divers, buried treasure, shells and squid, King Neptune, and a bunch of sexy-looking mermaids.

There was a swimming pool off to the side of the bandstand, where they held aqua follies in warmer weather, but tonight they'd put a wooden floor over it to make extra room for dancing. The bandstand was a huge open clamshell.

Herb and Max disappeared back stage to get ready for the performance, while the rest of us took a table beside the bandstand. Lucy sat nervously, smoking.

At eight o'clock Wal Harford and his Palais Entertainers kicked off the show, with Herb as a featured player. But it was pretty sedate stuff. Lucy didn't want to dance—she was too tense—so Molly and I cut the rug. Even though the band was square, with a couple of reefers in us it was kind of fun.

We danced for twenty minutes, then sat down laughing. The Blighter and Lucy had been at the table alone for that time, and when we returned Lucy was looking away from the table and frowning. The Blighter had his head down, looking at the drink in front of him.

Lucy went off to the ladies, and Molly went with her.

"How are you getting on with Lucy?" I said.

"I don't think she cares for me awfully much."

"Oh, she can be like that at first. You should have seen her and me when we first met!"

The Blighter smiled weakly and nodded.

By nine-thirty the place was full and the dance floor was crowded. A smiling MC came out and rambled on for a few minutes while behind him a couple of attendants dragged out bales of hay. Then he announced the first of the night's special attractions, Australia's new hillbilly singing sensation, "Tex" Perkal.

Max walked on stage in his cowboy gear, sat down on a hay bale, and picked a bass run on his guitar. The band fell in behind him, playing a little hillbilly swing. Max started singing in his croaky voice, a song all about riding through the hills of old Wyoming. The next one was about him riding the rattlers in Queensland, which in Max's case was just as farfetched as him being a cowboy from Wyoming.

He sang a humorous thing called "Don't Do Your Dough at the Races," then one about a bloke who's traveling down life's crooked road. This bloke sees the danger signs ahead but ignores them. He takes the wrong turn, goes down the bad road, and ends up in ruination. The band sang along on the chorus, in a kind of churchy harmony, about the warning signs this bloke had chosen to ignore: "Detour, there's a muddy road ahead!"

Even though it was a hillbilly tune, Max gave it enough oomph that people danced to it anyway. I sat it out, though. Something about the chorus was getting to me. Maybe it was just reminding me of Sergeant Jennings' dire predictions about what would become of me, or maybe it was the reefer in my system, but to hear the song tell it, one little blunder early on and you were history.

Max finished to great applause. Lucy stood up, smiled nervously and said, "I'm on soon. I'd better go backstage. Wish me luck."

I stood up and kissed her. "You'll be great, I know you will."

For the next thirty minutes Herb led a smaller combo made up of the younger blokes from the big band, most of them zoot suiters. They played strictly jump tunes, hard and loud. Molly and I had another dance. Jivers and jitterbugs dominated the dance floor, and for a while there it was like one of the big wartime nights at the Booker T.

Then the MC came back out and announced the special event of the evening, a guest spot by a wonderful new singing discovery, Lucy Chance.

They narrowed the spot to pick up Lucy walking in from the wings. An appreciative murmur went around the room. In that little pool of strong light, with the dark all around her, with her dark hair, dark dress, and glowing skin, she looked sensational.

She walked slowly across the stage, and before she even reached the microphone, she had the crowd onside.

She looked around at Herb, and they started into the distinctive opening of "Someone to Watch Over Me." Lucy got up close to the microphone and closed her eyes. The song was pitched low, and Lucy sang it with almost no vibrato, which made it seem like she wasn't singing so much as talking softly.

She kept her eyes closed as she sang, like she didn't even care there was a crowd looking at her, like the song was just a private wish of her own. Private, between her and me. Then I looked around the room. She had them all, even the waiters—every man and woman there looked just as certain that Lucy was singing directly to each of them.

Then Herb played a breathy, slow, big-toned tenor solo, just a few simple notes. Lucy sang one more chorus, still in that straight, soft, unaffected voice. There wasn't a man in the place, or a woman for that matter, who right then didn't want to be that someone to watch over her. Molly was looking at me.

Lucy finished the song, bowed her head slightly, and left the stage. They wanted her back, badly. But—shrewdly—she didn't do an encore, and the MC was forced to placate the crowd by promising to bring her back in the very near future.

Fifteen minutes later, Lucy, Herb and Max were all back at our table. Lucy was flushed and happy. Somebody from another table sent Lucy a bottle of champagne. We had a few more drinks.

At one point the Blighter was telling a story about his days in London during the war, and everyone was laughing. I turned to look at Lucy and saw she was looking daggers at him. The Blighter finished his story, and in the brief lull that followed Lucy turned to me and said, "He's laughing at us. All of us. At you too. You know that, don't you?"

"Eh?"

She nodded in the Blighter's direction. "What I said."

Lucy remained silent for a couple of minutes then stood up quickly. "I've got to pay my respects." Then she looked me dead in the eye, said, "Don't you do anything silly, will you?" and walked away.

I looked around the table. Molly was looking serious, but the Blighter seemed unconcerned. Max and Herb apparently hadn't even noticed. Max stood up and wandered off.

I turned to see where Lucy had gone. She was walking across the room, approaching a group of elevated tables. I saw her shake hands with some people, then she sat down next to Eric Prisk. She seemed to glance briefly back my way, but she didn't miss a beat, smiling and talking and being charming.

"*That* grub's here," I said.

Prisk beamed as he introduced Lucy to his friends around his table. I stood up and took a couple of steps towards them.

Molly stood up too, put her hand on my arm. "They're all radio people," she said. "Lucy wants to butter them up."

I stopped, exhaled slowly.

Molly withdrew her hand, and I sat back down.

"Bloody hell," I said, and slumped back in my chair.

Molly sat down, leaned over to me, away from the others. "I know you're nuts about her, Bill," she said quietly, "and it's not good to interfere, but can I ask you one question?"

"What?"

"Is it worth it?"

"Eh?"

"Is being in love with Lucy Chance making you happy?"

I had to think about it. "That's not easy to answer. But I can tell you this: what *does* make me happy is the thought that soon Lucy and I will soon have things sorted out, and then we can be together."

"By which you mean you'll have money?"

"With a bit of luck. I've got something on. If it comes through,

Lucy will be able to give up the old life."

Molly took a sip of her drink and said quietly, "She could do that now if she wanted to."

"What do you mean?"

Molly looked at the floor.

"What do you mean, Molly?"

"Ask her how much she has saved already. And while you're about it, ask her who owns the flat that we share."

"It's hers?"

Molly just looked at me. I didn't know what to say.

"She never told you about that, did she?" Molly said.

"Look, Molly, I thought you were her friend. If Lucy *does* have some money put away, then good luck to her. She worries about those things. She's had a hard life."

"So have we all. I've gone this far, so I'll keep going. I shouldn't say this, but the fact is, what Lucy cares about is money first, and singing songs in public second. You run a distant third."

"She loves me."

"Does she?"

"I know she does."

"Then I dare you to go to her with no money and no prospects. See how you fare."

There was a tap on my arm.

"William, old boy. Hate to interrupt you, but—"

I looked at the Blighter and he pointed over his shoulder.

"What?"

"By the door."

I looked again. The scar-faced goon, sitting at a table, very deliberately *not* looking our way. "Oh cripes," I said. "And see over there, there's that slimy mongrel Eric Prisk."

"Yes, but he's been here all night, whereas our friend over there just arrived. Which means that Munce and the other fellow won't be far away." The Blighter smiled apologetically at Molly.

"Awfully rude of us to talk shop like this, my dear, I know. You will forgive us, won't you?"

"Don't mind me."

The Blighter said, "I think we should leave immediately."

"Yeah, you're right." I stood up, took a few quid out of my wallet and said to Molly, "You and Lucy will have to make your own way back to town. Do you mind? Tell Lucy I'll ring her in a day or two."

"That's all right. Do you want me to call the police?"

The Blighter said, "No police. That won't help us at all."

I looked at my watch. "If we can get away from here in one piece," I said to the Blighter, "then I'm all for driving to you-know-where. I mean right now. Straight from here."

"Petrol?"

"The tank's nearly full, plus there's a jerry can in the boot, half full. I have plenty of coupons and we're both cashed up. I say let's go for it."

"I'm going to need something to drink."

"Can't you lay off it for a day?"

His face looked pained. "It'd be a frightful bore."

"All right, why don't you go out to the kitchen and see what they'll do for you. Go out the kitchen door. I'll meet you at the car. I'll go backstage, make my way out to the parking lot that way."

I left the table like I was headed for the brasco, then nipped backstage. No one challenged me. I found my way to the back door.

It was quiet outside. Across the river a dog was barking, and a truck was working its way up through its gears somewhere in the distance.

I walked around the building. The air smelled of the estuary, of salt water and shellfish and seaweed. And on top of that was the smell of reefer. The Chev was parked at the farthest end of the car park. There was no sign of the Blighter. Then a side door opened, and Lucy ran out.

"Where are you going?" she said.

"I left cab money for you and Molly. I've got something to do. It'll take me all night. Maybe tomorrow too. I can't explain, Lucy, but it's important."

She looked at me for a few seconds, then nodded. "All right, Bill. But promise me this. When you get where you're going, ring me. Will you do that?"

"Yeah, sure."

"Ring me before . . . as soon as you get there. All right?" Then she kissed me and ran back inside.

Half a minute went by, then the Blighter came out of the kitchen door.

"You're right, then?" I said.

He held up a large paper bag. "As rain."

"We can share the driving. With luck we can get to Toohey's hideaway tonight. Or near it, anyway."

The Blighter nodded. "Lead on, old boy."

Ten yards in front of us three men stepped out of the shadows, blocking our path to the car. We stopped. Aubrey Munce and his two offsiders. Just standing there.

Behind us a voice said, "I was rather hoping we could have a little chat before you left, Blighter."

We turned around. Eric Prisk, and a couple of blokes I'd never seen before.

The Blighter said, "Hello, Eric."

"Hello." Then he looked at me, stopped smiling. "Hello, Glasheen."

"Fuck you, you arsehole."

"Now, now." He faced the Blighter. "I was very much hoping that you gents would have something for me. You know, considering that you've already received a substantial down payment, made in good faith."

"Yes, I quite understand, Eric." The Blighter sounding like they were talking about a round of golf. "I'm awfully sorry, but I'm going to have to ask you to wait just a tiny bit longer."

"Ah, there's the problem, you see. Aubrey and his friends suspect that you're all bullshit, and try as I might, I'm having trouble convincing them otherwise."

The Blighter said nothing.

"It sounds awfully extreme, I know, but they're all for dealing with you and your uncouth chum right now." Smiling, sounding friendly as all get-out.

"Yes but you'd never get the register, that way."

"But they would argue that they don't really *need* the register, as such. They just need to make sure no one else has it. You see? In any case, I've done all I can, and I'm afraid I'm going to have to let you chaps sort it out among yourselves." Prisk smiled, then turned around and walked back inside, his two offsiders behind him.

Behind me a voice said, "We'd better take them away from here, away from the light."

I turned around. Munce was holding a gun. He motioned for us to walk, pointed towards the river.

"I've got a copy of the register in safe keeping," I said. "If anything happens to me, the register gets sent to the Commonwealth cops."

Munce chuckled. "You're an inept liar, Glasheen. In fact, you've just convinced me that you and the Blighter are indeed bullshit."

Someone pushed me in the back. "Come on, you bastard."

We walked a few yards across the grassy verge towards the water, surrounded by the trio of thugs.

"Hold it right there, hombres!"

Everybody turned around. Max Perkal stood there in his cowboy togs, Herb's gun in his left hand, his stockwhip in the other, a reefer in his mouth.

"What's going on here, pardners? You all right, Billy?"

Munce said, "Who's this clown?"

Max unwound the stockwhip, gave it a crack, and then flicked it at the nearest goon. It took the bloke's hat off, left him looking like a mug at a sideshow. The goon patted his bare head and looked around for his hat.

"What's the trouble?" said Max.

Munce said, "Listen here, you. I've got a gun. Understand? Now clear off." He pointed the gun at Max.

Max twirled Herb's pistol, gunslinger-style, then pointed it at Munce. "Have a go, any time you like, old mate."

"This is absurd," said the Blighter. "Come on, Aub. You can't start shooting *now*. None of us wants the police involved. Who would you rather deal with? Ray Waters or us?"

Max and Aubrey were staring at each other, each pointing his gun at the other. Munce's eyes were narrowed, but he looked calm and self possessed. A nasty piece of work, I thought. Max, on the other hand, was all over the shop, swaying and grinning like a simpleton, his gun hand unsteady, his eyes unfocused.

Then Max cracked his whip again, took off the other bloke's hat. "Anyone got a ciggy?" he said. "I can whip a lighted smoke out of your mouth. One of my best tricks."

Just then a party of laughing patrons came out of the club.

Munce lowered his gun and turned to me. "Tell him to put the gun away."

"Hey Max, it's copacetic," I said. "We're actually doing business with these fellers." I turned to Munce. "Aren't we?"

"You took the deposit but you haven't delivered the blasted register," he muttered.

"Wait a day, you'll get it," I said.

He was silent.

I nudged the Blighter and we walked over to Max, and turned him around. The three of us then started for the car, leaving the heavies standing in the shadows.

I said under my breath, "Quickly, before these mugs change their minds."

Max turned around and waved the Colt in the air. He called out, "Hey, Charlie," and laughed. "It's not even loaded!"

There was a burst of light from the barrel of the Colt and a deafening bang. A neon mermaid above the club exploded, and glass rained down on the roof. Max looked at me, his eyes wide. Then it was very still, except for the sound of dogs barking all over the district. A woman's nervous voice from the car park said, "What was *that*?"

I grabbed Max's arm and gave the Blighter a push. "Quick. The car."

More voices from the doorway. "Sounded like a gun." "Good God, they've shot the sign!" People were coming out of the club, talking excitedly.

The heavies melted away. We got in the car and drove off fast.

Max said, "Fucking bloody thing was *loaded*. Fucking irresponsible." He pointed it at me for emphasis.

"Don't aim it at me, for Christ's sake! Are there any more bullets in that thing?"

"I don't know." Max aimed it out the window and began to squeeze the trigger, squinting in readiness for the blast.

"For God's sake, no more shooting," said the Blighter. He reached over from the back seat, took the gun from Max and examined it.

"I could have hurt myself," Max said.

12

At midnight we were on the road, somewhere in the sticks between Parramatta and Penrith, headed west. We'd had coffee and sandwiches at Max's place when we dropped him off, and I was wide awake. The night was chilly and mist was gathering in the hollows and gullies, but the Chev was warm and running well, rolling along at fifty. There were very few cars out.

The Blighter sat quietly in the passenger seat, smoking Senior Service, sipping occasionally from his bottle. Every now and then he'd look out the back window.

"Relax, Blighter," I said. "We've left those arses a long way behind."

He didn't answer. A little later I looked across and he was asleep. I didn't mind. I had plenty to think about.

We drove through Penrith without seeing a soul, then over the river and up into the Blue Mountains. When I stopped to take a leak, the air was light and cold. Frost crunched under my shoes; otherwise it was dead quiet.

I drove on, hit fog again. I slowed right down, even though we hadn't seen another car for twenty minutes.

The Blighter woke up, peered into the fog.

"My God, where are we?"

"The Blue Mountains."

He lit a smoke. "Do you mind awfully telling me where we're going?"

"A little town called Henry Crossing."

"Never heard of it."

"It's an old mining town, supposedly over the other side of the mountains. But I'm buggered if it's on any map I've seen."

"Doesn't that give you pause?"

"I was told it was hard to find."

The Blighter turned and looked at me.

"I wrote down the general directions," I said.

"God, it's all a bit thin. And if and when we find Henry Crossing?"

"We track down this feller. You break his arms or whatever. I suppose I can tell you his name now. It's Bagshaw. Maurie Bagshaw. He lives right in the town."

After another fifteen minutes driving, my eyes went watery and my thoughts started swimming.

"You better take the wheel for a bit, Blighter."

"Certainly."

"You're not too pissed are you?"

He sniffed. "Scarcely pissed enough."

I pulled up and got out. "Jesus, it's freezing now." I got in the back seat and lay down.

The Blighter started off and immediately kangarooed it.

"I thought you told me you used to drive racing cars," I said.

"I'm rusty, that's all. Where do I go?"

I reached into my pocket for the directions I'd written down.

"Keep heading west. Go through Lithgow. About ten miles the other side there's a turn off to the right. No sign or anything, but there's an old broken-down farmhouse on the corner. Take that road, it's a dirt road, goes for about twenty miles. You come to a low bridge, and straight after that there's a crossroads. Take a right at the crossroads. Two miles past that there's a gate. You'll have to get out and open it. Go through, follow the road over the ridge. That'll take us out to another road running northwest. Should be sealed. If I'm still asleep then wake me up."

"Is that the destination?"

"No. There's more after that. Have you got it?"

"Of course I have."

I stretched out on the back seat and fell asleep. I could sense the car moving along the winding road, up and down hills, accelerating and braking, and the continually changing movement kept me from falling into deep sleep. But I had a sense of time passing. I half-thought, half-dreamed about Lucy and Eric Prisk, and what Molly had said, about Aubrey with the gun, the money buried in the backyard at Paddo, the long road still ahead.

Then I thought about Mum in Nowra, how I hadn't rung her for a few weeks. I pictured her face. She screamed, and Munce's gun went off. The ground underneath me just disappeared, I fell, and then they were throwing handfuls of gravel and kicking me. I tried to move my arm but couldn't.

I was on the floor of the car, wedged against the seat. Bits of stuff all over me. Windscreen glass. All was quiet and still except for a hissing sound.

"Weeping Jesus, what's happened?"

"We hit a blasted cow," the Blighter said.

I climbed off the floor. The windscreen was smashed. Steam was rising from under the bonnet. The Blighter was uncorking his bottle.

I got out and walked around the front of the car. There was a big ding in the grille, the bonnet was dented, and one headlight was out.

It was cold and dark.

"Where are we?"

"I'm not sure. There was a town about three miles back."

"There shouldn't have been. Did you follow the directions I gave you?"

"More or less."

"What was the name of the place?"

"Didn't really notice, I'm afraid. Something Creek."

"Christ, it's cold. What's the time?"

"Four o'clock."

I opened the side panel on the motor. The radiator was cactus.

"How big was this town? Was there a garage there?"

"There was a pub—and yes, I believe there *was* a garage."

"I suppose we'll have to wait till dawn, then go and see what we can arrange. Christ, I don't like our chances of getting a Chev radiator out here. Well, Blighter, this is another fine mess you've gotten me into."

"Really, old chum. You scarcely seem to need my help on that score."

"But how the fuck did we end up *here*, wherever this might be?"

"In your directions, you mentioned a bridge . . ."

"You missed it?"

He shook his head. "It was barricaded. Unsafe. So I doubled back, and worked my way round. I don't know precisely where we are, but I'd be very surprised if we were terribly far off our course."

"And this bloody cow. Why didn't you keep your eyes open? Shit, I should never have let you drive. All this bullshit about racing cars."

"Actually, Bill, had you been awake to see what happened, you might well be congratulating me now. Without some rather nifty ducking and weaving on my part—if I may say so—it almost certainly would have been considerably worse for us."

"Yeah, sure."

We sat in the car for a while, but it got so bitterly cold, after half an hour the Blighter got out walked around, gathered up some wood and assembled a temperamental, smoky fire, right next to the road. No car passed us the whole time.

We sat as near to the fire as we could, shivering. I didn't say anything. I was too miserable by then. Cold, and hungry, my eyes streaming from the wood smoke, I wished I was back at Darling Point, in Lucy's bed. The Blighter seemed comfortable enough, though, sipping his brandy and smoking his Senior Service.

"This cold is a bastard of a thing," I said.

He held out the brandy bottle to me.

I shook my head.

"It'll warm your blood."

I took the bottle from him, drank a big mouthful. I felt every drop as it worked its way down, burning at first and then spreading through my arms and legs, untangling my cramped muscles. The shivering stopped. I took another big swallow, and another after that, then handed the bottle back.

"I'm hungry as a bastard."

The Blighter held out his smokes. "They do go rather well together," he said. "And probably no worse for your health than Max's reefers."

So I took one, lit it. I coughed a bit, but persisted with it. My empty stomach stopped nagging. I laid down and went into a light sleep.

Some time after six the sky went from black to dingy gray, which seemed to be all the daylight we were going to get. We were in a long, low valley. The hills to either side were timbered with dark, scraggly gum trees, with huge rocky outcrops on the slopes. Nearer the road were cleared paddocks with thin, poor looking pasture. A narrow creek ran through the valley, overgrown with spiky willows. Thirty yards back behind the car, the dead cow lay by the side of the gravel road.

I stood up. "I'm going into town," I said.

"I'll come with you."

We trudged along the rough road, which wound down a long, winding slope through the gloomy valley. We walked a long way more than three miles, but didn't come to any town.

"So where is this bloody place?"

"It seemed like we went through it only a matter of minutes before we hit that wretched cow. But perhaps I was mistaken."

We walked on. A bitter wind came up. My nose was runny, my face and ears freezing cold.

We came around a long bend, and the bush seemed to get darker as the hills crowded in on the road. We passed a small un-painted timber cottage, with a scabby looking vegetable garden out the back. Then another cottage a little further along. Clothes hung on the line, and smoke was coming from the chimney. A dog barked at us. A woman came out of the cottage carrying a kettle. She spat on the ground and then started banging on the kettle with a wooden spoon.

"My God," said the Blighter. "The poor woman's completely demented."

We passed a whole row of similar cottages then came to a long wall with a large gateway set into it. A grimy painted sign over the gate read: "Cullens Creek No. 2." Beyond it were some old brick and iron sheds, a pit tower, and a small mountain of coal, with a railway siding right at the back. The road was black with coal dust, and for hundreds of yards around even the scrub itself seemed blackened.

As we stood outside the gate a group of about thirty men came straggling out. Lean and leathery, their faces smudged, wearing overalls and carrying gladstones. And completely silent. They looked at us darkly.

"Christ, it's *How Green Was my Valley*," I said quietly to the Blighter. "Or *Amos 'n' Andy*. They look none too cheery. What's up their arses, I wonder."

The Blighter nodded as they approached us and smiled. "Good morning, chaps," he called out.

One of the group muttered, "Bastards have got a hide."

They walked past us and on down the road. We let them get a hundred yards in front, then followed them around the bend and into the town.

Cullens Creek consisted of fifty or so dilapidated cottages, a few shops, a cafe, and a pub, an old Methodist church, and a one-room school, complete with a dozen scruffy brats who threw stones at the Blighter and me.

"Is this the arsehole of the earth, or what?" I said.

"If this isn't it, I'll wager it's just over the next hill."

We went straight to the cafe. They'd just opened up, by the look of it, but it was warm inside and smelled of frying bacon. I sat down, but the Blighter said, "I might have a look around."

"Suit yourself," I said. "I need some breakfast."

The Blighter shot through. A teenage girl in a shapeless cardigan shuffled out. Her expression, her every movement, seemed to say it was a pretty cruel life that had you working in a chew and spew in Cullens Creek. I was inclined to agree with her.

"Good morning," I said. "A bit cold out there today."

"It was colder last week. Do you want something?"

She said this without actually looking at me and seemingly without opening her mouth. I asked for bacon and eggs and a pot of tea.

She brought me the feed, which wasn't too bad. No one else came in.

By the time I'd finished my breakfast the Blighter still wasn't back. I paid up and went looking for a mechanic. At the other end of town I found a big shed with a rusted Vacuum Oil sign out front.

222

It was dark inside. There were bits of machinery everywhere, from every era of agriculture. A stump jump plough, a dismantled threshing machine, a wooden cart, various truck and tractor bodies, car seats, diffs, gearboxes, steering wheels, and various other rusted bits and pieces. At the back of the shed an old feller with thick white hair was bent over a tractor engine, peering at a spark plug.

"Good morning," I said.

He didn't straighten up, didn't turn around, didn't nod, didn't even blink, as far as I could tell.

I stood there like a gig for a minute or two. Then the old feller straightened up, carelessly chucked the spark plug into the darkest recesses of the shed, turned to me and said, "It's had the dick. What can I do for you?"

I told him about my car getting smashed up outside of town. He listened, but didn't acknowledge a thing I said. He had a burned-down rolly in his mouth; it seemed dead, but every so often he'd draw on it and produce bit of smoke.

I finished my sad story. He still said nothing.

"So do you think you'd be able to go and get it and fix it up for me?"

"Ooh." He shook his head slowly. "I'm a bit busy this morning." He nodded at the tractor.

"Well, I'm on my way through, and I'm in a bit of a hurry. It's kind of a . . . family emergency. I wonder if you could see your way clear to look at my car first?"

"Might not be able to fix it anyway. Chev, radiator gone, you say?" He shook his head like it was the biggest ask imaginable.

"But just say."

"Ooh, I don't know." He shook his head doubtfully. "Foskett was expecting his tractor back today."

"Look, I'm willing to pay a few bob more if I have to. I want to get on the road again."

In the end he rang up Foskett and made an arrangement. I paid him, up front, about four times what you'd pay in town, plus an extra charge for the towing, and a few quid extra—supposedly for Foskett to hire a tractor elsewhere.

I walked back to the post office and put through a trunk call to Sydney. Lucy's voice came on, thin and crackly over the line.

"Bill? Where are you?" I pictured her in her dressing gown in her nice, warm flat.

"I'm . . . in the bush. Hey, Lucy, you were terrific last night. Sorry I had to run. Did you get home all right?"

"Thank God you rang. Now listen to me, Bill. What I have to say is very, very important. Important for us."

"Oh yeah? Well good, because—"

"Now Bill, don't interrupt me. Just listen."

"Sure."

"Firstly, I know all about the register."

"Oh?"

"Don't ask me *how* I know, but I do. All right? Now tell me: have you got it?"

I didn't say anything.

"You still there, Bill?"

"I'm here."

"Well? Did you hear me? Have you got it?"

"Not yet."

"But you're on your way to get it, aren't you?"

"Yes. I expect to have it . . . soon. I mean, if it's there at all, that is."

"Good. Now this is what I want you to do, Bill. Get the register and bring it straight back here. Dump the Blighter. He's not working in our interests. Get rid of him and bring the register here."

"That bastard Prisk has gotten to you, hasn't he?"

"Listen to me, Bill. Don't try to be too smart, just do what I say. For *our* sakes. For us. Get the register. Ditch the Blighter. Come back here."

I stood there in the phone booth, thinking how small, how sweet, and how hard and faraway her voice sounded.

"Bill! Did you get that?"

"Yeah, but Lucy—"

"Don't tell the Blighter you've talked to me. He's not on your side. *Our* side."

"Lucy, you—"

"Bill? Not now. I have to go." She hung up.

I stood there holding the phone in my hand for a full minute, running through all the possible explanations of how the hell Lucy had become involved. And how long she'd been in on it.

I stepped out of the phone booth into the bitter wind and walked along the empty main street to the pub, the Rawlings' Family Hotel. From inside I heard a loud wave of hearty male laughter, then cheering. I went in and found the Blighter in the center of a raucous group of miners, smiling and laughing.

"Bill, there you are. Come over and join us. This is Billy, fellows, a great mate of mine and a damned good chap."

A voice said, "Come on over, mate," and a couple of others chimed in, "G'day, Billy."

I walked over, cautiously.

"Bill, the brothers here—you won't believe this—they thought we were *management* men. Snoops or scabs."

"What are you drinking, Billy?" someone said.

"Er, nothing. Thanks."

"That doesn't sound like a mate of Comrade Blighter's."

Much laughter.

The Blighter said, "Come on, Bill, have a drink with us."

"All right, a beer then."

I had the beer and then another couple. More men joined us, and by lunchtime there were about fifty men in the public bar— probably most of the adult male population of Cullens Creek.

Such conviviality wasn't the usual go at Cullens Creek, I found out. The miners had just downed tools that morning. They were on a two-day strike—"out the gate for forty-eight," as one of them called it. It was one of a series of wildcat strikes to back up their campaign for a thirty-five hour week and two weeks paid annual leave.

No bloody wonder there were power blackouts every other day in Sydney, I thought, with these work-shy bastards scurrying off to the pub at every opportunity. But I kept that opinion to myself.

At one o'clock I strolled back to the garage. It was shut. I hoped the Chev was at least inside by then—either fixed, or at least on its way to being fixed—but somehow I doubted it.

I went back to the hotel, found the publican and took a room upstairs. It was pokey and bare, but the old electric radiator warmed it up quickly. I crawled under the covers of the lumpy bed and fell into a dreamless sleep.

When I woke it was still light outside, but only just. I brushed my teeth, threw some water on my face, went back to the garage.

The Chev was there. The radiator was on the ground; it had a four-inch hole in its center. The mechanic came out from the back, wiping his hands on a rag.

"Any luck with the radiator?"

He took his time. "There's a bit of a problem. A couple of problems, really."

"Yeah?"

"Remember I said I was supposed to fix Foskett's tractor?" He nodded towards it.

"Yeah, I remember."

"Well, Foskett was still dark on me for putting *his* job back. And when I got out there to fetch your car, it turned out you'd killed his prize cow."

"Jesus Christ, the thing was wandering around on the road in the middle of the night."

"Maybe it was, but Foskett reckons he ought to be recompensed for it."

"I've already shelled out quids and quids. Foskett can go and get fucked."

The mechanic nodded slowly. "Look, mate. I'll tell you this for nothin'. You've come and you'll go. But I've got to do business with Foskett and all the rest of the cockies here, so I've got to stay onside with them, or else *I'll* have to go."

"Yeah, so?"

"So if you want me to fix your Chev you'd better square things with Foskett."

I waited for a moment, then said, "Christ. All right."

"I mean, *before* I do anything to the Chev."

"How much?"

"Forty quid."

"It must have been a hell of a good cow!"

"Yeah, it was, apparently. You can pay me. I'll pass it on to Foskett."

I handed over the money. "So when will you have the car ready?"

"As soon as I can find a radiator and a windscreen."

I had to pause for a moment before I spoke, because I was ready to deck the bloke. "And when do you think that might be?" I said quietly.

"I've rung up Grogan's over in Mount Hard. He's got a Chev out the back. The windscreen's all right and so is the radiator, except it needs a good backflush. I can send the young bloke to get them first thing in the morning.

"Can't he go now?"

He shook his head, like I'd just asked him to raise the dead.

"Crikey, *now*? It's a bit late."

I got my wallet out again. He looked at it, and then at me, smiling slightly.

"You really want to get going, don't you?"

"Yeah, much as I love Cullens Creek and all the good souls in it, I must push on. As soon as fucking possible."

The mechanic took a few more quid from me, said he'd see what he could do. I left him to it.

13

It was dusk by now. The street was dark, the shops were closed, and all was quiet except for the wind whistling in the telegraph wires. I went back to the Rawlings' Family Hotel, where the miners were still having a great old time, egged on by the Blighter.

I ordered a beer, then another. Six o'clock came, but rather than call time, the publican just shot the bolt on the front door, and things kicked on. I had another beer, found myself sitting at a table with a couple of miners named Sandy and Neville, wiry old blokes, with deep, dark lines in their skin.

They were brothers and didn't say a lot, like talking was too much of an effort to be bothered with. When they did talk it was brief, like a private language.

That suited me. I had plenty to think about.

But then at some stage, maybe I was on my third or fourth beer, Neville said, "You a member too, like the Blighter?"

"Eh?"

"A party member."

"Sorry?"

"The *Communist* Party," said Sandy.

"Not bloody likely," I shot back. "I wouldn't join that mob of spoilers."

Suddenly they were looking at me very closely.

"I mean—No, I'm not a party member myself personally, right at this moment."

"Not too sympathetic to the workers' cause, then?" Neville said.

"Don't get me wrong, I'm not on the other mob's side. It's just that . . . I'd better shut up."

"Go on, you're among friends."

"No, forget it."

"We're both party members, and our father was too. But we're not thugs. You can say what you think."

"Well, if you really want to know, I've had a gutful of it— bloody power workers are out one day, the wharfies the next, the bread carters this week and brewery workers next week and, with respect, you blokes every other day."

Neville nodded, looked at his brother.

"I've said too much, have I?" I said.

"No you haven't, son," Sandy said. "How old do you reckon I am?"

"Eh?"

"Guess my age. Have a go."

"Oh, I don't know. Fifty?"

He nodded. "How about Neville?"

I looked at him. "A bit older. I don't know, maybe fifty-five."

They laughed, like they were pleased.

"I'm thirty-five," Sandy said. "Neville's actually a couple of years younger than me, but he started work earlier."

I looked from one to the other. They weren't joking.

"Dad was a miner. We were born to it. But it's not easy work. It uses you up. It takes your body from you."

There was no stopping Sandy now.

"Most people won't even set foot inside a coal mine. The air's bad. It's wet, it's filthy, and you never know when things are going to go wrong. And if they do go wrong, you're in a tomb.

230

Nothing lives down there except rats, bats, and coal miners.

"I started when I was fourteen. Been down there over twenty years. Now my lungs are bad. I haven't got that much left in me. Everyone talks about the soldiers in the war making the ultimate sacrifice, and that's fair enough, but there are twice as many miners' widows in Cullens Creek as there are war widows, and plenty of blokes from around here went away to fight, too."

Neville said, "I don't know what happens over there in Russia. Maybe it's a workers' paradise or maybe it's as big a shithole as Cullens Creek. But we never got anything by waiting for the bosses to do the right thing, by being what the bosses would call 'reasonable.'"

I drank the last of my drink and stood up, feeling woozy. "I wish you well, but I've got to go and get a feed."

"Be buggered. Come and have tea with us."

"That's all right. I'll get something here at the pub."

"Yeah, food poisoning. Come on."

The Blighter and a few of the others came back to Sandy's place, too. The cottage—it was one of the ones we'd passed just out of town—was small and dark, but warm. Sandy's wife cooked lamb chops and potatoes. If she resented her husband dragging home a bunch of drunks from the pub, she didn't let on. The Blighter did his bit to keep things sweet by presenting her with a bottle of sherry and a string of compliments.

I offered to contribute a few bob to the cost of the meal, which was pretty good, but Sandy wouldn't hear of it.

"It's been a while since we've paid for any lamb or mutton around here," he said.

"You keep some sheep, do you?"

"No, but Foskett does."

A big laugh.

We sat in front of the coal stove, drinking beer. At eight-thirty I walked back to the post office to ring Lucy again. It was bitterly cold. The operator connected me, but it was Molly on the line, not Lucy.

"Billy, where are you? No, don't tell me! There are some funny things going on here."

"What?"

"A policeman was here, looking for you. Ray Waters."

"Yeah?"

"Harry Strettles was here too."

"What did he want?"

"Same as Waters. Then Max rang a while ago."

"What did he want?"

"He's had visits from Strettles and Waters. Herb has, too."

"They went to see Herb?"

"Apparently. Same question every time: where's Glasheen gone?"

"What did they tell them?"

"Max reckons nothing. Strettles got a bit rough with Max."

"Oh Christ. Where's Lucy?"

She paused. "She's not here." Another pause. "There's more."

"Yeah?"

"This morning there were two blokes in a car parked outside. It was like they were watching this place."

"Are they still there?"

"I don't know. And the phone's been acting strange since this afternoon. Funny clicks, like it's a party line, which it isn't. "

"Where is she, Molly?"

"I'm not sure. Did you have it out with her?"

"Sort of. Not really. I better go. Thanks, Molly."

I walked back to the cottage, my mind in turmoil. I stepped inside. Most of the miners had gone home; only Neville and a couple of others remained. Sandy's kids had been put to bed. I drew the Blighter aside, told him the guts of what Molly had told me.

"I don't understand why Strettles is involved," I said. "I told him sincerely I didn't have the register. Neither one of us even knew what it was back then."

"But meanwhile we've been telling all of Sydney the register is for sale. It's hardly a surprise, really."

"But why now? And why is Waters involved again?"

"It has to be Prisk. All he'd have to do is let it be known that you had gone to collect the register, and that he doesn't care *who* gets it for him, he's willing to pay for it."

"Waters and Strettles will think I've been playing the crafty bastard all along, while pretending to know nothing about anything."

There was a loud knock on the door. Sandy went and opened it.

A uniformed cop stepped inside. Middle-aged, with a pugnacious look on his face.

No one greeted him, except for Sandy, who said, "What do you want?"

He scanned the small room, stopped at me and the Blighter.

"And who would you be?" he said to me.

I looked around the room.

"Never mind them, they're not going to tell you," he said. "What's your name?"

"Glasheen."

"Do you own the Chevrolet at MacDonald's Garage?"

"Not exactly. I'm looking after it for the owner."

"And who's that?"

If he really wanted to know, he could find out easily enough, I thought, so there was not much point in lying.

"A bloke named Michael Toohey."

The name didn't seem to mean anything to him. "What are

233

you doing in Cullens Creek?"

The Blighter stood up. "Really, Sergeant, is this necessary?" he said in his poshest voice.

"And who are *you*?"

"Lieutenant Beaufoy Edward Hawley-White."

That stopped him for a second or two.

"William and myself are on our way to my family's property in Gunnedah to do a little kangaroo shooting."

"Yeah," I said. "We hit a cow last night."

"Funny way to come if you wanted to get to Gunnedah," the copper said.

"I was trying to find a shortcut and we got lost."

"Do you have any papers? Something to identify you?"

I gave him my driver's license.

He looked at it closely, then handed it back. He turned to the Blighter.

"What about you?"

"I'm afraid not, Sergeant. Not really in the habit, you know. But my family is quite well known in the Gunnedah district. You can easily check."

The cop looked at him. If it was true, and the Blighter really *was* a member of the squatter gentry, then as a lowly bush copper he was playing with fire. But he must have been thinking, what was someone like that doing in a coal miner's house?

He turned away from the Blighter and faced me. "If you've come here to stir up this commo riff-raff"—he gestured at Sandy—"then you look out! I'll give you plenty of trouble, believe you me."

"He's no commo," Neville said. "You can take my word on that."

Sandy chuckled.

The cop looked around the room, then back at the Blighter and me. "I don't want to see you still here tomorrow. As soon as

234

that car's fixed, clear out, you hear me?"

He went out, leaving the door swinging behind him. Sandy pulled it to, let out a big breath and said, "He's a fair dinkum mongrel, that bloke."

We heard a car start up and drive away.

The Blighter was looking serious. "A rightist?" he said.

Sandy nodded. "Used to be stationed up the Hunter Valley. He was one of the Rothbury strike-breakers. "

The Blighter turned to the brothers and said, "Excuse us a moment." He drew me aside. "When you rang Lucy's place, was it person to person or a normal trunk call?"

"First time it was person to person. Last time just a trunk call."

"If Waters' people were listening in, they could track down the operator who put through the call and find out you were here. And if Waters were to phone *that* copper ... We should push on to Henry Crossing tonight."

"The car won't be ready till tomorrow, at least."

Sandy came over from the other side of the room, "Don't want to eavesdrop, gents, but if it's transport you blokes need, then we might just be able to help you."

"You've got a motor car?" I said.

"A truck. Hasn't been started in a while, but it should get you over the range to Henry Crossing. Won't break any records, though."

"Is there petrol in it?"

"Yeah, a full tank. I didn't want to use it up until I was sure I could get some more. "

"What make is it?"

"An Oxford Cowley, 1927 model. Dad fixed it up before the war. He thought he was going to make his fortune selling cream and eggs in town. It has a good motor, although I have to tell you, it can be a temperamental bugger."

"I'll have a go," I said. "It's good of you to offer it."

Sandy shook his head. "Hang on, matey. We're not *giving* it to you."

"You're lending it to us?"

"Try hiring."

"How much do you want for it?"

"Just let me have a little talk with the others, would you?"

"What have they got to do with it?"

"Technically the truck belongs to the union. Dad said before he died that it was to be used for union purposes or sold for the good of the union, as we saw fit."

I looked at the Blighter. He shrugged.

The blokes went into a huddle. When they broke up, Sandy said, "Now, we've got nothing against you blokes. The Blighter here is a comrade, and you, Bill—well, you're a fellow traveler, in at least one sense of the word. So whatever you blokes are up to, we take it you're not acting *against* our interests. But by the same token, you haven't really said whose interests you *are* acting in, or what you're about. Not that we really want to know."

"So how much for the flaming truck?" I said.

"One thing at a time. On the face of it this wouldn't seem to be a trade union matter. Not directly, at any rate. And for that reason, applying socialist, or what you might call *collectivist* principles may not be the best way for us to handle it."

For a bloke who was supposed to have black lung, Sandy could certainly bang on.

"So what *would* be the way to handle it?"

"Let's apply a little capitalist thinking. Look at it as supply and demand. Now on the supply side, things are tight. There's only one truck, and we've got it. As for the demand side, well that's for you to decide. How badly do you need to get going?"

I didn't like the sound of this one little bit.

"So how much, Sandy?"

236

"How about you make us an offer?"

"All right Blighter," I said. "I've paid for everything till now. You can deal with this."

"Afraid I can't, old boy. I'm strapped."

"What? Two days ago you had a thou—you had plenty of money."

He looked at the floor, like a guilty schoolboy. "That was two days ago."

"What do you recommend we do then?"

"Pay the chaps what they want."

"All right, Sandy," I said. "You've outlined the capitalist solution pretty well. But I'm more a when-in-Rome-do-as-the-Romans-do kind of a bloke. I liked the sound of the socialist approach a lot more. You know, brothers sharing, and all that."

"I'm glad to hear we've raised your political awareness. 'To each according to his needs, and from each according to his capacity to give,' as we say. In that case, we will gratefully accept your donation to the miners' strike fund, and in return we'd be delighted to allow you full use of the Federation's truck while you're in the district."

Eventually we came to what the miners called an "agreement," which took half of my remaining traveling money. The deal concluded, we traipsed out to the back shed and by the light of a single kero lamp, examined the truck. It was bright yellow, but covered in chook shit.

"Of course, it doesn't have a self-starter," said Sandy. "But if we push start it once, it should charge up all right. We'll pump up the tires for you."

It roll-started easily enough. The seat was hard, the steering heavy, and the acceleration slow, but the motor sounded all right.

I had to apply all the force I could to work the foot brake. I stopped the truck and got out.

"All right. This'll do," I said.

Sandy said, "You'd better put on a pullover or two. It could turn cool tonight, and the old beast is a bit draughty. And you can bet quids it'll be cold at Henry Crossing. It's the arsehole of the earth, that place."

"I knew it was around here somewhere."

"And a word of advice. Keep your wits about you when you're there. Those bastards at Henry Crossing aren't nice like us."

Getting to Henry Crossing from Cullens Creek involved crossing a range of hills then winding down into the next river valley, Sandy told us. No great distance as the crow flies, but the roads between the two towns had not been well maintained, going as they did from one godforsaken place to another.

Henry Crossing had been a gold mining town in the last century, but not one of the bigger strikes. When the gold ran out, the miners and fossickers moved on—that's why it wasn't on the maps anymore. According to Sandy, there wasn't even a real pub at Henry Crossing nowadays. No copper, either.

The truck lumbered slowly over the hills. It was a wrestle just to keep the thing on the road. It took all my weight to make the brakes work, and the steering was so heavy I had to slow down almost to a stop to turn a corner. Not that it went that fast anyway.

An icy wind came into the cab at a dozen spots, and despite my exertions, my legs and back were soon aching from the cold.

The Blighter resorted frequently to his brandy and his Senior Service. I was so cold I started doing likewise. The cigs still tasted like shit, but I was finding a kind of comfort in them now, and the brandy, as well as warming the blood, somehow seemed to make a small but important difference.

The truck took it slow up the range, in low gear all the way. It got colder and colder. I kept hitting the brandy, smoking bungers, shivering, aching. Then it started snowing.

After forty minutes climbing the slope, we leveled out. The sky cleared briefly, and the moon lit up a black, empty plateau. We passed a windbreak of ancient pine trees alongside the road, then a farmhouse behind a low stone wall; a weak light shone from inside it. Everything was built low to the ground, hunkered down against the wind.

It took an hour to cross the plateau. The snow fell heavier than before. After a while our road joined a bigger road, also dirt and gravel. Another five miles and we passed a cattle-loading ramp, then crossed a ford, which we'd been told to look out for. A little way further on, a track led off to the right.

I pulled up the truck. The snow began to gather on the ground. The one working headlight lit up a dim cavern of road ahead, leading into the black scrub. There were no signs.

"It doesn't look too promising," I said.

The Blighter just shook his head and took a swig of brandy.

I released the handbrake and took off. After a few bends the track abruptly began to drop away. I felt the truck slide through the slush; my attempts at steering had little effect. I stood on the brake, then pulled on the handbrake. The truck slid slowly to a halt.

"This isn't going to be easy," I said.

I let off the handbrake and eased forward. As soon as the truck got up to ten miles an hour it started to slide down the muddy slope again. But I found that if I kept two wheels on the drier shoulder of the track they grabbed a little bit better.

For the next half hour we crept forward in low gear, the truck always threatening to take off. The track got steeper, then went into a series of hairpin bends. By then I was getting the hang of it, though—there was nothing to do except let the truck slip around as it wished, then pull up and edge round the hairpins. Even so, it was dicey. The snow was falling heavily now, and if the trek up the range had been a hard slog, going down was twice as slow.

And I was deeply tired. Despite the work I was doing to keep the truck on the track, I felt myself drifting off. My thoughts kept getting lost in the tangle of gum tree branches I could see in the headlights, and I was lulled by the slap of the windscreen wiper and the undulating revs of the motor in low gear.

A horrified shout from the Blighter pulled me up. The front wheel was barely a foot away from a black drop-off. That kept me awake for another few minutes, then I started getting cloudy again. I lit another smoke and said, "For Christ's sake, Blighter, the one time your chatter might be of use, you go quiet! Start talking!"

And he did. It was drunken, crazy bullshit—he hadn't had any sleep since the Colony Club, as far as I could tell, and he'd been on the slops the whole time—but it helped. He told stories, about the war, about women he'd fucked, about intelligence work—funny stories and horror stories. I laughed at them more loudly than was warranted, probably.

"Hey Blighter," I said. "What about that bullshit you told the copper about your family in Gunnedah? What was the strength of that?"

"It's perfectly true, dear boy."

"So why do you talk like a pommy?"

"I was banished to a boarding school back in the mother country at an early age. But underneath, I'm as Australian as you are."

"What a thought."

The Blighter took a swig from his bottle and threw it out into the darkness.

"The last of the brandy," he said.

Eventually the slope eased off and the bush started to thicken up around us. We passed a shack, and another one a little further on, then a snow-covered open paddock beside the road. We were on the valley floor.

"We're getting close," I said. "What's the time?"

"After two."

"We'll have to find this bloke Bagshaw's place. Wake him up if we have to. Then you do your stuff."

There were more shacks scattered around the place—run-down, rickety-looking structures. Which of them belonged to Bagshaw, though, I had no way of knowing. Les had told me it would be easy to find Bagshaw—everybody in Henry Crossing knew him—but that wasn't much use at two in the morning.

I kept driving. For quite some time everything was in darkness, then ahead of us we saw a dim light coming from a ramshackle building set back off the road. Smoke was coming out of its chimney; a beat-up truck and a couple of old cars were parked out front.

"Could that possibly be a pub?" the Blighter said.

"Impossible. But there's a light on at least."

I pulled off the road and parked next to the other cars.

I got out of the truck, and stumbled. My feet and hands were numb, and I felt icy cold deep inside. The Blighter got out, looked at the place, then at me.

"Here we go," I said.

As we walked to the door, I could hear voices. I pushed it open and stepped inside. It was a big room—dark and smoky, with a low ceiling. A bunch of men sat at a table playing cards under a low light, a few more clustered around a shabby billiard table. At another table, a woman was sitting on a feller's lap; he had his hand up her dress. Except for the electric light hanging from the rafters, it might have been a scene from the nineteenth century—a bushrangers' hideout, or a den of cutthroats. The men were unshaven and drunk—they were the roughest looking bunch I'd ever laid eyes on.

The conversation stopped as soon as we walked in.

"Who are these cunts?" someone said.

"Greetings, good fellows," said the Blighter. "We are but poor wayfarers seeking shelter from the storm. We have come many miles, but alas, I fear we can go no further on this dark night. May we tarry a while amongst you?"

There was dead silence. Then a voice said out of the dimness, "Fuck me. Is that you, Blighter?"

"Indeed it is. And by Jesus I need a fucking drink."

14

We were granted admittance. The bloke who'd recognized the Blighter—and vouched for him—was a deadbeat from the 'Loo. He used to drink at the Three Bells, he told us, but he'd left Sydney hastily after an incident he'd rather not discuss. I got the feeling that each person there had a bit of business they'd rather not discuss.

Once the cold stares and hard looks had eased off a little, we were given brandy, some roast lamb, and bread and butter. After we'd eaten, I quietly asked the Blighter's mate if he knew where I could find Maurie Bagshaw.

He looked at me strangely and nodded towards the table of card players. "That's him over there, the one facing this way. This is his place."

"He's the publican?"

"I suppose that's what you'd call him, if this place had a license."

I let some time pass, had another drink.

By the time the card game seemed to be breaking up, the Blighter had dozed off. I went over to Bagshaw's table. He smiled and gestured for me to sit down.

I told him Les Formica had given me his name. He nodded and shuffled his cards, smiling. I told him I was looking for Mick

Toohey's place. He nodded again. I told him I was one of Toohey's trusties, and that I was worried about him.

He kept nodding and smiling as I spoke. I told him I could probably find it on my own eventually, but if he would help me I could go straight there. Then I ran out of things to say.

"Got any money on you?" Bagshaw said.

"Not a lot."

"*Any?*"

"Some."

"Feel like a hand or two of poker?"

"Maybe."

"Then I'll tell you what: you put some money on the table, and I'll play you for it. Your money against mine. Until one of us goes bust. You lose, you fuck off and leave us alone. You win, I'll help you out. If I can."

I looked across the room. The Blighter was still asleep. But others were watching. I didn't like it.

"Yeah sure," I said.

Things went my way—for a while. The pile in front of me increased. Then things seemed to turn, like the tide running out. I had a couple of good hands that should have won, but Bagshaw bettered them, against the odds. I knew it wasn't the random flow of good and bad luck. There were two other blokes at the table, and every so often one of them would make an idle remark when he took a drink—"Send 'em down, Hughie!" or "Here's cheers!" He seemed drunk, but over time I sensed a pattern in his words.

I excused myself to take a piss and nudged the Blighter as I passed him, told him to join us when I got back. "Keep an eye on the bloke on my left," I said. "And make sure he knows you're watching him."

When I sat back down, the Blighter joined us, all good will and cheer. The flow of remarks from the other bloke at the table ceased, and I started to win a few. But Bagshaw still won a couple of big pots that I should have won. I watched his hands, but he was pretty slick with the deck. So I closed my eyes while he was dealing. It sounded all right. I concentrated hard, and then I heard it, the faint but distinct swish and click Jimmy the Gypsy had warned me about.

Just before Bagshaw went to deal, I said, "Mind if I cut the deck?"

He looked surprised for a moment then said, "Be my guest."

From then on, I cut after every shuffle, before a single card was dealt. By a little after five in the morning, I'd won the last coin of Bagshaw's stake.

Bagshaw stood up and stretched. "Well, young feller, you fucked me well and truly. Now it's home to bed and into mum. You can sleep on the mattresses over there in the corner."

"Bullshit. We're going to Toohey's. Now."

He glanced at me, then yawned again, elaborately. "Jesus, everyone's knackered. There's snow on the road. It's as cold as hell. Let's all have a sleep now and after a good breakfast I'll take you there."

"That wasn't the deal," I said. "You welching bastard."

Bagshaw straightened up a little.

The Blighter moved over beside him, threw his arm around his shoulder and gave him a friendly shake. "The impetuousness of youth, eh Maurie? Why not do as he asks?" He gave him another, rougher shake. "Eh?"

Bagshaw looked from the Blighter to me. Everyone else had gone home long since.

He sighed. "Well, I'm not going there. But I'll show you the way. It'll take you an hour to get there from here," he said. "If you can get through at all."

"We'll take our chances."

He sighed and said, "It's your funeral," then went behind the bar and returned with a pencil and paper.

"You go up this road towards Grimble's farmhouse and turn left at the causeway, about two miles along." He drew a map as he talked. "Follow that road all the way up to Liar's Bend. There's a crossroads. Turn left again towards Mount Disappointment." He drew on the map. "If you get all the way to Mount Disappointment you've gone too far. There's another little track leads all the way up the other side of the hill there, on through a place called Fool's Gully."

"Are you fair dinkum with these names?" I said.

He looked at me, all outraged innocence. "The gold prospectors last century named those places. Most of them went bad. If you don't like the names they chose, don't fuckin' well blame me. Anyway, Toohey's place is back up towards the ridge, at the top of the valley. Be careful of the old mine shafts if you're walking around up there."

I looked at the map. He'd drawn the turns and put an "x" where Toohey's cabin was supposed to be. It seemed clear enough.

"So what's become of old Misery then?" Bagshaw said.

Neither of us answered.

The track wound through a series of small farms along the bottom of the valley. We had to stop a number of times, while the Blighter got out to open gates. There were three or four inches of inches of snow on the ground. It was dead still.

We followed the twists and turns as Bagshaw had directed. The track started winding uphill, following the creek. It was slow going. The roadway was covered in snow, and I had to edge the truck forward at walking pace, unsure of what was track and what wasn't.

The road got narrower, left the creek then wound up the side of a deep gorge. As we came around a long lefthand bend, the headlight caught a hand-painted signpost at the side of the track: "THE DEVIL'S JUMP."

I stopped the truck and got out, my heart beating fast.

Dawn was breaking, but the stars were still out. We were at a kind of lookout. There was an almost sheer drop in front of us, and a steep hill behind us. Half a mile away across the gorge were rocky bluffs, and down below I could hear the rushing creek. Other than the track we were on, there wasn't a square yard of ground at less than a fifty-degree incline.

"Blighter, this must be the place. But there's nothing here."
I walked on around the bend. The track dipped into a hollow in the hillside. I followed it and came to the remains of an old wooden gate at the side of the track, overgrown with blackberry vines. A sign crudely written in red paint said "DANGER KEEP OUT."

I climbed carefully over the brambles, but still tore my jacket on the thorns. The remains of a path took me on through the bush and a little way down the side of the hill, until I reached a flat area maybe thirty yards wide. The ground was rough, little hillocks of rock and rubble overgrown with thistle and blackberry. In the center, bits of timber framing and rusty corrugated iron surrounded an open hole in the ground.

At the far end of the clearing—nearly hidden by ferns, leafless fruit trees, and thorny rose bushes—was a low, stone building.

The Blighter overtook me and went straight to the house.

He tried the door, then went to a window, put a rock through it, and climbed in. There was a banging noise inside, he swore loudly, and a minute later he opened the front door, holding a lighted candle.

"Won't you come in?"

The air inside was icy and bad. There were cobwebs and birds' and wasps' nests in the rafters, rat droppings and birdshit on the table. A brown snake had left last year's sloughed-off skin in the middle of the floor, and a few spindly weeds were growing up through the boards.

But you could tell the place had been done up well at one time. There were rugs on the floor and a couple of leather armchairs. Some trout fishing gear in a corner, a big fireplace. Over to one side was a kitchen area—an old wood stove and a table.

The Blighter handed me a candle. I went over to have a closer look at a framed picture on the wall. Five blokes in World War One gear, in a trench. There was the young Mick Toohey, his face not crooked then. The four fellers with him all looked sort of familiar, but not so that I could name them. Then I picked out Jack Carmody, wearing sergeant's stripes. Next to him a Mediterranean-looking feller, who I realized must be Les Formica. Then, to my surprise, unmistakably a much younger Joe Grimshaw. Finally I picked the other feller as Misery's old pal Cyril, the taxi driver.

"Oh, Jesus!"

I turned around. The Blighter had gone through a doorway at the other end of the room. I went after him.

Despite the icy cold in the room, it stank. The Blighter was standing with one foot either side of a pile on the floor, holding his candle up, and peering into a square hole in the stone wall.

An open safe.

He turned back to me, his eyes wide and mad. "It's empty."

I just stood there.

The Blighter stepped back, gingerly lifting his left foot over the pile on the floor, and nodded down at it.

"He was shot. A long time ago."

I looked again and realized it was a body. There were bones, blackened skin, and rotting clothing. I turned and walked straight out of the cabin, and sat down on a stump, shivering.

The Blighter came after me.

"Better have a cig."

I took one. He took a swig of brandy and handed me the bottle.

"Is it Toohey?"

"I believe so."

The sky across the gorge to the east was golden and clear now, though the sun hadn't risen yet. Our breath made clouds of steam in the air, and suddenly it felt colder than any time the previous night.

A mob of crows was complaining off in the distance, and further off I could hear the sound of a motor laboring uphill.

"There's a car coming," I said.

"Actually, I believe there are two." The Blighter looked into the distance for a minute. Then he pointed to where a short stretch of the road was visible, a quarter of a mile away. Two dark cars, fifty yards apart, were winding slowly around the bend.

"We have to go," said the Blighter.

"I don't think I can. I've had it. I really have."

He shook his head. "We can't stay here."

I stood up and we ran back to the truck. I got the crank handle from the cab to start it up.

"It's too late," the Blighter said, and ran up the hillside into the scrub.

I just stood there, unsure what to do. Twenty seconds later a big, muddied Oldsmobile rounded the corner. It stopped with a lurch, and Aubrey Munce and his two offsiders stepped out.

Munce was wearing an oilskin, a woolen beanie and heavy boots, and held a gun. As he limped awkwardly towards me I put up my hands and said, "The register isn't here."

"What a damned shame, Munce said. "But you're fucked anyway, Glasheen."

He lifted the gun and brought it down to point directly at my head. He looked along the barrel and tensed slightly, anticipating the sound of the gunshot.

When it came, Munce crumpled where he stood.

The other two fellers froze for a moment, then looked around and scurried back to their car.

The Blighter emerged from the scrub with Herb's Colt .45 in his hand. He went over to Munce's body, dropped the Colt and picked up Munce's gun, quickly examined it, then ran at the Olds, which was reversing crazily back down the track.

The second car came around the corner fifty yards away and pulled up. A blue Buick with Harry Strettles at the wheel, a bloke I didn't know sitting next to him.

The driver of the Olds tried to make a three-point turn, but when he put his foot down, the back wheels spun in the mud. Strettles took in the scene and quickly reversed back around the bend.

The Blighter caught up with the bogged-down Olds and fired twice inside. He waited a second or two, then ran off around the bend after Strettles' car, but returned only a minute or so later.

"They've gone, for now," he said.

He bent over Munce's body, felt his neck, then grabbed his wrists.

"Take the other end."

I shook my head.

"Quick, this has to be done." The Blighter was as sober as ever I'd seen him.

"Not by me."

"There's no other way. If you don't help me, it'll mean jail—for you, definitely, and possibly even for me."

We dragged Munce's body to the old mineshaft and dropped it in, then retrieved the two bodies from the Olds and did the same with them.

After that we pushed the Olds over the edge of the Devil's Jump. It was swallowed up completely by the thick bush down below. The Blighter pitched Herb's gun far into the ravine.

I got inside the truck. The Blighter walked off down the road. I waited, smoking cigarettes.

The Blighter came back after ten minutes and got in the truck.

"I don't know where the others have gone. My guess is, they're waiting for us a mile or two down the track." He turned to me. "Friends of yours?"

"It was Harry Strettles at the wheel. I couldn't pick the other bloke. Strettles used to be Joe Grimshaw's thug. I don't get it."

"He appears to have joined forces with Munce."

"But how did they find this place?"

"Ray Waters. He must be orchestrating it now. He could have got the records of your trunk calls from Cullens Creek. Maybe the copper there had an idea which way we'd gone, or maybe Waters made a lucky guess. Whatever, he must have tipped off Munce and Strettles. Even if they only left Sydney last night, they would have made it to Henry Crossing by this morning. And who else would they go to but Citizen Bagshaw?"

I looked at the deserted track back down the hill and got the shakes again. The Blighter handed me the bottle. I took a big sip, then breathed deeply. I looked at the Blighter, smoking his Senior Service.

"You killed three men almost in cold blood," I said.

He shrugged. "Would you rather I'd let Munce shoot you? I wouldn't worry unduly about them, Bill. They knew the rules and they had plenty of blood on their hands."

"Toohey's?"

The Blighter shook his head. "Not Toohey's, though."

I thought about it for a moment. "That only leaves Eddie Worrall. But that doesn't make sense either. Not if what you said was true, that he and Toohey were, you know, a pair of horses."

"They were indeed that. But you're wrong to credit Eddie Worrall with any degree of decency. He was a snake and a psy-

251

chopath. Once the blackmail had been well and truly set up, it must have occurred to Worrall that he could go it alone. Cut Toohey and me right out. He brought the register to Toohey earlier on VP Day. Toohey set the ball rolling. Then they came up here. When Worrall had the chance he killed Toohey. Toohey's obsession with secrecy made it easy for him. There were no witnesses. Toohey had let his guard down momentarily."

"He broke his own rule."

"Quite. Then Worrall would have gone back to town and searched the Durban Club, thinking the register had to be there somewhere. Munce and co caught him there and killed him."

It sort of made sense.

The Blighter sighed deeply. "All this is of only academic interest to us, however. Your friend Strettles is somewhat of a gunman, I take it?"

I nodded. "And he'll be thinking we've got the register."

The Blighter held up Munce's gun. "Rather a nuisance. We're quite out of ammunition." He looked at the road. "I don't fancy our chances going back down that way. I wonder if we might find a way out over the hill here?"

I turned and looked at the narrow track winding up the hill.

"Christ knows how rough it is under that snow," I said. "Or how long before it peters out completely."

"We'll see."

So I drove up the hill, not knowing when the track might die on us. In its wake, the truck left a perfectly clear set of tire tracks in the snow.

The Blighter kept an eye out the back for Strettles and his mate. For a while there was nothing, but as we got to the end of a long straight stretch, he said quietly, "They're coming."

They stayed a hundred yards behind us all the way up the hill.

"They think we're still armed," the Blighter said.

The track took us back onto the plateau. After a mile it

joined another dirt road. We drove on as the sun rose into a clear blue sky. The snow covering the paddocks glared brilliant white. I was shivering and aching, exhausted and colder than I'd ever been, with the smell of Toohey's decaying corpse still in my nostrils.

We were moving slow. Strettles' car was never less than a couple of hundred yards behind us.

"This is no good," I said. "Those blokes will be able sit there behind us until we run out of petrol. And that Buick will have much bigger tank than this old piece of shit."

We kept driving through flat, open country. We passed by a strange rocky hill a couple of miles off to the right. The Blighter looked around and behind us.

"I *know* this country," he said.

"Yeah? That's wonderful. Perhaps you can suggest a nice spot for a picnic?"

"Listen, Bill, there should be a side road along here somewhere."

"Yeah, great."

Five minutes later he said, "This one! Turn right here!"

It didn't look promising. "Blighter, we can't have much petrol left. I hope you know what you're doing."

"Take the turn for God's sake, Bill!"

I did, and so did the Buick. The road wound downhill until around a bend we came to a fast flowing creek. No bridge. No depth signs.

"Drive through it!"

"We don't know how deep it is."

"Drive through it!"

So I did. The truck sank to its axles and further. It pushed out a big wave, but the motor kept going. We bumped over the rocky creek bottom, and I could feel the swollen stream dragging us sideways. But the truck held on, and we made it across.

The Blighter turned and looked out the back window. He let out a war cry. "That's stopped them!"

A few more miles and we came to a paved road, and eventually to a garage and a cafe.

We filled the truck with petrol. I went to the public phone. I told the operator the number I wanted. I could hear it ringing at the other end. My heart was beating.

Lucy answered.

The operator told me to put my coins in, and when I did, said to go ahead and speak.

"It's me," I said.

There was a pause, then Lucy said, quietly but urgently, "Did you get it?"

I didn't answer.

"Bill? Are you there?"

"Yeah."

"Well, have you got it?"

"It wasn't there. "

"Oh, Bill."

"But never mind that. You've got to tell how come you're involved—"

"Not now, for Christ's sake, Bill. Oh, I've got to go."

"Hang on, Lucy, I need to talk to you."

She hung up.

I went into the cafe and ordered a cup of tea and a grill. The Blighter went into the phone booth. He came back a few minutes later smiling broadly, and signaled me to come outside.

"I've arranged some help."

"That's beaut, because I'm knackered."

"Just a little bit more driving and we'll be in the clear."

"I've had it, Blighter. I need a proper feed and a sleep before I can go on."

"Not yet Bill. Sooner or later Strettles will find his way around that stream. We've got to go on. I'll drive, if you like."

"I'd rather take my chances with the gunmen."

"Bill, pull yourself together. If we've managed to get to a phone, then there's every chance that Mr. Strettles has too. And if he gets on to Waters, it wouldn't be awfully difficult for them to track us and this damned yellow truck."

I shook my head. "I don't fucking well care."

The Blighter shook my shoulder. "Bill, listen to me. They will assume we have the register now. We're in more danger than ever. There are a hundred thousand men loyal to the Patriotic League. What if they get the word out to *them*? 'Find Glasheen. He's in a yellow truck.'"

The Blighter nodded towards the bloke behind the counter.

"That chap could be one of them. Or it could be the local butcher or newsagent, or cow cockie. We don't know. We've got to keep going."

I looked at the Blighter. He wasn't in any better shape than I was.

"I know I must sound like an absolute lunatic," he said, "but I haven't the time to make it sound more plausible for you, I'm afraid. But trust me, we've simply got to go."

I drained my cup of tea. "Right now?"

"Sorry."

"But I haven't had my grill yet."

"Here, I bought you a packet of Minties."

We drove on, I don't know how far, or for how long. The Blighter watched the country closely, muttering, "Yes, this is it," every so often. He directed me through a series of turnoffs, through flat farmland. I had no idea where we were, or even which direction we were headed. I couldn't have guessed the time, either.

We crossed the plain and into wooded hills again. The Blighter went quiet, looking out the back. "There's a car behind us."

He peered out the back for another minute then turned around quickly. "It's the Buick."

"We should have stayed at the cafe. Now we're fucking lost."

The Blighter didn't contradict me.

The car behind caught up and sat on our tail. I looked over my shoulder and saw Harry Strettles through the back window. He looked me in the eye.

We kept on. Suddenly the Blighter said, "That's it, there! Take this turn!"

The track led through an open gate. Just inside it and off to the side, a shiny black car was facing our way. Two men in suits were sitting in the front. I hit the brakes, but the Blighter told me to keep going.

I looked in the rearview mirror at the scene behind me. When Strettles saw the black car, he swung the Buick around and headed back out the gate. The black car followed.

Five hundred yards down the track, we came to a little cottage, half hidden behind an overgrown garden. Smoke was coming out of the chimney.

"Quick now," said the Blighter.

We walked up the short path. He banged on the door and turned to me. "Let me do all the talking. Understand?"

The door swung open, and a breath of warm air mixed with the smell of toast hit me. A big feller in a woolen pullover stood there, smoking a pipe. He looked at the Blighter, then at me.

I'd been drinking. I was upset. I was hungry. I needed sleep. I'd been a witness to a triple killing. I wasn't myself, not at all. But the feller standing in the doorway looked to me for all the world like the Right Honorable Joseph Benedict Chifley, Prime Minister of the Commonwealth of Australia.

"How are you, Blighter?" the big bloke said. "You'd better come in. You both look like you could do with a cup of tea."

15

I slept for a long time, though it was a strange, half-waking, half-dreaming sleep. I woke, still fully dressed, in a cold, almost dark room. Light was coming under the door.

I went out into the light and warmth. The big bloke with the pipe was frying eggs on the stove.

"How you going there, young feller?" he said. "Have a good rest, did you?"

"Yeah, thanks." I shook my head, trying to remember ... Who, why.

"Where's the Blighter?" I asked.

"Asleep in the other room. Like some eggs? There's tea in the pot there."

"Thanks." I poured a cup, lit one of the Blighter's smokes. "Where are we?"

"They call this area Pear Tree Hill."

"I mean, what's *near*?"

He pointed out the window. "Bathurst is about thirty miles that way."

"What time is it?"

"Three in the afternoon."

"Who are you, anyway?"

"Never mind me, son. I'll be off soon."

I took a deep drag on the smoke, let it out slowly. "There was trouble. We found Mick Toohey's body. Harry Strettles was chasing us—" I stood up quickly. "Is he still out there?"

"He shot through. But you'd better not say too much just yet. There'll be another feller along soon. He'll have a yarn to you about all that."

"Who are you?"

"I'm a friend."

"You look like Ben Chifley."

He smiled. "Do I?"

"Do you . . . do you know about the register?" I said.

He nodded. "You didn't find it, I understand."

"It wasn't at—"

He put his hand up. "No need to explain just yet, son." He put a plate of eggs and fried tomatoes in front of me. "There you go. Eat that."

I ate the food and drank another cup of tea. I started feeling better.

When I finished I took the plate over to the sink. "Funny how much you look like Ben Chifley," I said, "because I had a bit of run in with your—with Chif's opposite last week."

"Mr. Menzies?"

"Yeah, him."

"What was your assessment of Mr. Menzies, then?"

"He's smooth. *Bloody* smooth. Could talk the birds down out of the trees."

"So he'll be getting your vote, will he?"

"I don't think so. I'm a Chifley man. Always have been."

The big bloke smiled. "You're from Sydney?" he said.

"Yeah. Do you know who I am?"

He nodded. "The Blighter's been keeping us informed of . . . developments. But I would have picked you as a Sydney man, anyway. By your suit. And by those." He nodded in the direction of the couch. My jacket was where I'd thrown it. Petrol coupons spilled out of the pockets onto the floor. I looked from them back to him.

He smiled slightly, and shrugged his shoulders.

"What do I call you?" I said.

"Call me Joe."

"So you know all about the Lone Riders of the Lost Canyon or whoever they are, about the register and Mick Toohey? And that bloke Prisk?"

The big feller nodded. "We're democratic. My mob, I mean. Secret police and secret armies aren't our way. Nor are spying and manipulating and all that back room shenanigans. At least not yet, and may they never become so. But certain . . . elements out there don't feel the same way."

The other bedroom door opened. The Blighter came out, looking disheveled. He lit a smoke, rubbed a hand over his face, turned and said, "Good afternoon, gentlemen."

The big bloke nodded to him, "Afternoon, Blighter." Then he turned back to me. "We're a democratic party in a democratic country. If the people don't like us, we're out on our arses. But the voters of Australia don't get any chance to vote for or against the Patriotic League and their cronies. Much as I detest the coms in the trade unions, at least they're democratically elected. I have no time for secret armies and such."

I felt like saying, "Spare me, dad, you're not in Parliament House now," but I just nodded politely.

The Blighter coughed noisily, rummaged through his overcoat, found his bottle and took a sip. He looked up and saw me and the big bloke looking at him. He held up the bottle. "Anyone?"

The big bloke shook his head and went on. "So when we first came to know of the register's existence, we made a decision to try to get hold of it, if we could. It came to nothing. Then we heard that a certain youngster in Sydney seemed to be the key to it all. I had grave reservations about involving a mere lad in this sort of intrigue, but they told me that if anyone could turn up the register, it would be you. Whether you realized it or not."

He smiled sadly. "I'm sorry, Bill, for all the trouble we've put you through. And all for nothing."

"Maybe it wasn't all for nothing," I said.

The big bloke looked at me questioningly. "Would you care to explain what you mean by that, son?"

The Blighter was looking at me. There was the sound of a car outside. The big bloke went to the window, peeked through the curtain. "Here's Keith," he said. He came back and sat down opposite me and said quietly, "What do you mean?"

I looked from him to the Blighter, then back at him. "I mean, I know where it is."

"You have it?"

I shook my head. "The penny dropped this morning, up there at the Devil's Jump. The register has been under my nose the whole time. I suppose I'm not as clever as I reckoned."

There was a light tap on the door. The big bloke called out, "Just a moment, Keith, if you don't mind." He turned to me. "So what do you plan to do, feller?"

"Well, what about this story about the government being will-ing to *buy* the register? What's the strength of that?"

The Blighter leaned back, exhaled smoke and looked at the ceiling, a smile on his face.

The big bloke said, "I understand you're on the payroll al-ready?"

"Well, yes. I suppose I am, technically. But I was led to believe that, considering the register's national security significance and so on, the government might be willing to match what the Black Legion is willing to pay for it."

He sighed. "During the war, yes, we would have been," he said. "Even shortly afterwards, maybe. But now?" He shook his head. "With every conceivable allowance, I doubt if we could even sling you enough for a new zoot suit. If you were hoping for more, then I'm sorry, but you won't be getting it from the Commonwealth."

I nodded. "That's all right, Joe," I said. "No need to apologize. I'll cop whatever you think is a fair thing."

He looked at me for a moment, then looked at the Blighter, who was suddenly impassive. His voice became brisk and businesslike. "Let's be clear: the register is in your possession now?"

"No. It's in Sydney. I think."

"And you're prepared to hand it over to us?"

"Yeah, why not?"

He stood up, put on his hat and overcoat. "All right then. Well done. I'm going now, I can't be involved any further in this. Keith will fully debrief you. You can trust him." He put his hand out and we shook. He nodded at the Blighter, then walked over and opened the door.

He turned around, smiling. "Oh, and by the way, Bill. You wouldn't know this, but the Rationing Commissioners have a plan to issue a completely new set of ration coupons. New design, different colors. Much harder to counterfeit."

"Is that right?"

"It'll render all the existing fake coupons worthless."

I looked at him blankly.

"Just thought you might like to know," he said.

"Thanks, Joe. I'll remember that."

The big bloke nodded and left.

The Blighter quickly stood up, came over and patted my shoulder. "You really have the register?" he whispered.

I nodded.

The door opened. Keith was the gray-haired fellow who'd photographed me in Darlinghurst Road. He said good afternoon to us both, then took the Blighter aside. They talked for half an hour in the other room, then Keith came out, shutting the door behind him, and called me over to the kitchen table.

"Now, Bill, let me say first off, there's no need for you to say anything about any events which may have transpired over the past thirty-six hours. I have all the information I need about that. Understand?"

"I'm in the clear?"

"It's unlikely that your assistance will be required for any investigations which may ensue."

"But there were three blokes who—"

"Christ, son, I'm trying to make it easy for you, all right? Things will be taken care of. There'll be no whistles blown. Got it?"

"Yeah. What about Strettles?"

"A couple of Commonwealth men have had a long talk with him. He won't bother you again. At least, not over this matter."

I didn't say anything.

"Look, I can guarantee that. Strettles was right out of his class in this Patriotic League business. He never understood what the register was or what it could mean. Now he realizes there's nothing in it for him, he's moved on. But I want to talk about the register. I understand that you have it and are prepared to hand it over?"

"I'm pretty sure I have it, yes. And if I do, you're welcome to it," I said. "On one condition."

He raised his eyebrows.

"I want my name removed from every official file or record or scrap of paper associated with this business. So it looks like I was never here."

He nodded his head slowly. "All right. I can arrange that. I'll see to it myself."

"Thanks."

"So, the register is in Sydney?"

"Yeah. I think so."

"Would you care to tell us where it is?"

I shook my head. "I'll go and get it."

He was silent a moment. "Will you need some backup?"

"No. Just leave it to me. It'll take a day or two."

"Very well then." He wrote a phone number on a piece of paper and gave it to me. "Contact me the moment you have the register. No matter what time, day or night." He stood up. "You and the Blighter can take my car back to Sydney if you like. There's nothing to fear now, and you'll have the Blighter riding shotgun in any case. Is that all right?"

"Tickety-boo."

When he'd left, the Blighter said, "You've surprised us all once again, William. So where is it, after all this?"

"I might just keep that 'need-to-know' for the moment, Blighter, if you don't mind."

"Yes, probably the wisest course, old chap."

"Are you crooked on me?"

"On the contrary, I think you handled it all rather well. If the government men won't pay up, there's nothing much we can do. At least you've secured their cooperation and protection. They'll tidy things up for us. They'll warn off Ray Waters. So we're in the clear."

"Is Strettles really off our tail?"

"Good lord, yes."

"What if he decides to turn us in?"

"Strettles is a brute but he's not a give-up. And he didn't actually *witness* the various dirty deeds up there at the Devil's Jump. So be easy about it, Bill."

"All right."

"Now," he clapped his hands together, "Are you ready to travel again, do you think?"

I shook my head. "I've got to sleep, Blighter. It can wait a few hours can't it?"

"I suppose it will have to."

The Blighter had gone when I woke the next morning, and so had the car they'd left for us. There was a bottle of rum, a packet of smokes, and a note from him on the table. He said he was eager to get back to town, and it looked like I was going to sleep for some time, so did I mind terribly making do with the truck for now? The rum and smokes were to keep me warm on the return trip. Would I ring him at the Metropole the moment I got back?

I heated up a tin of baked beans and made a pot of tea. After breakfast I locked up and left. There was no one else around, so I left the key under the mat.

The truck kicked over all right. I drove out of Pear Tree Hill and spent most of the day retracing our twisted trail of the day before. It was cold again, but the rum and the smokes helped. I only got lost once, asked directions at a garage, and by late afternoon I was back in Cullens Creek.

The mechanic had fixed the Chev. It was battered and dirty, but it had a windscreen again, and a working radiator. It sounded good when I started it up.

As I was about to take off, there was a tap on the window. Sandy was standing there. I wound down the window.

"You're back then?" he said.

"Yeah. Came to get the car. You can have your truck back now, thanks."

"Did you find Henry Crossing all right?"

I nodded.

"There were some blokes through, asking about you and the Blighter."

"Yeah. I guessed."

"They got short shrift here."

"Thanks. I better shoot through."

But he stayed put.

"Listen, I was talking to Neville after you left. About you, ah, *hiring* the truck for all that money." He took a wad of pound notes from his pocket and handed it to me. "It was a bit steep. Better have some of it back."

It was about half what I'd originally slung him. Which made it still the most expensive truck hire in the state of New South Wales. "Thanks," I said. "How's your strike going?"

"It's over. We're back at work. For now. We're saving the big one for later."

I spent the night in a pub in Katoomba, left well before dawn and got back to Sydney just before eight o'clock. I had a long, large breakfast at the Hole in the Wall, drank a couple cups of coffee, then drove straight out to Darling Point.

Molly opened the door. She looked me slowly up and down. "You'd better come in."

"Is Lucy here?" I said.

She shook her head slowly.

"You know where?"

"Yes."

"And where would that be?"

"It's too late now, Bill."

"Where?"

"She's married a fellow, yesterday. Civil ceremony."

"Prisk?"

"God, no."

"Who then?"

"A fellow named Rupert Bowsher. A grazier."

"How the hell did he come into the picture?"

"He was always in the picture. He used to come to Sydney every few months, and he'd usually give Lucy a call."

"Has he got money?"

"He has now. Bags of it. And three thousand acres of good sheep country near Yass."

"What do you mean, 'now'?"

"Rupert was waiting to inherit the family property. His father finally passed away last Friday."

"There's a bit of luck. Lucy knew?"

Molly nodded. "He was always keen. But she told him months ago that he wasn't in the race without a substantial bank."

"That's what she told me," I said. "What about her singing and all that?"

Molly shrugged.

"I know Lucy—the real Lucy," I said. "She's not some grazier's wife in the sticks, I don't care how much dough he's got. It's not her. It's a mistake."

"Lucy thinks growing up in Botany was the mistake."

I sat down, lit a cig.

"You've taken up smoking?"

"Yeah." Not to mention blackmail and murder, I thought.

"You were right about Lucy," I said. "She was ratting on me all along."

"I never said she was ratting on you."

"Well, that's what it was. She betrayed me. She betrayed herself, really. I loved her. Still do."

Molly said softly, "But she didn't love you. And she never really said she did, did she?"

"She never said she didn't."

"She was keeping her options open. The way you asked her to. In the end it didn't go your way. You know how you rang on the weekend and told Lucy that your, ah, business deal didn't look like it was going to come good?"

"Yeah?"

"She was upset. Then Rupert Bowsher rang up that same day."

266

"He was first past the post."

Molly nodded.

"Yeah. Well. See you." I stood up to go.

"Bill, if there's *anything* I can do, any time."

"Yeah?"

"Yeah."

"Hang on. Do *you* love me?" I said.

"No."

"Oh."

"But I like you a lot."

I went to Paddington. There was a hole under the oleander bush where my jar of money had been. The house was deserted. The empty jar was sitting on the kitchen table, with a note.

Dear Bill,

Well, haven't there been some rough bastards around this old place? A bloke named Harry was here looking for you, and some other fellows after that, who didn't leave their names. I thought it best under the circumstances that Mavis and me and the little bloke nick off for a while.

I took the money you had buried in the back yard with me for safekeeping. I'll return it to you at the earliest opportunity.

Meanwhile, you'll be pleased to know I've decided to do something about my situation. With the price that rabbit skins are fetching, I got a feeling that a bloke who knows the ins and outs could do all right for himself. Of course, I'll need to get set up with a decent motor car and a tent and traps and what have you, so if you don't mind I might have to borrow a little bit of your money, which, of course, I'll repay with interest the first chance I get.

267

All the best
Cecil

P.S. In the meantime, if you ever happen to be down around the Murray River way, look us up.

There was no address on it, of course. I lit a smoke and sat there for a while at the kitchen table, wondering how bad I felt about the money. Not *that* bad, I decided.

I went out to the back bedroom. All my things had been gone through—the trunk, the money tin in the fireplace and the rental paperwork. I gathered what remained, locked up and left.

I went to Darlington and let myself in to Carmody's place. A couple and a mob of kids were sitting at the kitchen table.

"Oh. You must be Mrs. Sprague's brother," I said to the man. "Sorry to barge in on you."

"Who are you?"

"I *was* the rent collector."

"Are you still?"

"I don't know. I need to have a look in the ceiling."

He looked at me for a couple of seconds, then said, "Go ahead."

I brought the ladder in and placed it under the new manhole Carmody had installed. The work he'd been so keen for me to see.

I climbed up into the attic and struck a match. Over in the corner, sitting on the rafters was a two-foot-square section of tongue-and-groove flooring, with a wooden box sitting on it. I crawled over to it and found it was unlocked.

I struck another match. Inside the box was a neat stack of large envelopes. I took them out. The first one I peeked inside appeared to contain legal documents. Others were full of letters. The last one contained a thick bundle of large photographs. One sheet had a section torn from the bottom corner. I put every-thing in the box, dragged it over to the manhole, and called Mrs. Sprague's brother to help me down the ladder with it.

He gave me a funny look. "You're taking that with you, are you?"

"Relax, sport," I said. "The old feller who used to live here wanted me to have this. I know that for a fact."

At the door he said, "So what happens about the rent?"

"I don't know. I've sacked myself as rent-collector. Sooner or later someone will be around, I suppose, wanting it. Until then . . . suit yourself. Shout the kids an extra paddle-pop or two."

I rang Max Perkal from the phone on the corner. He was still asleep, his mother said. I asked her to wake him and told him I'd be around in a few minutes.

Max greeted me blearily when I carried the box in.

"What've you got there?"

"Never mind. Can I use your room for an hour or so?"

He scratched his head. "Yeah, I s'pose so."

"Thanks. Leave me to it. And hey, Max, we've got to talk about our petrol coupons."

"All right. I'll get Mum to make you a cup of tea."

I closed the door and started on the papers. First the legal documents. They appeared to be the title deeds to Toohey's rental properties. I put them all back in their envelope, then took out the sheets of photographic paper.

Each photograph was of a page of closely written names and addresses. There were forty-three of them. The register. I scanned down the first couple of pages, then put them all back in the envelope.

The next envelope contained another bundle of photographic sheets. The first one was a letter addressed to a colonel in Orange, New South Wales, signed by Major Eric Prisk. The next was addressed to a navy admiral in Glen Waverly, Victoria. It was substantially the same letter, also signed by Prisk. I went through the rest. Different addressees, same basic letter. I read and reread them, then studied the register again.

I found Max in the kitchen with his mum, listening to a race broadcast. The race finished, to neither's satisfaction.

"Max, would there be a decent camera in the house, by any chance?"

He shook his head. "Try Herb," he said.

I rang him. He made a call, then rang me back. I drove to Elizabeth Bay and collected a camera from Herb's mate.

On the way back to Max's I stopped in at the City of Sydney Library, and asked the woman behind the counter where the old *Sydney Morning Heralds* were kept. They were all bound, she said. Did I know what dates I wanted? I told her I wasn't sure, could I just see all of them for 1944 and 1945. She suggested crankily that if I used the index, I'd probably save both myself and her a good deal of trouble. What index, I said.

She led me over to a shelf, pointed to a row of blue books. "*Herald* indexes, year by year," she said. "Whatever you're after, it should be listed there."

The first one I picked up covered the first half of 1945. There were eight entries for Prisk, with the title of each news story, the date and page number. I jotted down the details, then checked the second half of the year, then went back to 1943 and 1944. I went back to the counter with my requests, and stayed in the library reading until closing time.

Back at Max's that night, I read the list of names and addresses and each individual letter once more. By the time I'd finished, I had it figured out.

I met the Blighter next day in the bar at the Metropole. He greeted me warmly, and we went outside to talk.

"Well?" he said.

"Yeah, I got it."

He clapped me on the shoulder. "Well done, Bill, excellent work. You have it with you?

"No."

"Never mind. So where the devil did you find it?"

"It was stuck in the ceiling of a house in Darlington. The register has been sitting there since the evening of VP Day, is my guess. Mick stashed it away before he went bush. Not even Eddie Worrall knew. While I was out trying to deliver Mick's message to you at the Mansions, Mick probably got his mate and trusty Cyril, the taxi driver, to take the register and some other stuff to this place at Darlington, to be looked after by another old trusty."

The Blighter smiled, nodded his head. "Well, this has all worked out rather splendidly, then. With Munce and his boys gone we can sell the register to Prisk with no complications at all." He clapped his hands. "It's perfect!"

I shook my head. "But I don't want to sell it to him, Blighter."

His smile disappeared. "Why ever not?"

"It's hard to explain. I wanted that money for a reason. That reason's gone now."

"Lucy Chance?"

I nodded.

"I am awfully sorry, Bill. You were rather gone on her, weren't you? Odd isn't it, the way the affections work? The other lass, Molly, was much nicer to you, although I take it you had no special feelings for her."

"Oh, Molly's all right. Anyway, Blighter, I don't have the heart for it anymore, with people dead and all that. Fuck Prisk. I don't want his money. Let the government bloke have the register. They were paying our wages after all. I'm sorry, Blighter. You were counting on the dough, weren't you? "

He took a while to answer. "Well, one rarely has enough, of course. But I suppose the point is, if you can do it once you can do it again. It's like the cloak-and-dagger work—it doesn't do to become too attached to any particular outcome. Oh, I'd be lying if I said I wasn't disappointed, but I understand. Mind you, if I thought there was any chance of persuading you otherwise, I'd give it a jolly good try."

"There isn't, Blighter."

"No, I rather thought not. Oh well, once more into the breach, eh?"

"Yeah."

"So what precisely was on the register then?"

"Well, that's a long story, Blighter, and I don't feel like going through it right now. I've arranged to meet the government bloke tomorrow at the house on Oxford Street. I'm going to give him the stuff then. Meet me there, if you like, I'll give you the mail. Nine o'clock."

I was there early. At five to nine the Blighter arrived.

"G'day Blighter," I said. "Have a seat. There's a pot of tea made."

"Thank you, old boy. So, William, it's here?"

I tapped the large envelope on the table in front of me.

The Blighter nodded. "Jolly good. Well, better say it now, I suppose." He sighed. "Bill, I'm awfully sorry, but there have been some changes to the procedure of this morning's meeting."

"Have there?"

"I know how much you wanted to do the right thing, and I have tremendous admiration for you. Really, I do. And I sincerely wish I had just a fraction of your integrity."

"Yes?"

"But alas, I haven't."

"It's too late, Blighter. The Commonwealth copper will be

here any minute," I said.

"Probably not. I took the liberty of postponing the arrangement. On your behalf."

"Oh."

We sat there for a moment. The Blighter took a swig from his flask then looked at me apologetically.

"So, Bill, I'm going to have to take this, and I do hope you don't attempt to stop me." He reached over and picked up the envelope. He got out the bundle of photographic prints, untied the ribbon which held it together, and started flipping through the sheets.

"What am I supposed to tell the government bloke?" I said.

"You can tell him whatever you like, Bill. I expect to be out of the country very soon. Of course, I'd *prefer* that my reputation not be any more tarnished than it already is, but I realize it would be quite out of order to expect you to cover for me."

"Were Cec and Mavis your people, Blighter?"

"Not originally. They became so." He nodded and looked at me. "Sorry Bill. I told you it's a ghastly, deceitful business."

"Forget it. Lucy too?"

"She made contact with Prisk at my urging. She already knew you, of course. But Lucy was never fully under my control. She never really reported on you, if that's any comfort."

"I rang her from Cullens Creek. She wanted me to dump you by the wayside as soon as I got the register."

"The vixen!"

I pointed at the envelope. "So what happens to that stuff then?"

He looked at me. The back gate banged. Footsteps.

"I think you know the answer."

Eric Prisk entered the kitchen. The Blighter didn't even look up.

"Sorry Blighter, I got restless waiting in the car."

"Take a seat, Prisk," I said.

He remained standing, looked at the Blighter and said, "Well?"

The Blighter didn't return his look. "Here it is," he said. "I was just about to acquaint myself with it in detail."

"Never mind that, Blighter. Let's make the exchange with no further ado."

Prisk took a long envelope out of his pocket, withdrew a thick pile of ten pound notes and held it out to the Blighter.

The Blighter looked at the money in Prisk's hand, looked again at the pile of photographs. He passed it over, took the money from Prisk.

"I'll need to check that it's all here, Blighter."

"As will I, Eric."

Prisk sat down and started going through the pile, while the Blighter counted the money.

"What do you reckon, Prisk," I asked. "Worth it?"

He ignored me. He flipped through the sheets, first the register of patriots and then the letters. Then he went through the letters again. He looked up and said to the Blighter, "It's not all here."

The Blighter looked at him blankly.

"Ah, gentlemen," I said, "I believe I may be able to shed some light on that matter."

They both looked at me.

I turned to the Blighter. "It's not how you thought it was, Blighter."

"Really?" He was smiling, ready to say something sarcastic, but interested just the same.

"The register never was the main thing. You said Prisk was the go-between? That was bullshit. He was the prime mover. Il Duce. Worrall and Toohey were blackmailing Prisk, first and foremost, and the Patriotic League as an afterthought. *You* were the go-between, Blighter."

I turned to Prisk. "And Worrall was *your* special friend, wasn't he?"

Prisk stood up. "What's this lout playing at, Blighter? Are you part of this?"

"Afraid not, Eric. I rather think we should attend to what William is saying, as he does appear to be holding the aces."

Prisk looked at me again.

"So, Worrall . . ." I said. "He was—?"

"He was my private secretary," he said quickly. "For a brief period."

"Yeah. So he had access to your confidential stuff. A bit of a scallywag, I gather?"

Prisk didn't answer.

"You see, Blighter," I said, "the way I understand it, this goes back to '44."

The Blighter picked up the pile of photographs on the table and started looking at them. Prisk sat there staring at me.

"If you read those letters, the story is pretty plain. Prisk pulled strings and organized a bogus army commission for himself. Just to make himself feel good, I suppose. But it went to his head, and he started seeing a glorious future for himself. So he contacted some fellers he knew, from the *old* secret army, back before the war. Other people, too—returned men with a grudge, old-fashioned conservatives, RSL fellers. Not to mention people who hear him on the radio and write letters to him saying, 'Good on you, Eric, we're with you, sport. Let's kick the reds in the bum!'

"Prisk travels around the country. He tells the old secret army crew not to lose contact with their people, that big things are brewing.

"So, to cut a long story short, the new, improved secret army—the Patriotic League, as they called it—was really Prisk's idea. He sent out letters to his key contacts, proposing the national federation of secret armies. I don't know how many letters

Prisk sent out. But Eddie Worrall quietly copied a dozen of them. They're all basically the same, with different addressees. Worrall copied the letter and Prisk's mailing list. That's the register we've been fighting for."

My mouth was dry. I stopped to take a swig of tea before I went on.

"Anyway, Prisk here cools down after a while. The secret army business starts looking like the ridiculous, overgrown boy-scout jamboree that it really was. And Prisk pals up to Bob Menzies. Pig Iron Bob and his mates say, 'Ever considered running for parliament, Eric? You're our sort of chap.' Which sounds good to Eric."

I stared hard at Prisk, who was looking grim. "How am I doing? Warm? Yes, I thought so."

I turned back to the Blighter. "To hell with this secret army bullshit, Prisk thinks to himself now. But Eddie Worrall has meanwhile passed the material on to Mick Toohey, his, ah, very special friend and a bloke who knew how to run a lurk. And who knew from personal experience how badly some people want to keep their secrets quiet. Worrall and Toohey set about blackmailing Prisk and all his cronies. So far, Prisk and his friends probably hadn't done anything all *that* criminal. But if it got out, it would be embarrassing as hell, especially to Prisk. And maybe seditious too, who knows? Ask a lawyer about that one. Whatever, Prisk was desperate enough to call Aubrey Munce and associates in, to clean up his mess for him.

"Worrall was a rat who'd betrayed a trust once before and was more than ready to do it again. He killed Toohey, then Munce killed Worrall. Prisk was way out of his depth by then, and scared shitless."

Prisk didn't say a thing. The Blighter looked from me to him. I went on.

"Things went quiet. Maybe Prisk and Munce and the King's

276

Secret Brigade of Oddfellows hoped that the register and the letters really were lost at this point. But they weren't. After a while an old feller named Jack Carmody, who'd been quietly minding the register the whole time, guessed that Toohey was no more. He took it upon himself to write to a crim named Joe Grimshaw, sounding him out, hinting that he had some valuable material for sale, and would Grimshaw be able to broker it for him. He signed the letter with my name. I think he planned to guide me through the rort step by step, for our mutual benefit. But in his excitement he walked in front of a truck and got killed before he could tell me about it. Leaving me in the hot seat, and completely oblivious."

The Blighter took a sip from his flask. "Admirably done, Bill."

"Now Major Prisk here understandably has the shits, because the package you gave him, Blighter, is a little bit light on."

Prisk sat there, his mouth closed, his jaw working. Then he said, "What are you playing at, Glasheen? I paid that money in good faith," he said.

I turned to the Blighter. "Like I said, Worrall copied a dozen letters. There are only eleven there." I turned back to Prisk. "And you can stick your money up your arse. That's between you and the Blighter."

"So what do you want, then?"

"I don't want anything from you. I passed the last letter on to some friends in the Miners' Federation. It's up to them what they do with it."

Prisk stood up and turned to the Blighter. "Are you going to let this young bastard get away with that?"

"Get away with what, Eric? As far as I knew you were paying for the return of the register. Which you now have. I had no idea about this other stuff until now." The Blighter stood up. "Well, Eric, to my mind our business is complete. I'm sorry if it didn't

yield all you hoped for. But really, old chap, you'd have to con-
cede that I've fulfilled my part of the bargain."

Prisk walked out without another word.

The Blighter watched him go, then turned to me. "Can I en-
tice you to share a celebratory drink at the nearest public house,
Bill?"

I shook my head. "You can get fucked."

"Oh, Bill, don't sulk. Everything has worked out rather well,
don't you think?"

"I made another copy of the register, Blighter. I'm passing it on
to the government feller anyway," I said.

"Even better! William, old boy, you're a natural at this."

16

I met Keith the next day at City Tatts. I gave him the copy of Prisk's mailing list. I made no mention of the letters, nor did he ask me about them.

The cop looked at the register, shook his head and said, "Not much is it? All that trouble, people killed. For this."

"You know any of those names?" I said.

He looked down the register, nodding occasionally and smiling. "A few."

"What'll you do," I said, "arrest them?"

He smiled, took a sip of his beer. "I don't think so. Not unless they assassinate Chifley or Evatt or someone."

"So what'll happen, then?"

He shrugged his shoulders. "Give it a year or two, and either we'll all be goose-stepping down George Street or else the League will have quietly gone underground, and you'll have a hard time convincing anyone they ever existed."

"I don't understand that."

"That's how it is. Do you know how many federal coppers there are keeping an eye on them?"

"I wouldn't know."

"Me and two other fellers. Three of us in all."

"And the Blighter?"

Keith chuckled. "Yeah. And the Blighter."

"But . . . why?"

He pushed his hat back on his head. "No one's really that interested anymore. During the war, when the Russian commos were our allies and the fascists were our enemies, sure. But now? Mr. Menzies is telling us that the commos are the big threat. And people are listening."

"But what about Chifley? I thought he was, you know, taking a personal interest in the Sacred Knights of the Runny Nose and all that."

"He *was*. Now he's caught in the middle. He has to prove to the Liberals and everyone else that he's not soft on the commos."

"What about you?" I said.

"I do what I'm told. But I don't have much use for those red bastards. If you get anything on *them*, by the way, let us know. I'm sure we could do some business."

"I don't think so. But speaking of which, did you do what you said, remove my name from the records?"

"Completely."

Then he paid me up. After subtracting the wages in advance that the Blighter had already given me, it turned out I was owed just under forty pounds. I blew it all on a nag that same afternoon.

Max, Herb and myself met and pooled all the counterfeit coupons we had left. I took them up to the Hi Society Milk Bar and after a bit of to-ing and fro-ing, sold them to the Abercrombie Street Mob at a pretty good price, considering.

Then Max and I went up to Burt's to clear out the records from the jukebox. Danny, the local lout came up to me the moment I arrived. "Hey Bill, there's been a bloke down here asking questions, about the jeans and the records and all that."

"Rationing Commission?"

"No, not that. He's reckons he's a, you know, scholar."

"Yeah, sure. What would a scholar want with you?"

"He says he's writing something about bodgie Yanks and black marketeers. How do you like that? 'A field study of deviant groups,' he called it."

"Fair dinkum? What did you tell him?"

"Nothing much. He asked about where we buy our clothes and that. What we think about things. About coppers and girls and having jobs and all that. I told him we were called bodgies. He liked that. Wrote it down straightaway."

"What else you tell him?"

"That wearing blue jeans and jiving to 'The Devil's Jump' are the big G.O. around here."

I stayed on at the Oxford Street place, but it was kind of lonely there with the Underwoods gone, without the aroma of May's cooking, and without the little bloke getting around the joint.

A week after the meeting with Prisk, the Blighter turned up there unannounced.

"G'day Blighter. You're still here. What's on the go?"

"There are some loose ends to clear up. Rather necessary, I'm afraid."

"Yeah, what?"

"Firstly, would you by any chance have any brandy?"

"Sorry."

"Then I suggest we adjourn to a public house."

Ten minutes later we were set up in the back bar at the local.

"What's on your mind, Blighter?"

"Awkward situation, Bill. Concerning those chaps up there at the Devil's Jump."

My heart kick-started, and I felt a stab of fear go through me. "Are we in trouble?"

"No, not at the moment. I've been thinking things through. The way I see it, Toohey's death has nothing to do with us. You may or may not know this, but they 'officially' found the body the day after we were there. Supposedly after an anonymous tip-off. You might be asked to appear at the inquest, but more likely not."

"I'd rather not."

"Of course. But I've no doubt that you could handle it appropriately, should it happen that way. No, it's the others who are the worry."

"Are they going to find them too?"

The Blighter put his hands up. "Settle down. There's no reason for those bodies to be found, *ever*. But let's just for argument's sake imagine that somehow they were found, and that we were called to give an account."

"Go on."

"Well, as I see it, one could make the case that killing Munce was self-defense. The other two, though, are rather a moot point. Munce was the only *armed* one among them, and he was disabled by the time I dealt with the others. Might be hard to explain to someone who wasn't there. And the cloak-and-dagger boys have made it clear I'd be on my own if it came to that."

"But you said they'd never be found."

"And nor should they be. But, well . . . I certainly don't mean any offence by this, Bill, but to my mind the weak link in the chain is *you*. You saw me kill those chaps. You know where the bodies are. Indeed, you know everything. And—please don't take offence at this—you have shown a tendency to be, well, *stricken* by conscience on occasion."

He looked me in the eye.

"Now, I know you're as staunch and trustworthy as the day is long. But over time, who knows what might happen?" He leaned back. "As I say, it's damned awkward."

"I see."

"Now, Bill don't look like that! I wouldn't kill *you*, old chum. Good lord, no, one simply couldn't do it. But I do need some sort of guarantee, nevertheless."

"Such as?"

"Well, I know you wanted so awfully to remain above the sordid commercial side to the affair, but I'm afraid I'm going to have to insist that you be a party to the blackmail. You were, after all, damned keen on the idea in the earlier stages at least."

He dropped an envelope on the table.

I picked it up and lifted the flap. A bunch of ten pound notes.

"Just put it in your pocket, will you, Bill, and everything's settled."

"How much is there?"

"Nothing like half the take, of course. But probably enough for a decent motor car. I see the old Chev is looking rather shabby these days."

Eric Prisk kept his job on the radio, but the heat went out of his rants, and he never so much as mentioned the coal miners, not even at the height of the big coal strikes over the next couple of years. And he never did manage to win pre-selection for the Liberal Party.

The Filthy Blighter dropped completely out of sight. I heard he'd gone to South Africa. But someone else said he was up the bush roo shooting, and someone else was sure he was off on a big game fishing expedition with Jack Davey. One feller said he'd heard the Blighter was in Berlin doing something *very* hush-hush for the British government.

Two weeks after I last saw the Blighter I drove round to Mrs. Sprague's.

"I won't be collecting the rent any more," I told her, "Sooner or later someone will be around chasing it up, I suppose. You better take these." I handed her the title deeds to the place.

She took them from me, looked at me but said nothing.

"They won't give you ownership, exactly, but without them it'll be hard for anyone else to prove ownership. For a while, anyway. Might give you a rent break for a year or two. Maybe you could save up and buy a place at Padstow or something."

She stood there staring at me with her mouth open. Then she smiled. "Well, thanks. What can I say? That's . . . really decent of you."

"Nah, it's nothing to me. You may as well do yourself some good if you can."

"Well, thanks."

"All right. See you then."

"Just a second," she said. "Why are you looking so down in the mouth?"

"Am I?"

"Yeah."

"No reason."

She stood there a moment, then said, "Would you like to come in for a cup of tea? The kids are down the road."

Mrs. Sprague was over thirty, maybe even over thirty-five, but she wasn't such a bad sort for all that. She had a quiet smile on her face. "Well, make up your mind. This offer's not good for ever."

"Thanks anyway," I said. "But I'd better be going."

The next day the Rationing Commission announced the issue of completely new, redesigned coupons. You could exchange the old coupons for new ones, but they were looking pretty closely at all the coupons that were handed in. Max and Herb were astounded at my foresight, even a bit suspicious, but they were grateful nonetheless. The Abercrombie Mob probably weren't too thrilled about it, but I didn't feel any need to seek them out to discuss the matter further. I did one last tour of the rental properties and handed out the title deeds to all the tenants, told them if they could do any good with them, then go for it. Except for the gypsies. Fuck them, I thought, they're good for a few bob yet.

Mum died in August at her sister's place. She'd had cancer all along. Uncle Dick was with her for the last month. I got there the day before. She went quietly, and we buried her at Nowra.

I saw my brother at the funeral. He indicated that if I ever got in serious trouble, then *maybe* I could contact him, but if our paths never crossed again, then that might not be such a bad thing either. I didn't argue the toss with him.

Back in Sydney that night, I had a few drinks and a feed at Paddo, but I couldn't face going home, so I went down to the Trocadero to kill a few hours.

Molly Price was there. She got rid of the bloke she was with and took me back to her new flat, a little one-bedroom place in Hinders Street, where she offered me solace in the time-honored way.

I woke next morning in Molly's bed. It was gray outside. I got up quietly, went out and bought a newspaper, came back and made tea and toast for us and went back to bed.

At ten o'clock we were still there. Molly had gone back to sleep but I was wide awake, thinking. I tried to take my mind off things by studying the form guide. I circled a selection or two, but really my heart wasn't in it.

Molly snuggled into me, then opened her eyes and looked at the form guide on my lap.

"Don't back Torchlight," she mumbled.

I looked at her. "It's the favorite."

"It won't be trying."

"Really? What would you suggest, then?"

She propped herself up on her elbow, brushed a lock of blonde hair out of her face, squinted at the paper and then pointed. "That one. Hasty Whisper."

She laid back down. I sat there feeling slightly miffed. Then after a minute I looked up the early market. Hasty Whisper was a hundred to one.

I shook Molly's shoulder. "Do you know something?" I said. She nodded.

"Who's your source?"

"Don't ask."

"The info's good?"

She nodded again. "The best."

I thought about it for another moment.

"Do they know that you know?" I said.

She shook her head, sat up. "I don't think so. The chap who told me . . . He had his mind on other things at the time."

I picked up my watch from the bedside table. Still three hours before the race was run. To pull it off properly I'd have to place smallish bets with as many different bookies as possible so as not to ring too many alarm bells. I could use Max and Herb as stooges.

I felt my heart pick up a bit. I got out of bed. I still had most of the money the Blighter had given me in my jacket pocket. I got it out and counted it.

Molly was watching me.

"There's a hundred quid in the tea caddy," she said. "Why don't you put that with it?"

"How do you know what I'm planning?"

She didn't answer.

"All right," I said. "And if this comes off, Molly, how about we take some time off? Together. Maybe we can pick up where we left off on VP Day . . . What the hell, the war is over."

She smiled. "Sure."

286

I rang the others. After lunch the four of us went out to Randwick. We let the first three races go by, then placed our bets. The best odds we got were sixty-six to one, the worst twenty to one. Five minutes before the race the price shortened to tens, then to eights, but by that time we were in the stand, all our money invested.

Max and Herb were edgy, smoking non-stop, looking left and right like nervous sharpies. The horses began to assemble behind the starter, and Max and Herb went down to the fence to watch the race up close. I stayed put.

It was a warm afternoon. I watched a flock of seagulls circling in the sky to the south. I was still staring at them when the race caller said those words I always love to hear . . .

"Got them away to a good start."

ABOUT THE AUTHOR

Peter Doyle was born in Maroubra, in Sydney's eastern suburbs. He worked as a taxi driver, musician, and teacher before writing his first book, *Get Rich Quick*, which won the Ned Kelly Award for Best First Crime Novel in 1997. He has since published two further books featuring protagonist Billy Glasheen, *Amaze Your Friends* and *The Devil's Jump*. He also wrote the acclaimed *City of Shadows: Sydney Police Photographs 1912–1948*. He teaches writing at Macquarie University, Sydney.